HOW L.
ANGEL

BY
A. G. MACDONELL

To
MY MOTHER

What a piece of work is a man! how noble in reason!
how infinite in faculty! in form and moving how
express and admirable! in action how like an angel!
in apprehension how like a god! the beauty of the
world! the paragon of animals!

HAMLET

PART I

WHEN the Greek-owned steamship *Glory of Bangkok* foundered in the summer of 1913 off the Moluccas, there were only four survivors, three men and an infant boy. The men, curiously enough, were all missionaries, returning from a missionary congress in Singapore to their respective cures of Melanesian souls. Whether a life-long devotion to the gospels induces an extra toughness of fibre, or whether the example of St. Paul off the coast of Malta, as recorded in Acts xxvii. 27-44, creates a will to live among sea-faring parsons, or whether the incessant side-stepping of hungry cannibals founds a natural habit of athleticism, are questions that admit of no certain solution. Let it simply be recorded that after the Greek captain and Levantine crew had departed from the foundering ship in the only available boat, after the first-class passengers had taken the only available life-belts (not knowing that they were stuffed with sawdust and Greek parsley gathered by a romantically-minded purser on the slopes of Mount Olympus), and after the steerage passengers, mainly Arab pilgrims and Chinese plantation labourers, had resignedly committed their souls to a variety of heathen and unavailing gods, the three stout clergymen, temporarily pooling their chances of Divine Assistance, got hold of a large spar of wood, went over the

3

side, and swam for the tempestuous line of white spray which seemed to be evidence of a reef. Luck, Resolution, and three separate versions of the Prayer for those in Peril on the Sea, pulled them through, and dawn found them lying asleep after their exertions upon a small, sandy beach which divided the Flores Sea from the eternal forests. They were awoken by the wails of the fourth survivor, the baby boy, who had managed to make the journey by Luck alone, and they had to take immediate stock of their position.

Their first obvious asset was the possession of three strong and hardy physiques. The Reverend Eustace Smith had played cricket for Eton, had been Keeper of the Field, Keeper of the Oppidan Wall, had won the Weight and the Hammer for Cambridge in the Sports, and at fisticuffs had been the terror of the hooligans of Bermondsey during the short period of his curacy in that district. Twenty years among the natives of the Solomon Islands had neither impaired his wind nor noticeably increased his girth, and he was unquestionably a fine figure of a man.

Monsieur René Forgeron, one time pastor of the Protestant Church in Aix-en-Provence, was very much smaller but almost as strong. He was thin and sinewy and brown, and his small hands contained a latent strength that had surprised the chief of the Waitorowaitoro Cannibals just before they cracked his spinal cord at the neck in 1904. Monsieur had spent eighteen years in the Marquesas Islands.

The third of the survivors was Pastor Hans

Schmidt, who had left a little old mother in far-away Schwartzburg in the Thuringian Forest, to spend a lifetime converting the Samoans to the general principles of Lutheranism. If Hans Schmidt had been a soldier he would have become a splendid-looking sergeant-major; had he remained in civil life in Schwartzburg, the dark brew of the Löwenbrau would have blown him out like a huge melon. As it was, twenty years of strenuous endeavour in Samoa had left him strong and burly and barrel-chested.

Their next obvious asset was a thorough familiarity with life in wild and tropical places. They knew exactly what to do and how to do it, and so in the time-honoured fashion of Alexander Selkirk, Ben Gunn, and that curiously named Robinson family from the Helvetian Republic, and with vastly greater efficiency, the three strong pastors set to work.

The unfortunate *Glory of Bangkok* had been driven many hundreds of miles out of its course before took place the final catastrophe which caused, as catastrophes to Greek-owned ships are apt to do, such grave suspicions and distrust at Lloyd's, and the island upon which the survivors had clambered was far from the track of white men. In 1913 the works of Mr. Conrad had not yet obtained the wide publicity which has since made Carimata as well known as the Isle of Wight, Macassar as anti-Macassar. There were no Conrad cruises, no *Ten Days in Lingard's Country*, no *In Search of Almayer*. But, if the tourist element was conspicuously lacking, the scenery and climate was very much the same then as now, and it was in an atmosphere of immense mirrors, unbroken lustres,

gathering shadows, sleeping waters, polished and
dark surfaces, and scented mantles of starlight and
silence, that the three reverend castaways set to work,
swiftly and efficiently, to provide board and lodging
for themselves and the baby.

Their operations followed the tradition. The wreck
broke up and flotsam came ashore, planks, barrels,
sails, spars, and all the other odds and ends which,
in the hands of heroes, have from time immemorial
turned into huts, stockades, ovens, canoes, beds,
chairs, brass-swivel guns, and anti-malaria medicines.
Natives came to observe and stayed to talk, for
between them the three parsons were fluent in every
language between Singapore and Pearl Harbour.
Small barterings followed and, little by little, trade
and friendship grew, until a peaceful and prosperous
settlement lay shimmering above the unending murmur of lagoons and southern, palm-fringed seas.

No white men came that way, or piratical dhows,
or news of catastrophic battles, or tidings of the
gallant new world. It was very quiet, and the missionaries were happy and the boy grew up.

It was an extraordinarily fortunate circumstance
that the three men were very like each other tempera-
mentally, for otherwise life at such close quarters,
with no other white society available, would have
sooner or later resulted in an explosion. But all three
men were placid and mild and sympathetic. They
understood each other's difficulties, humoured each
other's whims and weaknesses, and instinctively
accommodated themselves into a sort of automatic
harmony, so that their friendship year after year was

as tranquil and serene as the turquoise shield of ocean. Thus Smith and Schmidt never dreamt of mentioning the battle of Waterloo unless they were alone together, in which case Smith invariably called it "Blücher's victory at Plancenoit." Forgeron would have hurled himself into the lagoon with a stone round his neck, rather than admit that George Washington had ever existed, and a tacit understanding between Frenchman and Englishman obliterated from the entire archipelago the memory of the redoubtable Captain of Köpenick, and the unfortunate headway which had been made by King Edward VII in his work for the establishment of an Entente between England and France. Herr Schmidt, seeing clearly that exceptional circumstances required exceptional concessions, invariably spoke of Alsace-Lorraine as if it was part of France. The Reverend Eustace, in the same spirit, often told some capital anecdotes against Canute and the Danish invaders, and, while careful not to suggest anything against the Saxon Kings, often warmly praised the civilizing influence of the Norman Kings. And if no concession of similar magnitude was forthcoming from Monsieur René, the other two knew perfectly well that they must make allowances. The French, as a nation, are not taught to do very much in the conceding line, and both the Nordic pastors were delighted at the way in which Monsieur René sometimes spoke a little English or German.

It was a blessing that all three were Protestants. A Jesuit in the fold, or an Agnostic, would have been the very devil. As it was they spent many a happy

evening sneering at the Doctrine of Transubstantia-
tion, and enjoyed many a hearty laugh at the pre-
tensions of the Holy Father. The choice of names for
the infant boy provided a capital example of the
harmony in which they lived. The only thing they
knew about the tiny castaway was that his drowned
parents had been English, and it was obvious, therefore, that the choice of his new surname, in case he
never recovered his old one, should be left to the
Anglican clergyman. Naturally he selected Smith.
That left the two christian names to be chosen, and
long and earnest were the discussions over the palm-
oil candles and round the fragrant sandalwood fire.
It was agreed in principle that one christian name
should be typical of the genius of France, the other of
the genius of Germany, and both should be literally
Christian. Hans Schmidt assented to this second
clause with an acquiescent but heavy sigh. More than
ever he regretted the comparatively late conversion
to Christianity of his Fatherland, especially as
Monsieur René would strongly dislike any attempt
to bring the nationality of Charlemagne into the
question. No. Herr Schmidt shook his great head
and mentally ruled out Siegfried, Nibelung, Wotan,
and all the rest of the mighty Germanic epic. The
poor little babe would never bear the name of
Tannhäuser Lohengrin Smith.

Many combinations of names were anxiously
tested from the social, historical, religious, psycho-
logical, and phonetic points of view. Some passed one
test and failed at another; some passed two, three,
even four, only to fail at the last hurdle. Thus

Rabelais Wilamowitz-Möllendorf, though beautifully representing Gallic wit and Prussian learning,
would be an overwhelming social handicap through
life. Pascal Huss, socially impeccable, might revive
round the head of the innocent youth echoes of
Jansenist controversy and fanatical reform. Napoleon
von Moltke was historically out of the question.
Bourbon Hohenzollern would turn any head from
the quiet contemplation of the principles of bourgeois
democracy to which all three missionaries were
firmly attached, while, on phonetic grounds alone,
Bach Balzac was impossible. Other combinations
which were reluctantly discarded during those long
summer evenings, full of fire-flies and phosphor-
escence and the glow of distant volcanoes and the
low murmur of native traders crouching beyond the
Tuans' palisade, were Gambetta Goethe, Heine
Dreyfus, Villon Winckelmann, Grimm Delysia, and
Wagner July-fourteenth. All were rejected, and it
was not until the autumn was far advanced, bringing
with it all that wealth of autumnal tints in which, so
far as the Archipelago is concerned, Mr. Conrad
subsequently pulled off his well-known corner, that
the three genial men of God made their final decision. The child was to be called Hugo Bechstein
Smith.

The years passed. The missionaries grew in age
and wisdom and riches. To their sacred duty of converting the local rustics to one or other branch of the
Protestant faith, they had added a second duty, that
of making money for little Hugo, and in this they

succeeded more and more with every year. As in everything else, the reverend gentlemen fitted perfectly into commercial co-partnership. The work was divided into three separate departments. The Reverend Eustace Smith, red, round-faced, jolly, interviewed the customers, and stood them drinks at an improvised bar-counter with a real brass rail, which an up-country chief had bartered for an old bowler hat that had come ashore one spring on the wings of a storm. The Reverend Smith also went out in search of new customers, at first with a small bag of samples and later, as business grew, in a palanquin carried by natives and followed by hired sample-bearers. His geniality, popularity, and childlike business abilities brought to the firm innumerable clients. It was Pastor Schmidt's duty to keep the accounts, work out the costing, prepare the annual balance-sheet, hide the reserves, hide the existence of an inner reserve, and invest the credit balance in gilt-edged securities, in whatever form gilt-edged securities could be found in those parts. The actual bargaining, the handling of the innumerable clients, was left to Monsieur Forgeron, who soon showed an aptitude for this class of work that was surprising in a child of the indolent, dreaming, vineyards of Provence.

Rumours from the outer world seldom rippled across the gulf of burning ocean. Once or twice white men fleeing from justice passed by in stolen junks, and once an Australian desperado held up the tiny settlement with a pair of impressive revolvers while his companion ransacked the huts, or rather bungalows, for booty. Unfortunately, like the ex-king of Mar-

quesan cannibals, the desperadoes underestimated
the strength of Monsieur Forgeron's small fingers,
especially when operating from behind in the manner
approved by the apaches of the Vieux Port of Mar-
seilles, and it was but a poor consolation to these
gentlemen from Ballarat that they were subsequently
buried beyond the palisade with three different sets
of Protestant rites.

But apart from these rare incidents, life was uneventful. The outbreak of the World War, the guns of
the *Emden*, the sinking of Cradock's Squadron, of Von
Spee's Squadron, the pursuit of the *Dresden*, the
signing of the Armistice, not a murmur of any of them
reached the tiny settlement. Even the news of the
visit to Malaya of Mr. Somerset Maugham came to
them from island to island, from tribe to tribe, from
lagoon to lagoon, in so strange, so garbled, so fetish-
ridden a form that it seemed to the missionaries to be
some relic of old tribal lore, some epic of ancient
battles, symbolical perhaps of the irresistible advance
into the forests of the fighting white man, the lordly,
the terrible, the demi-god. Monsieur wrote a learned
paper on it, to be incorporated ultimately, if circumstances permitted, as an appendix in a later edition
of Frazer's *Golden Bough*.

All this time Hugo was growing up, and in 1929 he
was seventeen years of age. He was of middle height
and dark and slender. His face was almost as fine in
profile as a girl's, with beautifully shaped features.
Masses of black hair tumbled across his forehead,
and tangled themselves into his grey-blue eyes.
When one of the clergymen periodically cut it for

him and insisted on his brushing it, the curls fell at
once into perfect natural waves. His teeth shone
brightly whenever he smiled his quick shy smile, and
in fact, he looked exactly what he was, a sensitive,
intelligent, quicksilvery sort of young man who might
turn into anything or nothing, and nobody would be
much surprised at either.

The three missionaries had given him a remarkable education. He was tri-lingual in English, French,
and German, and could speak in addition at least a
dozen native dialects. He could sing, with restrained
delicacy of tone and feeling, in a charming little light
tenor, *Die Lorelei, En passant par la Lorraine, Knocked 'em
in the Old Kent Road,* the *Spring Song* from *Die Meister-
singer von Nürnberg, Malbrook s'en va-t-en guerre,* and the
Eton Boating Song, as well as chant a great number of
local ditties, accompanying himself on an alligator-
skin drum. He was intimately acquainted with a
large number of fragments of French, German, and
English literature, for, of course, his worthy teachers
had to rely entirely upon their memories. Two complete plays of Racine he knew by heart and Act I of
Voltaire's *Zaïre,* and, less perfectly, a sermon by
Bossuet, and the plot and general outline of eleven
novels by Balzac, six by Anatole France, and *Madame
Bovary*; he knew the essential contents of Ranke's
History of the Popes, the first volume of Diel's *Frag-
mente der Vorsokratiker* (4th edition), and Klette's great
*Beiträge zur Geschichte und Litteratur der italienischen
Gelehrten der Renaissance.* He had a working knowledge
of Shakespeare in German, and had learnt to recite
at least one of the great Shakespearean speeches in

English, the one in which Cymbeline is exhorting the Scots to attack Harfleur, beginning:

> To-morrow and to-morrow and to-morrow
> Sleep that knits up the ravelled sleeve of care
> Creeps in our petty pace from day to day.
> Not all the drowsy syrups of the world
> Have fallen into the sere and yellow leaf.
> And so once more into the breach, dear friends,
> And he that fears his fellowship to die with us
> Seeking the bubble reputation
> Even in the cannon's mouth,

and so on.

"That's all I can remember," Smith used to say, snapping his fingers vainly. "I shall be forgetting my own name next," he often used to add.

Hugo's English literature, apart from this one speech of Cymbeline's, consisted mainly of parts of the *Pickwick Papers*, a rather confused synthesis of *Esmond* and *Wuthering Heights* which the Reverend Eustace was always inclined to muddle up with each other, and a minute knowledge of the earlier Sherlock Holmes stories. Pastor Schmidt had given him a useful grounding in arithmetic, Monsieur René in elementary science. History had been taught him on the same tactful lines on which the three friends conducted all their affairs. That is to say, he was to look askance at Catholicism, Mahomedanism, Anabaptistry, and Cannibalism; he was to regard Spain, Russia, and Austria, and less often Holland and Turkey, as the enemies of progress, civilization, learning, and light; he was to understand that Spanish, Russian, and Austrian armies, and less often

Dutch and Turkish armies, were invariably defeated on land and sea. Napoleon was the greatest example of an Administrator, Frederick the Great of an Art-Patron, George III of a Monarch. And so it was throughout the arts and sciences. And if the Reverend Eustace sometimes found it difficult to think on the spur of the moment of an English composer to put beside Beethoven, or a canal-builder to parallel de Lesseps, it was part of the unspoken gentleman's agreement that on these occasions an additional half-hour might be devoted to the evening's cricket instruction.

On the practical side Hugo learnt new things every day. He picked up very quickly the arts of the forests by which alone human life in the forests is maintainable. He could shoot a macaw with his blow-pipe, skin it, fry it over a fire, lit in any one of half a dozen ways, and serve it up with butter sauce and mushrooms on a palm leaf, all inside eleven minutes. He could follow a trail, trap an alligator, or cast a balance-sheet with equal readiness. He could run, swim, row, climb, with the agility of any native, and by the time he was sixteen he could put his foot on Uncle Eustace's brass rail with the best of them, and his fast bowling was already a source of great and legitimate pride to the Reverend Eustace. With a short run—"Never more than eight yards, my boy"—an easy, high action, and enormous strength in fingers, wrists, arms, and shoulders that were incessantly employed in leaping from tree-top to tree-top in the forests, Hugo's off-break came fizzing off the coco-nut matting wicket like a snake. On summer evenings the little settlement would ring with the sound of bat upon ball, the panted ejaculations of the native fieldsmen, and the deep voice of Uncle Eustace calling out, "When in doubt put four men on the leg-side and bowl at the leg-stump." Uncle René would lie in a long chair and marvel silently at the complexities of the English character, while Uncle Hans would be so absorbed in making his estimates of the probable native demand for home-brewed beer during the winter months that he could hear nothing.

It is possible that the Reverend Smith enjoyed the evening's cricket even more than Hugo. He threw himself into it with enormous gusto, whereas Hugo, although a keen player, sometimes felt that he would prefer to be hanging head-downwards from a eucalyptus tree, or stalking the local rabbits with a blow-pipe. But Uncle Eustace was a single-minded enthusiast. After the game was over, he would often call the native fieldsmen into a circle and give them a detailed account of the innings which he had played for the M.C.C. and Ground against the Colchester Garrison, in 1901, or describe, to the accompaniment of a low ripple of native admiration, the six wickets for eleven runs which he took when bowling for the Bermondsey Clergy against the Young Amateurs of Surrey.

Once Monsieur Forgeron had found him sitting in a state of some perplexity on the beach, staring at a list of names which he had written in the sand with a stick.

"Can I assist you in the solution of some problem, my dear Eustace?" Monsieur Forgeron had enquired.

"I fear not. I greatly fear not," the Reverend Eustace had replied. "I am drawing up a cricket eleven to play for the World against Mars."

"Dear me!" exclaimed the other. "I had no idea cricket was played in Mars."

"Nor, so far as I am aware, is it," rejoined Eustace, thoughtfully adding the name V. Trumper to his list.

"Then what is the exact significance of your team-building, if I may venture to coin the expression?" asked the Frenchman.

"It is an attempt to arrive at a team which would play against Mars, if Mars actually did play cricket."

"I must admit myself to be possessed of a truly opaque mental density," said the puzzled Latin, "but even if we were to assume that cricket was played in Mars, and that a satisfactory date for the match could be chosen, and a uniform code of rules agreed upon, there would still remain the matter of transport."

"I am quite aware that such a match is impracticable," agreed Eustace, whereat the Frenchman gave a cry of comprehension, as a man in a church-tower will cry out on identifying in the confusion below him some familiar landmark, a house or a statue or a much-frequented pub.

"Ah!" he exclaimed, "then you are engaged upon a work of imagination?"

"Precisely."

"And your team is an ideal team, a vision, a grail, an unattainable perfection of a team—in your own idiom, a regular corker?"

"That is so," conceded the Reverend Eustace, a little sheepish at being detected in close association with anything so un-English as an ideal.

"Tell me," went on Monsieur René thoughtfully, "is this pastime of building imaginary cricket teams a popular one in your country?"

"Exceedingly," replied the Reverend Eustace. "Nor is it confined to cricket teams alone. The English have from time immemorial been much stronger on imagination than some people think, and it is not uncommon in England to see men arguing with gentlemanly warmth the merits of their respective teams to represent the World against Mars at lacrosse, hockey, Rugby football, golf, lawn-tennis, and chess."

"And is it always Mars?" asked the Frenchman, a little wistfully. "Is it never Venus?"

"Certainly not," replied Eustace with quiet dignity, as he scratched out "Stoddart" with his stick and substituted "Shrewsbury." "That would not be in accordance with the best standards of good taste."

Monsieur went slowly back to his work, murmuring something of which the words "England" and "Parthenogenesis" were alone audible.

The one art which Hugo could never master, which made him blush all over every time he was set down at his little sandalwood desk to work at it, was Uncle René's art of Salesmanship. Hugo suffered squirming, wriggling agonies during these hours of tuition, and his shame and shyness if anything increased with time rather than diminished. It was the only dark patch in the happy sunshine of Hugo's life. He grew to look forward with misery and loathing to the weekly hours on Sales Resistance (for Uncle René was years in advance of his time), on Mass Suggestion, on Individual Approach, on the cultivation of the Gimlet Eye, on Hundred per Cent Results, and all the rest of the Syllabus of Efficiency and Modernity. Hugo was always glad to turn from Curves of Extractable Wealth to Uncle Eustace's oft-heard lecture on "The Straight Bat: Its place in Cricket and Character."

One morning when Hugo was nineteen, or as near nineteen as could be guessed, the three missionaries sent him off on a hunting excursion with one or two natives to act as trackers, beaters, and carriers, and gave him permission to camp out for the night if he found that sport was good. Hugo received the unexpected news with enthusiasm, for it meant missing a talk on Arnold of Rugby and the Public School System and also a lecture in the afternoon on "The Spanish Prisoner Trick," in Pastor Schmidt's new series of twelve lectures on "The Practical Philosophy of Worldly-Wisdom." Hugo had found the first three lectures of the series intolerably dull, the ones on Fraudulent Prospectuses, the Law of Libel, and the principles of Optical Dynamics underlying the Three Card Trick.

The prospect of escaping into his beloved woods and wandering at pleasant random among the giant trees (which Hugo, not having met any Californians, was sure must be the biggest in the world), filled the

lad with merry glee, and off he went, whooping and
singing, with a platoon of faithful natives.

But he left behind him a conclave of gravity and
importance.

For the subconscious harmony which prevailed
among his adopted uncles to such an extent that it
almost amounted to telepathy, had suggested to each
of them simultaneously that the time had come when
a Line had to be taken on the subject of Woman.

So the lad was sent out hunting, three gourds of hot
arrack-punch were filled, three pipes put on, and the
debate opened.

The first definite note was struck at once by the
Reverend Eustace.

"The Line we ought to take is to take no line about
it whatever," he maintained. "In England, and after
all the boy is English, women, as women, are not conceded to exist at all in the lives of boys of his class
until they are a year or two older than nineteen——"

"I beg your pardon?" interrupted Monsieur René
courteously. "But did you say nineteen or ninety?"

"Nineteen," replied Eustace. "Between the ages of
nineteen and twenty-two, they are put in the position
of being able to meet, very occasionally, if they are
flightily-disposed, a class of women called tobac-
conists' daughters."

"In France, Joy's Daughters. It is all the same,"
murmured Monsieur René, and Herr Schmidt
nodded wisely.

"Nothing of the kind," exclaimed the Reverend
Eustace warmly. "That sort of woman does not exist
at all in England, not officially, that is to say. And no

boy of Hugo's class ever, I say ever and I mean ever, has anything to do with them."

There was a blank silence after this *ex cathedra* utterance, broken at last by Monsieur's bewildered question, "Then up to the age of twenty-two——"

"Precisely," said the Reverend Eustace, interrupting deftly.

Herr Schmidt looked distressed. There were many things he wanted to say, but he was rather a slow thinker and slow talker, and he was usually a few sentences behind in any conversation.

Monsieur René smoothed his neat black beard with his small fingers and gazed abstractedly at Eustace. Eustace squared his shoulders very much as Wellington squared his infantry at Waterloo, ready to defend his position to the end.

"And after twenty-two?" asked the Frenchman at last. "What happens then?"

"He meets some nice girl of his own class, County folk preferably, and marries her."

"But how if Hugo never meets her? He may be stuck here for life."

The Reverend Eustace waved a strong brown hand. "My dear fellow," he said, "with your shrewdness of judgment and clearness of observation—both such typical characteristics of your nation——"

"Thank you, thank you, my dear Eustace," murmured the Frenchman, deeply moved by this tribute.

"You cannot have failed to notice," proceeded Eustace, "that all the symptoms point to our deliverance from exile at an early date. Praise be to God," he added gloomily, and all three men sighed deeply.

"Tourists are pushing north and west and east in all directions. I hear of them almost daily on my business round. Sooner or later one of them is bound to call at this island, and our long captivity will be over."

"Prosit," murmured Schmidt heavily, shaking his head and lowering a pint of punch. "When that day comes," went on the Englishman, "our duty to Hugo is plain. We must provide him with money and send him back to civilization."

"Take him back, you mean, don't you?" said Monsieur.

The Reverend Eustace looked a little confused. "I should, of course, have said take him back."

"He will then meet lots of girls." observed Pastor Schmidt.

"Not until he is twenty-two," replied Eustace firmly, "and then only of the County families, and they don't really count as girls."

"What do they count as?" enquired the Frenchman with interest.

"You know perfectly well what I mean, René," replied Eustace.

"It all seems very queer," said the German. "In Thuringia it was not like that. At least not when I was young. It may be different now."

"Germany is Germany, Hans," Eustace reminded him. "As I was saying; when Hugo returns to England he will pursue the normal life of a normal Englishman, and there is no need to put ideas into his head that any other life exists."

"Can you blot out the memory of all this?" René

waved from the lagoon to the palm-groves and from the palm-groves to the steamy swamps.

"A year or two at Magdalen will soon put that right," replied Eustace with a good deal less confidence. The landscape was looking particularly oriental at the moment.

"It cannot be done. René is right," said Hans.

"But you don't understand Englishmen," protested Eustace.

"Hugo is not exactly typical," replied Monsieur drily. "For one thing his French accent is impeccable."

"Hugo is a cosmopolite," boomed the German.

"But I say," the Reverend Eustace fairly wriggled in his chair, "you don't see what the implications are. You haven't followed this thing to its logical conclusion. If we agree to your proposals, we shall have to talk to Hugo about women."

"That was the idea," said René gently.

"But gentlemen can't discuss women."

"Why not?"

"Because they would cease to be gentlemen, of course."

"For myself, Friend Eustace," said Schmidt, with his jolly laugh, "I don't think I've been much of a gentleman since I first landed in Samoa forty years ago."

"And you know," said René with a sly smile, "the French are never gentlemen."

"That may be so," said Eustace, tugging at his great black beard in perplexity, "but it is difficult for me to forget that I am an Old Etonian. Warre's," he added, automatically.

Schmidt gurgled with simple fun. "It is difficult for us to forget that you are an Old Etonian, my dear Eustace," he exclaimed, and the three missionaries laughed heartily.

Then the Anglican priest re-knitted his brows.

"I see that I'm in a minority," he said, "and of course I give way. Under protest, be it noted, but still, definitely I give way. It is agreed, then, that we give Hugo some instruction about women?"

"Agreed," murmured the other two.

"I think, then, that it would be best," proceeded Eustace with a rather nervous cough, for he was not quite certain how this proposal would go, "if you left the matter in my hands. I used to be tolerably up in my 'Idylls of the King,' and I feel certain that with a little concentration I could marshal the main facts in the story of Sir Gawain, Sir Bedivere, Sir Gareth, King Arthur, and" he coughed again, "of course, Sir Galahad."

Emboldened by the silence with which this proposal was received, Eustace went on with a rush, "And I would naturally not fail to point the moral from these stories."

"What moral?" asked René silkily.

"Moral," echoed the bewildered Schmidt. Eustace's fears were being realized early.

"The —er—moral that Woman, as Woman, ought to be worshipped."

"Oh, I'm with you there," remarked René, casually, throwing himself back in his chair. "For a moment I couldn't see what you were driving at."

"Woman's place is in the kitchen," announced

Hans Schmidt, once citizen of Schwartzburg in the Forest of Thuringia.

"Woman's place is on a Pedestal," replied Eustace Smith strongly.

"Woman's place," said René Forgeron, knocking out his pipe, "is in Bed."

"Women exists to be worshipped," began the Reverend Eustace in the third of his lectures to Hugo on this intricate subject. He and his pupil were strolling through a cool glade, for the missionary found his thoughts flowed more smoothly when he was taking exercise of some kind. "And this worship is expressed in England in a number of different ways. For example, a woman's name is never mentioned in, the smoking-room of a club. Then again gentlemen always open the door for women and allow them precedence in passing in or out. They also remove their hats on meeting a woman, unless she happens to be their mother, wife, or sister. They fetch and carry for women, including their mothers when they are old, and their wives when they are new. Sisters are optional. The only exception to this form of adoration is that no man need feel it his duty to carry a brown-paper parcel in the street of a town for any woman."

"May I make a note of that, please?" asked Hugo timidly. These new lectures thrilled him as none of the earlier series on such things as Double-Entry and Political Economy had thrilled him, and he was anxious to miss none of the points of this fascinating subject.

"By all means," said the Reverend Eustace, and he waited till the lad had jotted down a few notes on his home-made papyrus with his cuttlefish-ink fountain-pen. He then proceeded, "It is difficult to paint in adequate language the chivalrous attitude towards women of the old public-school boy, especially, I think I may say, of the Old Etonian. But perhaps it is unfair to single out our school for special mention, for I have known many chivalrous gentlemen from Oundle, Ardingly, Hurstpierpoint, Winchester, Framlingham, Mill Hill, and even one, so far as I can recollect, from Harrow. Or am I thinking of St. Lawrence College, Ramsgate? At any rate, my point is that it is the public-school system which is directly responsible for this old-world chivalry. The modern Sir Galahad would never dream of using such words as 'dash' or 'confound' in front of a woman, of smoking a cigar in the drawing-room, of walking on the inside on the pavement, of serving his hardest service at lawn tennis, of allowing a lady to pay her own tram fare. In short, the Englishman looks upon all women as objects of veneration until he marries one of them and settles down."

"In what way does he look at them then?" asked Hugo.

"After that he does not look at other women in any way at all. He is a married man."

"Then I suppose," ventured Hugo, "that he spends the rest of his life worshipping his wife."

"In effect, that is the case," said the Reverend Eustace, "although, of course, the passage of years may bring a certain—how shall I express it—slacking-

C

off in the small, outward details of fetching and carrying. In England women do not expect, indeed do not
like, their husbands to be over-demonstrative. Over-
demonstrativeness during the period of betrothal and
up to, say, four months after the actual wedding
ceremony, is permissible. After that it becomes bad
taste."

Hugo sat down on a large stone and jotted a few
more notes on his papyrus. It all seemed very confusing to him, but he expected that he would find
everything perfectly clear by the time he reached the
end of the course of lectures.

"Women," continued the Reverend Eustace, "are
by nature shy, modest, and retiring. The sight of
violence and, above all, of bloodshed is apt to make
them faint. Nor are their intelligences much stronger
than their nerves. A woman could no more drive a
motor-car than she could sit in Parliament; she could
no more conduct a business establishment than she
could fly; she is fitted neither for work in an office nor
for the rigours of exploration and travel. And it is
fortunate that an omniscient Deity has planted in
their bosoms"—he coughed awkwardly and blushed
a little—"no ambition to shine at politics, at commerce, at law, or at medicine. No, Hugo, the Englishwoman's two ambitions are, firstly to remain
on her pedestal and"—he lowered his voice and
glanced furtively round—"though I would not dream
of saying this in front of our two worthy friends,
secondly to become the mother of Empire-builders
in the greatest Empire the world has ever seen."

"Is that all?" asked Hugo.

"That is all."

"Women," said Pastor Schmidt slowly, leaning forward at his desk—the German missionary did all his best thinking at his desk—"present the simplest problem in a very simple world. You choose a woman—anyone will do, provided she is of a reasonable age—and you marry her and you put her down in a kitchen, and there you leave her. All women are happy in a kitchen, provided it is their own kitchen. You see her from time to time, and you complain if the soup is cold, and then the soup is hot again, and you are both contented."

There was a pause.

"*Das ist alles?*" asked Hugo after a bit.

"*Das ist alles,*" replied the good pastor. "We will now go on from where we stopped last time in the Real and Nominal Prices of Commodities. At the same time and place, the real and nominal prices of all commodities are exactly in proportion to one another. Let us consider this theorem."

Monsieur René lay back in his long chair and settled a cushion behind his head. It was the attitude in which he did all his deepest thinking.

"Women," he said dreamily, "are divine."

"Like the God of Luther?" asked Hugo in surprise.

"Not in the least like the God of Luther," replied the Frenchman with a gay laugh. A macaw, vermilion and cobalt and black, rose from the trees in startled indignation and flew across the lagoon, trailing a reflection of splendour on the water below.

"Divine as that bird is divine," went on the missionary, "divine as all things of beauty are divine." He fell into a deep reverie from which Hugo did not like to disturb him. When Monsieur did at last speak, it was to ask, "Which course of lectures are we on at the moment? I've forgotten."

"The Woman Problem," replied Hugo, preparing his papyrus and fountain-pen.

"There is no Woman Problem," murmured the Frenchman. "There is only Life, and Woman holds the Key. All women are exactly the same. All women must be made love to all the time. That is the secret. One may hate you for making love to her, but you must do it. Another may despise you, but you must do it. They may hate you, despise, distrust, pity you, laugh at you or weep for you, but at least you will not have committed the most fearful of all crimes and so they will never trample you down into the deepest of hells."

"What is the most fearful of all crimes?" whispered the bewildered and rather frightened Hugo.

"To ignore her. Listen. You will think that each one is different. It is you who are at fault for not being different. Kiss one woman and she is pleased. Kiss another and she is cross. Why? Because you did not understand that the same kiss will not do for both. It is you who must be subtle, because they are not subtle. It is you who must change with every woman, for they are unchanging as the eternal hills. And above all, above all things in this world, you must make them smile at you, for they will smile at someone. If they smile at you, life is Paradise. If they smile at someone else, it is Hell. So you must spend your whole life making them smile at you. Believe me, child, it will be time well spent."

"Even after marriage?" enquired Hugo.

"Oh, marriage!" replied Monsieur off-handedly, "I wasn't thinking about that. I was talking of Love. Happiness consists not in marriage or in success or gold or the esteem of one's contemporaries, but in loving, and being loved by, as many divine ladies as possible in one's brief journey through this mortal valley. Constancy, fidelity, monogamy, call it what you like, is the quality of a man who is incapable of happiness anyway. Once allow yourself to slip into the miserable trick of monogamy, and your life is as good as over."

"As good as over," repeated Hugo, writing furiously.

"The good God," resumed the missionary, "sent Woman into the world to try us, to tempt us, to dazzle, infuriate, bewilder us, to inspire and to lead us, to amuse us, to bully us, to torment us, in short to enchant us. Very well. Be enchanted."

He closed his eyes, and a long silence fell upon the air. The macaw came back across the lagoon to its home in the palm-trees. The distant murmur of the surf at the outer reef vibrated through the shimmering haze, and the smoke of fires went straight up to heaven.

"*C'est tout?*" whispered Hugo.

"*C'est tout, mon petit.*"

That singular state of society which is called, for

want of a better name, but not by any means for want of a worse one, Western Civilization, was creeping relentlessly nearer to the peaceful settlement.

The three missionaries could feel it coming. A hint here, a rumour there, a story of white men seen in uncharted waters, an epidemic of influenza, a great clot of oil slimily fouling a pale pink reef of translucent coral, a dying albatross with a charge of shot in its snow-white breast, the annihilation of an island tribe by another tribe which was armed with Mills bombs, and everywhere a steady diminution of trade, were symptoms which, each by itself inconclusive, together made a cumulative certainty. Civilization was at hand and even the backwaters of the Moluccas were, at long last, to share in its blessings.

The first real, concrete impingement of the West was not, as might have been expected, a tradingship. Indeed it was almost exactly the opposite. For one of the earliest ripples which arrived at Kalataheira was the Trade Depression. Business slackened off incomprehensibly. Nobody could account for it, not even the oldest inhabitant of the neighbouring islands. A lack of confidence, a sort of commercial paralysis, seemed to have settled on the archipelago like a fog. One ancient witch-doctor, who was more than a little suspected of Quackery, professed to have seen the cause of the depression in a vision which had been revealed to him, alone among men, on account of his integrity, his notable virtue of character, and his kindliness of heart. He offered to sell the secret of his vision for a mere bagatelle, a couple of sacks of salt or a dozen brass rods, to anyone who was interested in political economy and the theory of distribution. A number of native students paid up and squatted in a circle round the veteran seer.

"It has been revealed to me," he began, "on account of my integrity, my notable——"

"Yes, yes, yes," cried the students. "Get on with it."

"Very well," said the seer, rather hurt by the interruptions. "The cause of the trade depression is this. For the first time in history the world has got all the goods that it wants, and so it is ruined."

"Say that again," said one of the students.

The witch-doctor ignored him. "There is so much coffee in the world that no one can drink coffee. There is so much rubber in the world that no one can use rubber. There is so much tea in the world that no one can drink tea. All goods are so cheap that no one can afford to buy them. Not until they are too expensive to buy, will people be able to buy them. The only way to improve trade is to put up barriers to trade——"

At this point a stone was thrown, and the meeting broke up in confusion. The witch-doctor, ancient though he was, charlatan though he might be, had still a sufficient command over magic and spells to conjure up a capacity to cover the hundred yards in nine and four-fifths seconds, and so get away with his life. But his reputation was gone for ever, and he was compelled to support a declining old age by turning tipster at local race-meetings.

To return. The first Western ship that arrived at Kalataheira was not a trading-ship. It was a beautiful white steam-yacht, and it came slowly up the coast outside the coral reef.

The three missionaries raced down to the reef and waved improvised flags and shouted wildly and gesticulated. No wonder they were excited. After twenty-one years of exile they were to be rescued at last. Piccadilly, the Cours Mirabeau at Aix, the dusty little Square at Schwartzburg, the old familiar haunts, the sights and sounds of their youth, Home, Home was beckoning to them at last. With tears of emotion rolling down his cheeks, honest Pastor Schmidt watched the yacht come gently to a halt; Monsieur René was frankly crying as the boat was swung out on the davits; the Reverend Eustace had to hum the *Eton Boating Song* for all he was worth to conceal the lump in his throat. Home, Home at last.

Hugo goggled with excitement at the beautiful, swan-white, iron ship, so different from the praus and dhows of the Moluccas, and at the smart rowing of the boat's crew, and the smart blue and white and gold uniform of the officer, and the American flag at the stern of the pinnace. This at last was Life.

The American officer came ashore. The missionaries fell on his neck, René literally, the other two metaphorically. Great bowls of arrack punch were brought out, long chairs stretched, punkah-boys set to work, and the whole apparatus of hospitality set in enthusiastic motion.

The Reverend Eustace and Monsieur René explained the situation of the little colony, punctuated with much slow head-nodding from Herr Schmidt.

They wanted four passages home, preferably to Europe, but failing that, to America. They were prepared to pay for the passages, either in money on arrival, or else in kind, pearls, ambergris, gold dust, gold bars, turquoises, or any of the numerous portable securities in which Herr Hans had invested the profits of long years of successful trading.

The officer, on his side, explained the situation of the yacht. It had been chartered, he said, by a powerful literary club, The Joseph Conrad Society of Boston, with its two affiliated subsidiaries, the Joseph Conrad Society of Milwaukee and the Joseph Conrad Korzeniowski Society of Chicago, to tour the Archipelago in search of the spirit of the Master, and also local colour for lectures, addresses, learned papers, etcetera, which were to be written and read during the forthcoming winter. At Singapore, however, the entire party, which consisted of thirty-one lady and four gentlemen novelists, sixteen critics, and twenty-eight mixed poets, had been seduced, in the metaphorical sense, from the admiration of Conrad by a book about Northern Siam by Mr. Alec Waugh. With the impulsive decision which is so characteristic of the citizens of the United States, the party immediately departed for Northern Siam, whether in search of local colour or of Mr. Waugh himself was not known. Before they left they instructed the captain of the yacht to cruise the Archipelago with the very extensive cinematograph apparatus that had been thoughtfully provided by the Society, to shoot half a million feet of typically Conrad country, return to New York and have the film developed and ready by the time the party got back from Siam by P. & O. and Cunarder.

It was in pursuance of these instructions that the yacht had come cruising past the lovely settlement at Kalataheira, "shooting" diligently as it went. As there was accommodation for one hundred passengers on the yacht and not one single passenger, the captain was delighted to put four first-class suites at the disposal of the castaways and to load their boxes of gilt-edged securities into the hold. He also agreed to wait for three days in order to allow the missionaries to wind up their affairs, for an American, however keen a hustler he may be, has always time for courtesy. It would give him an opportunity, he explained, of scouring the country in search of potatoes, an article of provision which had recently run out on board the yacht.

By the end of the third day everything was ready. The packing-cases had been stowed under hatches; farewells had been exchanged with the natives; Monsieur René's wives and Herr Schmidt's wife had been paid off; the ladies of the Dorcas Society, and the members of the Mothers' Union, and of the Women's Rural Institute, had combined to present the Reverend Eustace with a dozen pairs of plaited bedroom slippers; a great banquet had been eaten; speeches had been made; and Monsieur René, who had recently brought off a local corner in potatoes, was able to make a deal with the American captain that afforded a very handsome profit indeed. The three missionaries were in the highest of spirits.

"Home again, Hans," cried the Reverend Eustace

boisterously, slapping the big German on the back.

"Yes," replied Hans.

"Back to London village, Eustace," shouted René across the lagoon, as he superintended the loading of a pearl-chest into the yacht.

"Yes," replied Eustace.

"Two months and you will see the Champs-Élysées," boomed Hans over the steaming punch.

"Yes," replied René.

Late in the evening the passengers went aboard. The lagoon and the deserted settlement and the fireflies and the homing parrakeets lent themselves to a first-class piece of descriptive writing, and the Society's caption-writer was hard at work under a stars-and-stripes awning on the main deck.

It had been a long and tiring day, both emotionally and physically, and the four passengers went straight to their suites. At midnight the anchor was weighed, and by the time Hugo came down to breakfast next morning the yacht was slipping easily along through the Jilolo Strait, a hundred and fifty miles from Kalataheira. At ten o'clock the chief steward came in some alarm to the captain. The three Reverend gentlemen had not slept in their bunks, nor was there any trace of them in the yacht. Each had left a letter pinned to the dressing-table in his stateroom, addressed to the other two. After some hesitation, due to his American sense of delicacy, the captain opened the three letters. Each missionary had committed Hugo to the care of the others, and swum back to Kalataheira.

PART II

CHAPTER I

THE voyage of the steam yacht *Joseph Conrad Korzeniowski* (the novelist's Polish surname had been added out of deference to the large number of Polish members in the Chicago branch of the Society) was uneventful. Many photographs were taken of lagoons, reefs, volcanoes, half-castes, amateur beachcombers, English novelists from Yorkshire in search of material for novels, ambergris, canoes, and fat German hotel-keepers who were often indistinguishable from the Yorkshire novelists, and many note-books filled by the caption-writers.

Hugo explored the ship from end to end and, when that pastime had been worked out, had to fall back upon the library for entertainment. It contained the complete works of the Master, of course, and also those of Sinclair Lewis, Theodore Dreiser, and the plays of Eugene O'Neill and Shakespeare, and the poems of T. S. Eliot, Ezra Pound, Vachel Lindsay, and Browning. There were twenty-five copies of each volume.

Hugo made one or two attempts to engage the American officers in a conversation about the subject that was causing him so much bewilderment, Women and How to Treat Them, but it was useless.

At the first hint that this was the topic to which the young castaway was working up, these lean, brown, clean-shaven men shut their strong jaws with a click, and a look of intense silence came into their clear eyes. This puzzled Hugo a good deal. He had thought that the divergent views about Women of his three clerical instructors covered the whole field. But already, in his first step into the great world, he was encountering a fourth theory, a theory of absolute silence. Poor young man! He could not be expected to appreciate, even dimly, the deep sensitiveness which so hampers, in the Courts of Love, the best and highest type of American gentleman.

The yacht steamed through the islands, and eastwards to Panama, slipped through the cuts and locks of the canal, and turned northwards on the last lap of its two years' cruise. There was only one more halt between Panama and New York, and that was the British port of Nassau, Bahamas, where a cargo was to be loaded for the private consumption of the members of the Joseph Conrad Society of Boston with branches at Milwaukee and Chicago. For even the highest-browed of North American literary ladies like a nice drop of Scotch now and then, and even though Prohibition has been officially abandoned, it is still so much more satisfactory to buy direct from one of those sweet English baronets at Nassau than to pay an increased price to a man who is probably called Thugs Bernardone or Fugs Alighieri or Bugs Buonarotti.

Hugo went ashore while the wooden cases, each marked "New Testaments," were being stowed away

in the hold of the yacht. In spite of all his tri-
nationalism, he felt a thrill as his foot touched Imperial soil and his eyes rested upon the Union Jack
flying over a vast warehouse. He was home at last.
His foot was on his native asphalt and his name was
Smith. For an hour he wandered, entranced, along
the broad, sunny streets, looking at the shop-windows,
and listening to the astonishing variety of Scottish
accents with which the air was laden, and gaping
at the colossal motor-cars in which Pittsburg coal-
owners and peroxide damsels whizzed past, until he
came to a thoughtful halt outside a house on which
the following notice was displayed:

UNIVERSAL NATIONALITY PROVIDERS, INC.

and underneath in smaller letters:

BEEN BUZZED OUT? WE'LL BUZZ YOU IN AGAIN

In the window there were specimens of fifty-six
varieties of passport. Here was an opportunity of
saving an infinity of time and trouble.

The yacht's captain had told him all about passports and visas and Ellis Island and Quarantine, and
had warned him that the least he could expect would
be a couple of months' detention while the authorities discussed his curious, undocumented existence.
Apparently a great war had been fought by the
Americans in order to make the civilized world
free for democracy, and one of the most important
results had been that every person in that civilized
world was fettered for life to a document. Without
that document it was impossible to move from one

D

country to another, and in many lands of the new free world it was impossible to work, play, buy, sell, marry, divorce, or die without that document.

"Suppose," Hugo said to the yacht captain, "a man without such a talisman were to arrive in your city of New York, as it might be me. What would happen to him?"

"It would depend on whether he had the makings of a good citizen or not," the captain had replied.

"And what are the makings of a good citizen?"

"There are only two. The Possession of some Money, and a signed statement denouncing Anarchism. You are in possession, if not of money, at any rate of goods that are easily convertible into money. And I am sure that even if you have anarchical inclinations, you will have sufficient tact to say nothing about them until you are admitted into the country."

"But suppose I had no money," persisted Hugo. "I trust I do not incommode you with my questions," he added, with one of Monsieur Forgeron's graceful bows.

"You do not incommode me in the least," the captain had replied. "If you arrived in New York without money or papers, you would be deported. That is to say, you would be sent back to the country from which you started."

"But if I had no papers, how would I land in the country from which I started?"

"You would not land. You would be sent back to New York."

"But in that case," said Hugo wrinkling his brow

in perplexity, "I would go backwards and forwards between the two countries for the rest of my life."

"That is so," replied the captain.

"But there must be cases in which that has actually happened."

"Certainly there are."

"And there really are people going backwards and forwards on ships like that?"

"Yes."

"At the expense of the steamship companies."

"That is the regrettable feature," conceded the captain, who held a block of shares in the White Star Line.

"There doesn't seem to be any sense in it," said Hugo after a long pause.

"The passport system," replied the captain austerely, "is the world's best defence against Bolshevism."

Long and earnestly Hugo gazed into the window of the Universal Nationality Providers, Inc., and at last he opened the door and went in. The public offices of the Corporation consisted of one large room with a counter at one end, furnished with three hard chairs, a carpet, and a signed photograph of Mr. Volstead. Behind the counter sat a girl. She was dark and tall and elegant; her hair was expensively waved; her manner quiet and assured; her dress black with neat white collar and cuffs. She looked, in fact, more like the daughter of a hundred earls than a simple stenographer.

"I beg your pardon," began Hugo, removing his hat, clicking his heels, lowering his eyes, and bowing

from the waist, thus combining the essential features
of the three sets of manners which he had learned.
"Can I buy a nationality here?"

"Buy an incognito you mean, don't you, Michael?"
replied the lady astonishingly. A faint smile turned
for a moment the corners of her tiny mouth.

"I beg your pardon," said Hugo again, this time
blankly.

"I haven't seen you since we danced together at
Heron Castle, Michael," went on the soft easy voice,
with a curious emphasis on the word "danced."

"I'm afraid," stammered Hugo in confusion,
"that you are mistaking me for someone else. My
name isn't Michael and I haven't been to Heron
Castle."

The faint smile fluttered again. "And you never
made Lord Gallowglass drunk on green chartreuse,
I suppose?" she murmured.

"Certainly not."

"Or made love—rather successful love," she
coughed a tiny cough, "to his daughter?"

"I didn't even know he'd got a daughter."

"Not even Deirdre? Oh, Michael! You used to say
Deirdre so beautifully."

"Are you the daughter of a lord?" exclaimed Hugo,
with wide-open eyes, "Then why are you working
in a—in a—in a——"

"Shop?"

"Well, yes."

"Michael, my sweet," remonstrated the elegant
girl, coming round to the client's side of the counter,
hopping nimbly on to it and displaying what seemed

to Hugo to be about seven yards of beautiful pale silk legs. "Surely you know that the only way that the British aristocracy can make money is by trade and by this." She waved a white hand, tipped with five orange flames, round the whole of Nassau, Bahamas, and brought it to rest for an instant on the photograph of the hero of the Eighteenth Amendment to the Constitution of the United States.

"But I assure you," remonstrated Hugo, "that my name is not Michael."

The girl sighed. "You were so sweet last time," she said wistfully. "But I presume you know your own business best. You wouldn't care to kiss me, I suppose?"

Hugo recoiled in alarm. All the teaching of the Reverend Eustace surged down upon him like a bank of fog. Here, if anywhere in the world, was an occupant of the top story of a pedestal, and on to a pedestal Hugo instantly hoisted her.

"Thank you, no," he said, "Thank you very much, but no. I really couldn't. I mean, I do thank you very much, but all the same I really couldn't."

To his surprise the girl broke into a gay laugh.

"You are a wizard, Michael," she cried. "You're the best of the whole lot, damn my soul if you aren't."

"Quite," said Hugo. It was all he could think of to say.

The daughter of Heron Castle suddenly tucked her black satiny dress tightly round her knees, lifted her legs above the counter, pivoted smartly through an angle of 180 degrees, hopped down to the ground on the private side of the counter, and became once more the business woman.

"And what can I do for you, sir?" she asked with a genteel expression on her face.

"I want a nationality," said Hugo, relieved by this sudden change of tactics.

"Have you any particular preference?" asked the saleswoman briskly. "I have here a very pretty line in Guatemalan citizenship at a hundred and ten dollars fifty. Or we could fix you up as a Liberian negro, with a pedigree stretching back as far as the maternal grandmother, and a failed B.A. of the Institute of Wheatology, Houston, Texas, for seventy-eight dollars and ten cents."

" But I don't want to be a Liberian negro," protested Hugo.

"There is no sort of compulsion to become one," replied Lady Deirdre equably, pulling out card after card from a small lacquered cabinet. "I can do you a very jolly Catholic priest who has been expelled from Goa for simony at twenty-seven dollars. And here is a perfectly sweet Siamese major-general with five medals and eleven grown-up daughters. Very useful if you thought of going in for the white slave trade."

"But I want to be an Englishman," said Hugo, horrified at the unconcerned reference to unspeakable vice which fell so smoothly from those near-coral lips.

"It's more expensive," said the girl. "We've got to be so careful to get our references right. They're so particular in England."

"It doesn't matter about the expense."

"Wouldn't an Ulsterman do just as well? They work out much cheaper."

Hugo hesitated. The three pastors had been unanimous in their praise of Ulster, its dockyards, its stern civic virtues, the double-decked anti-rain cape to which it has given its name, and its detestation of the Church of Rome. But the call of blood was too strong.

"No," he said firmly, "it must be an Englishman."

"Very well," said the girl. "It will cost you three hundred dollars. Let me see. You'd be about twenty-one, Michael, wouldn't you? Then you'd better have been born after 1907. That makes your birthplace Hawke's Bay, New Zealand."

"I don't quite understand," said Hugo.

"Those born before 1907," explained the beautiful saleswoman patiently, "we usually put down as born in Kingston, Jamaica. No one can check the certificates, as all the records were destroyed in the fire and earthquake of that year. Those born after 1907 are sent to New Zealand because of the earthquake of 1930."

"What a wonderful command of detail you've got," exclaimed Hugo in admiration.

"What a wonderful command of self you've got," retorted the girl with a flash from her dark eyes that made Hugo jump. She went on in her professional tones, "Then if you'll come back in an hour's time, everything will be ready for you. By the way, if you have no special preference for names, I would suggest Howard Macaulay Jenkinson. All three are unobtrusive and all three typically English."

"My name is Smith," cried Hugo loudly.

The flame-tipped hand was held up as if in bene-diction, or in traffic-stopping.

"Oh no, no, no, no," she cooed, "you can't do that."

"Smith," replied Hugo.

"Oh, please, Michael."

"Smith."

"But——"

"Smith. And what's more—Hugo Bechstein Smith."

"Very well," Lady Deirdre said coldly. "In an hour's time then." She returned to her desk without another glance at him. Hugo filled in the hour with a visit to the yacht for some of Mr. Forgeron's gold-dust, and a visit to the bank where he changed the gold-dust into paper dollars. Owing to Pastor Schmidt's solid grounding in financial theory, he was enabled to check the rate of exchange to a fraction of a cent.

When he returned to the office of the Universal Nationality Providers, Inc., he found that the efficient daughter of Lord Gallowglass was ready for him. A dark blue passport stamped with the great golden arms of the United Kingdom of Great Britain and Ireland was lying on the desk. On the inside of its cover was inscribed the majestic plea on behalf of the bearer which begins with the words "We, George Nathaniel, Earl Curzon of Kedleston, Viscount Scarsdale, Knight of the Most Noble Order of the Garter, a Member of His Britannic Majesty's Most Honourable Privy Council, Knight Grand Commander of the Most Exalted Order of the Star of India, Knight Grand Commander of the Most Eminent Order of the Indian Empire. . . . His Majesty's Principal Secretary of State for Foreign Affairs. . . ." and later on came to the statement that Hugo Bechstein Smith, by national status a British subject, by profession an agent, was born in Hawke's Bay, New Zealand, on April 1st, 1910; that his domicile (in French *domicile*) was London, his height five feet ten inches, the colour of his eyes brown, his hair brown, his face oval. There was also a photograph of him. Attached to the passport was a birth-certificate signed by the rector of St. Swithin's, Hawke's Bay, New Zealand; a marriage-certificate, dated 1906, of Howard Macaulay Jenkinson Smith, gas-fitter and plumber of Kingston, Jamaica, to Wilhelmina Caroline Nibbs, spinster, of the same city, signed by the vicar of St. Dunstan's, Kingston. And there was also a lock of yellow hair tied with pale blue ribbon and labelled, in faded writing, "Dear wee Bechy, aged six months," and a photograph of an exceptionally repulsive child of about four wearing a broad velvet collar, a tunic with a belt, and buckled shoes. On the back was written, "Little Bechstein," and below was printed, "Macmahon & Sons, High Art Photographers, Hawke's Bay." Lady Deirdre was nothing if not thorough.

Hugo handed over his money, pocketed the documents and was about to go out, when Lady Deirdre whispered, "Michael." Hugo stopped nervously, and the girl, with a swift glance round, went on in the same undertone: "It's not strictly professional, but for old time's sake I've made you up a couple of smaller identities in case they come in useful." She slipped a couple of envelopes furtively across the counter and added, "One's a Los Angeles Kidnapper and the other's a Welfare Worker who's come to the Bahamas to study the Factory Acts. There's nothing to pay for them."

"It's very, very kind of you," said Hugo earnestly.

"I haven't forgotten that night at Heron Castle, even if you have, Michael," was the soft reply. At the door Hugo was struck with a sudden idea.

"Wherever did you get that photograph of me that's in the passport?" he asked.

The girl trilled with blackbird laughter.

"Very good, Michael," she replied. "Very good indeed. *Bon voyage* and—*au revoir.*"

Outside in the sunlit street, Hugo stopped and pondered over the extraordinary behaviour of the girl. He had been exceedingly civil. Indeed he felt that Uncle Eustace would have warmly approved his action. But somehow—Uncle René might have been a little sad, a little disappointed at the failure of his pupil to pursue an acquaintance so suddenly, if mysteriously, begun. As for Uncle Hans, he became utterly discredited within an hour of Hugo's arrival in civilization. Who could imagine that divinely beautiful girl in a kitchen? Why, the thing was sacrilege. Uncle Hans would have done better to have stuck to his accountancy and his costing. Hugo was struck with an idea. He would go back and invite Lady Deirdre to dine with him. At dinner he could see how the land lay, and could decide whether it

was possible to combine the respectful adoration of
Uncle Eustace with a trifle of the more intimate
notions of Uncle René in a way that would bring
discredit upon the teachings of neither.

But Hugo was naturally so inexperienced in the
ways of the world, that he did not like to return to the
shop without a better excuse than an invitation to
dinner—little knowing that there are few better ones
—and he loitered on the pavement in a state of some
indecision. Happily a casual, almost unconscious,
glance at his passport provided him with the required
excuse, and he went boldly back into the shop.

There was a demoniac gleam in Lady Deirdre's eye
as she looked up and saw him come in, but she said
nothing.

"I say," began Hugo without ceremony. "This is
all wrong. It says brown hair and brown eyes, and
mine are black and pale blue."

Lady Deirdre yawned elegantly but ostentatiously.
"You can overdo the Simple Simon stuff, Micky,"
she remarked.

"What do you mean?"

She exploded in righteous annoyance. "Who the
hell looks at passports, you fat-head?" she demanded.

"Then what's the good of having them?" enquired
Hugo in surprise.

Lady Deirdre sighed heavily and looked at the
ceiling.

"Anyway," went on Hugo, "will you dine with me
to-night?"

Lady Deirdre did not move a muscle of her indolent,
bored attitude, but she sprang to attention mentally.

"Trying to seduce me again?" she asked. Hugo broke out into carnelian blushes and a strong perspiration simultaneously, and he began to stammer.

"Hit it first time, have I?" went on Lady Deirdre calmly. "Well, you've got a cheek and no mistake. Think you can come back after two years and pick me up where you left off? Hop it, laddie, hop it. I wasn't born yesterday."

In a state of burning confusion, and a fog of astonishment, Hugo backed out of the shop and bolted.

That evening Hugo transferred his belongings to an English ship returning with empties to Liverpool, said good-bye to his American friends on the yacht, and set sail for Home.

The last thing he saw as the ship steamed out of Nassau harbour was a gigantic picture of himself on a hoarding.

CHAPTER II

FELIDA CALIENTE was in a great rage, a roaring, cyclonic sirocco of a hot rage. She was, in fact, as cross as cross could be. And she had good reason, for had not her handsome young husband just deserted her? Had he not departed at five o'clock that morning leaving nothing behind save only a hundred and seventy-four suits and a note on the pin-cushion? And it was not as if he had deserted her for another woman. That would have been all right. A divorce case, with, say, Aurora Minnehaha as co-respondent, or La Tigrita de los Andes, or even this new copper-brunette from Lapland, would have been admirable for all parties concerned. The armoured-car pursuit across New Mexico, the serving of the writ by the sheriff from a helicopter at Phoenix, Arizona, the briefing of Clarence Darrow, the hotel in Reno, Nevada, and the final, passionate kiss of farewell in the court-room after the pronouncement of the divorce, all these had been exploited a thousand times for the benefit of the American public. But there was always room, as Scheherazade had found, for a thousand and first, and Felida would have made the most of it, and so would Arthur Ed. Dowley, her publicity agent. And this scum, this miserable wart

53

upon the Body Celluloid, this international Plague-Spot, had sneaked away, with a couple of old school chums, to go snouting about for old ruins in Yucatan. Where was the publicity in old ruins unless it was you used them as backgrounds for the big shot? The Coliseum in Rome, Europe, and the Eiffel Tower in Paris, Europe, that was all you wanted. So what in hell's name was the sense in digging up some more? And in Yucatan of all places? With a couple of fellows? She might have guessed that Mike was nothing but a hot-ziggety-dam highbrow from the way he whistled Sousa in the lapis-lazuli bath up at the shack in Beverly Hills every morning.

Thus Felida on the subject of her defaulting husband, and in the best American that she could lay her tongue round. It was not very good American, that most expressive and picturesque of languages, but then Felida was only three years out of Foch Street, Kennington, London (Europe), and more could not be expected of her. Her real name was Maud Princess Mary Maggs, from which it can be deduced that her parents were stout upholders of the Throne.

Felida's career had been rather like the Wrath of God, slow to start with and pretty fierce once it had got under way. At eighteen years of age a typist in a city office, she had only yielded to the blandishments of the junior partner on condition that he got her an introduction, produced in advance, to someone in the film world or the theatrical world. The junior partner was so overwhelmed with Maudie's dazzling beauty, for she really was exquisite, that he hustled around with a vigour that he but rarely displayed in the office, and in a short time he produced a middle-aged manufacturer of woollen yarn from Bradford who was toying with the idea of financing a revue. Miss Maggs persuaded him to toy with her as well, and the junior partner retired in high dudgeon to his desk with nothing for it but to reflect on the perfidy of women. The revue was a triumphant success and not even the acting of Miss Maggs—now Miss Felida Caliente—could prevent it from running for a year. During this year the beautiful actress refused no fewer than one thousand one hundred and forty-one offers of a change from her wool magnate, but she remained strictly faithful to him. Nor was it until the offer arrived from Hollywood which she had been so passionately longing for, that she deserted the Bradford citizen and departed for the Far West. It took exactly seventeen months from that first coy kiss behind the addressograph in the city office for Felida to reach her goal, stardom and an eighty-room shack in the Beverly Hills.

She was about five feet six inches in height. Her nose was deliciously tilted, her chin firm, very firm, her cheeks soft and curved. Her mouth was hard, but its hardness, and indeed its shape, was easily camouflaged beneath a cupid's bow which was a triumph of the cupid's-bowmaker's art. A crown of rippling glory surmounted it all, now golden, now raven black, now platinum, and now tawny like the coppery glow of Carimata. All that was alluring. But the secret of Felida's triumphant career was the extraordinary wizardry by which she made herself appear slim to her public and plump to her adorers.

This, then, was the World's Adored, who had been so shamefully let down, betrayed, ruined, by Michael Seeley, formerly of Eton College and Oriel, Oxford, and now the latest comet to blaze on to the universal screen. Michael Seeley had been a vast success even before he married Felida. Afterwards, there was no holding him, and his salary was prodigious. Between them, husband and wife, they were touching about a million dollars a year, and as soon as they had undergone the regulation tour of Europe with its visits to the Old Home, its scattering of largesse to the mob, its receptions by Paderewski, Bernard Shaw, the Prince of Monaco, and the British Navy, its offer of the throne of Albania, its opinions of the London Policeman, and its reasoned appreciation of the art of Dame Sybil Thorndike, as soon as Mr. and Mrs. Seeley had complied with all these formalities, it was confidently predicted, particularly by Mr. Dowley, that their joint salaries would easily pass the million mark. And here was that goddam bum (to quote Madame again) falling down on it. Everything was set for the tour. Staterooms, railway trains, hotel suites, Rolls-Royces, all these had been chartered. Sixty cages of pets, from a snow-leopard down to a pair of "nude" mice, all of them the lifelong and inseparable companions of the great film actress, had arrived from the Natural History Corporation of Thirty-second Street. For a love of animals is essential to anyone visiting the Nordic countries. Eighteen orphans of veterans of the Great War had been collected and were ready to be shoved into the steerage at a moment's notice to be sent gratis round the battlefields. Kindness to children is a certain winner, even in Latin countries. Typewritten slips had been prepared by Mr. Dowley for Felida to study and memorize on the voyage, containing statements such as: "I think the London police are too marvellous." "It is lovely being at home again." "Yes, the Prince of Wales was our ground-landlord in Kennington. He was always most considerate." "I think the art of Dame Sybil is too marvellous." "The talkies have come to stay." "After all, there's no place like England."

All this had been done and much more. Seventy-eight thousand dollars had been expended by Mr. Dowley on advance publicity. Mr. Shaw had been insulted six times by cable in order to provoke him into giving a reception for the film stars. Their names had been entered for the Dunmow Flitch, and Piero della Francesca, Felida's four-year-old champion racehorse, had been entered for the Derby. (The rejection of the latter by the obviously anti-American caucus which controlled these things, caused a good deal of bitterness in Hollywood.)

And now Michael, formerly president of the Oriel College, Oxford, Archaeological Society, had gone ruin-hunting in Yucatan with a couple of stiffs.

Felida gazed at Mr. Dowley. Mr. Dowley gazed at his pointed, patent-leather, suède-topped, button boots. Both had temporarily exhausted their vocabularies.

At last Mr. Dowley observed gloomily, "You'll have to go alone."

"Yus. I mean yeah," Felida hastily corrected her-

E

self, and went on primly, "That's O.K. by me, big baby boy."

"I'll get out a story how Mike is on some real romance," said Arthur Ed. Dowley.

"How do you mean real romance?" snapped Felida. "I'm his real romance, you cow-faced pimple."

"I mean some story about his being treasure-hunting, or in a secret mission for the Queen of Roumania, or been offered the Presidency of Ecuador."

"All right, O.K.," replied Felida, relapsing into listlessness. With the realization that the position was hopeless, all the snap had gone out of her. She didn't care a row of dimes what Artie said about Mike.

The publicity agent went out of the hotel-suite in a thoughtful mood. He came back in forty-two seconds like a thunderbolt, waving aloft the latest edition of an evening paper and too full of emotion to speak. All he could do was to stand in the door-way, ankle-deep in carpet, and gibber like one of Felida's lifelong pets.

"What the hell?" murmured the actress languidly.

"Double-crossed," the publicity agent shrieked at last. "Look," and he thrust the paper at her.

"Michael Seeley slips leash," said the headline: "Quits John Bull's Former Rum Store Under Alias," and much more in the same dark monosyllabic vein. For the Lady Deirdre added to her slender income by occasional, opportunist journalism, and although there was a strong vein of sentimentalism in her, it was not strong enough to permit even a magic night at Heron Castle to obscure the main chance.

It was at crises like this that Mr. Dowley was at his best. In the humdrum, everyday business of persuading five continents that Felida was an unparalleled, God-given genius, he did not rise above the general level of his professional colleagues. But when the emergency came, when the Old Guard had to be flung in or held back, there was no one like Artie. He took off his coat, his collar, his tie, his dickey, and his cuffs, sat down at the telephone, and got to work.

He called up a friend at Nassau, John Bull's Former Rum Store, and verified that an Englishman named Smith had sailed for England on the previous night in a returning rum-runner called the *Pride of Glen Livet*. He called up the office of the secretary of the Admiralty and offered a hundred thousand dollars for a month's hire of a United States destroyer complete with personnel and cleared for action. Unappalled by the emphatic words with which this generous proposal was turned down, he tried the office of the United States War Stores Disposal Board, in case any destroyers or light cruisers might have been inadvertently left over from the World War, he tried the Bethlehem Steel Corporation, the United States Navy Yard at the Federal Prohibition-Enforcement Department, and Tammany Hall. All was in vain. Those who possessed warships were niggardly sweeps, while those who had the heart to help lacked the essential material. But Arthur Ed. was invincible. Officialdom had failed him. Very well, he would try unofficialdom. Within an hour he had clinched a bargain with Pugs D'Este, Autocrat of All the Hi-jackers from Penobscot Bay in Maine to the

Laguna del Madre at the mouth of the Rio Grande. Artie was to put up eighty thousand dollars—forty down and forty on completion—and Pugs was to provide a small, fast motor-ship with eleven of a crew, three six-pounders, two hotchkiss machine-guns, and a hundred and twenty automatic pistols.

That night Felida, accompanied by a hastily acquired chaperone, alleged to be called Madame la Duchesse d'Argentat et Dôme, and Artie, went on board the motor-ship at the port of Newhaven, Connecticut. The eleven gentlemen who were contracted to navigate, run, and fight the vessel, bowed low with the profound courtliness of the Old World when Beautiful Youth and Titled Age stepped on deck, and Artie, supreme organizer in emergency, had even contrived for some pressmen, photographers, and a representative of the Mayor of Newhaven, to be present on the quay, so that it was to the white blaze of magnesium, the drone of cameras, and the rotund phrases of mayoral goodwill, delivered by proxy, that the great chase began. The press of five continents, for Artie had found time to circulate a news-story that afternoon, waited breathlessly for news.

The sixty cages of pets, inseparable from their mistress, travelled on the s.s. *Aquitania*, and the escape of a mottled Peruvian lizard on the third day out caused a certain amount of misunderstanding in the vicinity of the cocktail-bar.

CHAPTER III

Mr. Arthur Ed. Dowley was a small man with very black hair and deep, lustrous brown eyes, and a complexion which is usually described by lesser lady novelists as "olive." Actually, it was a pale yellowish-brown. His upper lip was adorned by a small black moustache. A native of that portion of the ancient land of Persia which marches with Azerbaijan and Armenia, his name had originally been Arfa-ed-Dovleh, and the first rung in his business career was the office of camel-holder to merchants, professional men, thieves, tax-gatherers, and soldiers, in the bazaars of Tabriz. Thence he had worked his way up by energy, intelligence, and perseverance to the post of seller of news at a street corner in Ispahan. These news-sellers correspond to the newspaper-boys of our own country, who have supplied from their ranks so many of the financial magnates whose names appear in the Birthday and New Year's Day Honours Lists. From news-seller it was only a step for young Arfa to become clerk to a lawyer of doubtful integrity, and it was a remarkable piece of good luck for the youth that, when the lawyer had to fly the country for refusing a bribe from the Minister of Justice on the grounds that it was not large enough, he deemed it prudent to take his clerk with him. For the lad already knew too much. Escaping from Bushire on a pearling schooner, the lawyer and clerk worked their way before the mast, with extreme discomfort, to Karachi and there they set up a small business for the purpose of selling gold-bricks, shares in diamond-mines, concessions to bore for oil in Luristan, second-hand fountain-pens, umbrellas, cricket-bats, mining machinery, and, in short, anything that they could persuade anyone to buy. Young Arfa showed such extraordinary aptitude at the game that he was deported by the British police within six months, and he found himself alone with his wits against a hostile world at the age of eighteen. But Arfa's wits were a formidable asset, and as he was by nature resilient he was not unduly cast down by an occasional rebuff, and even when he was deported from Sydney, Australia, on the vague charge of knowing more about company law than some Australians, he still faced the world undauntedly. As he used to say afterwards, no one was ever so lucky with his deportations as Arfa-ed-Dovleh. For by a providential coincidence each one was bringing him nearer to the Golden Coast of California. At last, he had to leave Auckland, New Zealand, in such circumstances that there was practically no alternative but to skip out by the very first boat that came along. It happened to be a steamer bound for San Francisco, and young Dovleh was not discovered among the cargo until the fifth day out from port. His native charm and ready wit secured him an amnesty from the wrath of the captain, and he was put into a white coat and appointed a saloon-steward to serve drinks to the first-class passengers. At San Francisco the intrepid young man swam ashore to evade the enquiries of the immigration authorities, and, striking southwards at random, arrived at Los Angeles almost simultaneously with the first great boom of the Motion Picture. He instantly saw the possibilities in this new form of entertainment and, changing his name to Arthur Ed. Dowley, an alteration so small that it could not reasonably offend the susceptibilities of his ancestors, he flung himself into the fray. Within twenty years he was the most famous publicity director in the whole of Hollywood.

Mr. Arthur Ed. Dowley would have made an admirable chief of staff to the first Emperor Napoleon. Once he understood what had to be done he went and did it, just as Marshal Berthier had been wont to do. It is true that Arthur would have looked a bit queer in a blue pelisse trimmed with grey astrakhan, tight white breeches, big black boots, spurs, and an ostrich feather in his hat. But the point is that just as keen an organizing brain can lurk behind a pair of velour spats as beneath a strip of gold lace, and it is the results that count.

The hi-jacker's flier caught the *Pride of Glen Livet* with the utmost ease, a little to the west of the thirtieth degree of longitude, and politely requested her to heave-to. Captain MacRory, who recognized Pugs d'Este's boat immediately, had no objection whatever to being hi-jacked while steaming in bal-

last. Moreover he had every reason for being civil to
Signor d'Este. They had concluded many a happy
little deal together in the good old days. With a
genial wave, therefore, he hove to and within half an
hour Hugo had been transferred, packing-cases and
all, protesting loudly and vehemently, to the motor-
ship. The instant he had set foot on the deck of his
new and unexpected transport he was hurried down
to the saloon. There, proud, erect, beautiful, flashing,
and furious, stood Felida.

"Well?" she said.

"It's all jolly fine to say 'Well,' " retorted Hugo
with spirit. He was extremely cross at the compulsory
transhipment.

Twilight was coming on. The saloon was full of
shadows and sudden spurts of westering sun which
only made the shadows darker. A golden shaft
whizzed through a port-hole and struck Felida's
hair into a mass of golden waves. The ship heeled
slightly, the shaft vanished, and the cabin suddenly
seemed grey. But Hugo was in no mood to appreciate the difference between the Glowing and the
Drab.

"It's all jolly fine to say 'Well,'" he repeated
angrily. "What's it all about?"

"Yucatan!" sneered the beautiful creature mysteriously, with a toss of her head.

"I'm not a catan," retorted Hugo indignantly. "I
don't even know what a catan is."

"You're the funny boy, aren't you?" she replied.
"Hey, what's the game?"

"I don't know who you are, madam, and I don't

know what you're talking about," said Hugo. "I've been taken by force off the ship on which I was perfectly——"

"Cheese!" was the cryptic and inelegant reply. "Look here, bo! You may be able to double-cross all your other little sweeties. Probably you do. That's their affair, not mine. But you needn't think you're going to double-cross me. Because you're not. And here's another thing I want to make perfectly clear from the start. Renting this ship has set me back eighty thousand dollars. That's coming out of your little sock. Do you get me?"

"I do not get you," replied Hugo with asperity, "and I don't want to get you."

"Look here, Michael," began the lovely lady.

"My name is not Michael. My name is Smith."

"Oh yeah?"

"Hugo Smith. I've never seen you before, and so far as I know you've never seen me before. You're mistaking me for someone else, just like the girl in that office in Nassau did."

"And who did the girl in Nassau mistake you for?" asked Felida, in the gently ironical tones which a cat might use towards a vainly escaping mouse.

"For a man called Michael."

"You surprise me," murmured Felida. Or rather it was as near a murmur as her voice could achieve.

"I was surprised myself," conceded Hugo.

"And so your name isn't Michael Seeley," she near-crooned, "and you aren't married to me, and you weren't booked for a publicity trip to Europe with me, and you haven't tried to double-cross me and get to Europe alone, ahead of me. Oh no. Oh, dear me, no."

"The proper place for a woman like you," said Hugo angrily, realizing with a sudden flash of insight how exceedingly deep was the wisdom of Uncle Hans, "is in a kitchen."

This was a most unfortunate remark, for the Maggs entourage in Foch Street, Kennington, had been sharply divided years ago on the question whether little Maudie should work up through the ranks of kitchen-maid and cook to the status of butler's wife, or through those of filing-clerk and stenographer to partner's mistress. The word "kitchen," therefore, struck a most unwelcome chord in the heart of La Caliente, and the small, shadowy saloon was filled with the invective of Hollywood and Kennington, in the proportion of about one part of the former to nine of the latter. Hugo was astounded. He had been under the impression that his mastery of the English language was fairly complete, and here were a hundred words and phrases that the Reverend Eustace , had not taught him. He sat down at the table and stared in bewilderment. The lovely lady was certainly cross. Hugo thought that perhaps he had been a little brusque. A twinge of conscience assailed him. After all she was a woman and, though it made no difference to a true cavalier, a beautiful one at that. The wisdom of Uncle Hans clearly required a little delicacy on occasions. Remorse followed the twinge. Hugo sprang up from his chair.

"Madam," he ventured deferentially, at the first moment when the dainty cupid's-bow ceased to discharge arrows of venom and blasphemy, "I humbly beg your pardon. The fault is mine entirely, and I offer you the profoundest apologies."

Cupid's-bow shot a last short flight of shafts, each a genuine Bargee's Despair, and Hugo hurried on:

"But, honestly, I do assure you that my name is not Michael anything, and I have never been married in my life. This is my first visit to America or Europe or anywhere else except the South Sea Islands. I've lived there all my life till just the other day."

There was a sort of ring of sincerity in Hugo's voice as he said this, and for the first time a wrinkle of doubt marred the white purity of Felida's brow.

"Hey, Artie," she called out in a rasping soprano that made Hugo jump, "switch on the lights." The lights were obediently switched on, and Felida stared at the young man.

It was a long scrutiny, and at the end of it she suddenly barked again, "Hey, Artie," and Mr. Dowley shuffled in. A long cigar, unlit, sashed in a splendour of scarlet and gold, added a touch of colour to his normal black and white of hair and platinum, morning-coat and diamonds.

"Evening, Mr. Seeley," said Artie, with a subtle mixture of affability and deference.

"Is it Mike?" said Felida.

"Eh?"

"Is it Mike?"

"Why, sure it's Mr. See——" The little Persian's voice died away as he turned to Hugo again, and he scrutinized him in some perplexity, walking round him several times and finally coming to a halt and rubbing the top of his head with a podgy palm.

"Well?" said Hugo.

"Well," said Arthur Ed. slowly, "if you told me that was Mr. Seeley, I'd say 'Why, sure it's Mr. Seeley.' But if you said 'Here's a guy that's mighty like Mr. Seeley,' I'd say, 'Yeah, he is mighty like Mr. Seeley.' Do you get me?"

"No," snapped the divine Caliente.

"What I mean is," explained Mr. Dowley laboriously—long acquaintance with film stars had accustomed him to making laborious explanations—"that he's as near being Mr. Seeley as it's possible to be without being him."

"Then it's not Mike," shrieked Felida.

"Nope," replied Mr. Dowley, pulling an automatic pistol out of his coat-pocket and laying it on the table, "but he's going to be."

Silence descended upon the cabin. Hugo was completely mystified. Felida, who found any feat of mental gymnastics quite beyond her powers, was puzzled. Mr. Dowley chewed his cigar thoughtfully, and gazed at the pistol.

The powerful motor-flier throbbed and vibrated as it tore its way across the long Atlantic rollers towards the islands of the Azores.

"Boy," said Mr. Dowley at last, "we've lost a fellow like you, almost exactly like you. But we've gotten you instead, and you'll do fine."

"I don't think I quite follow."

Arthur Ed. sighed patiently. This newcomer to the circus was running true to form. He might not be a film star, but he had some of the essential qualities. He needed laborious explanations, if possible in monosyllables.

"Meet Miss Felida Caliente," he said with a be-jewelled wave. "The World's Adored, the Queen of Beverley, etcetera, in private life Mrs. Michael Seeley. She and him were scheduled for a publicity trip in Europe. He beat out, hopped it. Seventy per cent publicity value of trip gone——"

The World's Adored started as if she had just de-tected a cobra making a bee-line for one of her famous ankles. Some words had penetrated into the central portions of her mind, words that she understood.

"Seventy per cent, you great bum," she shrieked. The Neapolitan gentleman who was at that moment responsible for the safety of the ship, peered out into the gloaming and wondered who was the sacred son of a bastard who was letting off the fog siren on a clear evening.

"It's all right," said Arthur soothingly, bringing all his Oriental charm to bear. "I should have said forty per cent. You represent sixty per cent, Happy Domesticity thirty-five, and him five."

"Hm!" was the Beauty's non-committal reply.

"Forty per cent publicity value gone," Art. Ed. continued his exposition. "Must get it back. You come along. We get it back."

"But still I don't see——"

"From now on you are Mr. Michael Seeley."

Hugo smiled politely and bowed to Felida.

"I'm afraid that, greatly though I appreciate the compliment of being offered the honorary position of

this lady's husband, and deeply though I envy the
gentleman who is actually privileged to hold it,
nevertheless I fear I must decline."

"Oh no," said Mr. Dowley affably, nodding at the
pistol. "Oh, dear me, no."

"What do you mean?" faltered Hugo, his heart
giving an unpleasant thump.

"Just that. It isn't an offer. It's an order."

"But you can't force me to—to—to—pose as this
lady's husband."

"Can't we?" was the quiet reply.

"But—but—but——" said Hugo, and was ruthlessly interrupted by the lady herself, who had by this
time grasped the great idea.

"Artie," she cried. "Hot ziggety dam, but you're
the cockroach's waistband. Boy, you're a marvel.
Bloody hot stuff," she added, with a relapse into
memories of earlier days.

"Thank you," said Artie modestly.

"But——" began Hugo.

"Listen to me," said Mr. Dowley, fingering the
pistol meditatively but with an obvious familiarity.
"For the next twenty-eight days you're Mr. Michael
Seeley, film star and husband of this lady. At the
end of that time you're free, and I'll give you five
hundred pounds for your trouble."

"But I don't want——" began Hugo.

"Boy," said Mr. Dowley, "nobody's asking you
what you want or don't want. I'm telling you some
facts. We're going to draw up a contract, and if you
break it, I'll sue you in the courts and shoot you in
the eye. Got that?"

"Yes," said Hugo faintly.

"And I'll take charge of all that baggage of yours as soon as we're through the Customs," went on the inexorable publicity wizard, "and I'll keep it for you. You won't be so keen to walk out on us if it means leaving all that stuff behind." .

"It's a scandalous outrage," exclaimed Hugo angrily.

"That is so," was the affable reply. "And now we'd better get to work. This boat won't be long in making Cherbourg, and we're going to tranship there to a big liner, the *Gigantania*, and there's a lot to learn. Sit down."

In a daze Hugo sat down. Artie pulled a great sheaf of typewritten papers out of his pocket.

"Now," he said, "what do you think of the London policemen?"

"I don't know," said Hugo. "I've never seen one."

"You think they're too marvellous," said Artie reproachfully.

CHAPTER IV

THE mammoth liner *Gigantania* came slowly to Southampton Water. On all sides there were signs of festivity and rejoicings. Hundreds of small flags fluttered from the masts of moored ships; bonfires flung great palls of smoke skyward from the Isle of Wight; aeroplanes wheeled and circled overhead, dipping and tumbling and whirling in an ecstasy of hospitable enthusiasm; a destroyer dressed ship; the shore was black with crowds, waving distant handkerchiefs and shouting inaudible cheers. The tugs tugged. Pinnaces, rowing-boats, canoes, dinghies, shot dangerously hither and thither. Even the sun shone.

Felida Caliente was coming home.

The Mayor of Southampton was on the quay, wearing his chain of office and holding a silk hat in one hand and a beautiful speech in the other. Behind him were the massed corporations of the Corporation. All, in fact, of the well-oiled machinery for welcoming a film star was running easily and smoothly.

"Isn't the Prince of Wales here?" were Felida's first disappointed words after the speeches were over. Arthur Ed. nudged her sharply with his elbow and she went on, hurriedly, "He was our landlord in the old days down in Kennington. He was always most considerate."

Whereat the crowd, listening with rapt attention at the mouths of the hundred and forty-one loud-speakers, cheered delightedly, and hoped she would say something about Princess Elizabeth.

After the quayside reception was over, the Mayor had to hurry away to preside over the Drains and Sewers sub-committee, and Miss Caliente with her famous husband, her famous manager, Mr. Dowley, and her bosom friend, the Duchesse d'Argentat et Dôme, were escorted to the largest hotel in Southampton for a cup of real English tea.

Hugo was in a daze. His movements were mechanical, his answers to questions were vague and irrelevant, his smile was fixed as if modelled in wax by a rather inferior sculptor, his brain was in a confused whirl. He spoke to no one, answered no questions, acknowledged no salutations. Indeed, so aloof was his behaviour that it was agreed, by all the worthies of Southampton, that never before had a film star of such surpassing "tone" and elegance and superiority landed in that hospitable port. Mr. Seeley was written down in fifty thousand hearts as the ideal of Anglo-American social culture, and the phrase "typical Boston" was often on fifty thousand pairs of lips during that day.

But it was an unconscious elegance that Hugo was displaying, a totally unpremeditated air of superiority. He had gone through many phases of emotion since Mr. Dowley had made his original

F

proposition in the saloon of the motor-ship and backed it with his automatic pistol. Incredulity, fear, and alarm, had chased each other swiftly across the cerebral stage; then had come sulkiness and useless anger; then a gradual appreciation of Felida's matchless beauty; and then the well-known reaction which modern psychologists write unintelligible books about, and invent grotesque names for, and get made Ph.D. at Heidelberg and the University of North Dakota in consequence, but which ordinary people simply describe as, "Well, damn it, why not?"

"Well," said Hugo to himself, after the fiftieth repetition of the statement that he thought the art of someone called Dame Sybil was simply marvellous, "damn it, why not?"

He had two alternatives before him. He could either land alone in England and search, alone, for the family from which he sprang, and when he had found it, or rather if and when he had found it, make friends with them and with their friends. That was Plan One. Or he could start his new life in the middle of a host of ready-made friends and acquaintances. That was Plan Two. In Plan Two he would be a centre of interest and attraction from the very start. There would be not a moment's loneliness. And, furthermore, he would be in a position to worship, at very close range, an exquisitely lovely goddess in the true spirit of Galahad and Uncle Eustace. For Hugo was bound to admit that the more he looked at Felida, the graver became his doubts for the second time within a few days of the essential wisdom of Uncle Hans. To banish Lady Deirdre or Felida to the sordid society of pots and pans and grease-papers and dripping would be a monstrous iniquity. Surely Schwartzburg in Thuringia could not have known such loveliness when it formulated its below-stairs doctrine. No, thought Hugo, Uncle Eustace is the boy. He knew what he was talking about when he made me raise that enchanted pedestal. Plan Two is the game.

Under Plan One he might be alone for months, or even years before he found any of his relations. And when he found them, they might all be in lunatic asylums, or Chairmen of local Tory Associations, or both, or in prison, or in debt; they might be Dukes who would disclaim all responsibility for him, or even cast him into jail as an impostor. (The Reverend Eustace had been very fond of telling a long story about a man who had come from Australia and had claimed to be the heir of something or other, and had instantly been sent to quod for a huge space of time; Hugo had never listened very carefully to the details, but that was the gist of it.) How much better it would be to land among friends and look about cautiously for his family, than to plunge into a vortex of loneliness.

"Damn it," said Hugo again, "why not?"

But even his comparative willingness to go through with what Arthur Ed. had started as compulsory, did not prevent his feeling a little lost in the Southampton hotel. Fortunately he had no duties to perform, no speeches to make. Miss Caliente held the floor. It was her day.

Half-way through the function at the hotel, a

black-coated gentleman of quite extraordinary deference approached Hugo and whispered that he was
wanted outside if he could spare a moment. It was
nothing of importance. A very trivial affair. Indeed
it was a scandal, the black-coated gentleman suggested, with a delightful kink in his spinal cord, that
Mr. Seeley should be bothered with such a trumpery
affair.

In the corridor of the hotel a man was standing. He
was a very quiet man, brown and clean-shaven,
dressed in navy-blue with gold buttons and gold
braid on his peaked cap.

"Mr. Seeley?" enquired the quiet man.

Hugo gulped and admitted it verbally for the first
time. "Yes," he said, crossing his Rubicon and
burning his boats simultaneously.

"What is in your luggage?" went on the quiet
stranger, fixing him with a deadly eye.

"Gold-dust," replied Hugo, "and ambergris, and
pearls, and sandalwood idols, and——"

"Quite so," said the stranger, unfolding a large
sheet of paper. "Then why has your agent declared
only a hundred and seventy-four suits, four hundred
and sixteen pairs of shoes, two hundred and sixty-
two silk shirts, twelve hundred ties, ninety-four autographed photographs, seventy-four albums of press-
cuttings, and a picture in oils, hand-painted and
autographed, of the Queen of Roumania?"

"Let me look," said Hugo, taking the sheet of
paper. It was signed at the foot "Arthur Ed. Dowley,
for Michael Seeley."

"Mr. Dowley had no authority to sign for me," he

went on quickly, handing back the declaration, and
pulling Pastor Schmidt's stock-book out of his pocket.
"This is my declaration for the Customs, and here is
my estimated valuation of the total."

The customs-officer looked at him keenly.

"Very well, sir," he said at last, "will you please
come with me?" and he led the way through the
town to a gigantic shed right down the middle of
which ran a low counter in the shape of a very flat
oval. Hugo's forty-eight packages lay on the counter,
and in the middle of the flat oval stood half a dozen
men, each and all of whom might have been a twin
of the man who had come to the hotel, so quiet were
they, and so brown and so cleanly shaven. And so
bright were their gold buttons. And so formidable
their appearance.

"Will you sit there, sir?" said the senior officer,
pointing to a bench, "while we check your valuation
of your belongings."

Hugo sat down. The only other occupant of the
bench was a small man, with a gay, pink complexion,
and a white moustache, and pale blue eyes. He was
very thin and wiry, and a bowler-hat was pulled well
down over his widespread ears. An eye-glass dangled
on his concave waistcoat, and a scowl overshadowed
a face which might in happier moments have been
the countenance of a small and elderly seraph.

"Damned scandal these Customs," he opened at
once as Hugo sat down. "They ought to accept a
gentleman's word."

"Quite," said Hugo. He recalled very vividly that
evening by that lagoon—how many centuries ago it

seemed—when Pastor Schmidt had opened his seventh lecture in his "River of Trade" series with the words, "In a Customs-house few men, and no women, are quite sane."

"Take my cigars—" went on the man.

"Thank you," said Hugo, but nothing concrete, or rather nicotinous, materialized.

"Take my cigars. A hundred of them. How can that upset the Budget? What effect can that have on the Balance of Trade?"

"I quite agree," said Hugo. "It's absurd."

"It's the sort of thing that is ruining the country," cried the little man with rising anger. "I've got to pay taxes to support those fellows; then I've got to pay taxes on a trumpery box of cigars; and finally I've got to waste valuable time waiting till they check over all those infernal packing-cases, simply because in a fit of absent-mindedness I forgot to declare my cigars. I shall write to *The Times* about it. I don't mind the money. It's the waste of time."

"I don't mind the time," replied Hugo with a smile. "It's the money that worries me."

"Why, have you got a lot of stuff?" demanded the fiery little gentleman.

"I'm afraid all those boxes are mine," said Hugo apologetically. The eye-glass shot miraculously into place.

"Good God, sir, what are they? Geological specimens?"

"No—er—not quite. Er—pearls, and gold-dust, and mother-of-pearl——" He broke off, astonished by the curious purple glow that was spreading, like a sunset over Eastern seas, across the little man's face. A babbling noise accompanied the phenomenon, as of a turkey-cock that is hampered by a rather severe stammer.

"And you, an Englishman," exclaimed the man between bubbles, "are reluctant to pay duty on these imports! Have you no sense of patriotism?"

"I don't really mind paying," said Hugo, "if I've got to. But I'd sooner not. I'm a Free Trader, you see."

"A what!" shrieked the little man, so that the tin roof rang, and the echoes curled and eddied to the farthest ends of the shed, like a soul crying out in a desolate place.

"Oh, well, it doesn't matter," said Hugo soothingly. He was anxious not to be drawn into controversy, especially with a person who seemed to be so amply covered by Pastor Schmidt's wise aphorism about sanity in a Customs-house. "But as for patriotism, at least I'm bringing all this stuff into England which wouldn't come in if it wasn't for me. I mean, all that is solid net gain to the country," he waved towards the packing-cases. "Nothing has had to go out of England to pay for it."

Seldom can pacificatory remarks have met with such a prompt cross-counter to the button. The little man bounced to his feet, grasped his umbrella by the middle, goggled down at Hugo, and asked, with a perfectly monstrous calm:

"Are you a Bolshevik?"

"N-no," stammered Hugo, not knowing in the least what a Bolshevik was.

"Or a German?"

Here Hugo was on firmer ground.

"My second name is Bechstein."

"I might have known you were a Hun," cried the little man with a bitter sneer. "Who else would want to stab England in the back like this? Your forty-eight packing-cases are forty-eight stilettos, plunged in the back of the Old Country. I at least paid for my cigars."

Hugo was bewildered. "I don't quite see——" he began.

"You see perfectly well, sir," interrupted the other. "You are engaged in a dastardly attempt to ruin our Balance of Trade. You are bringing gold into England without sending something out of England to pay for it. If there were a thousand people like you, which please God there aren't, bringing your pestilential free gold into the country, we should be ruined to-morrow. Yes, sir, ruined. I at least pay for my cigars and thus create wealth in England. You, sir, ask nothing for your gold and so create poverty. Do you know what you are, sir? You're a Traitor. Do you know what I am?" He swelled himself out by some mysterious power, whether by auto-suggestion, or by creating an illusion around him like an Indian juggler, or by the reception of some Divine Afflatus, until he towered over the unfortunate Hugo like the King of all Frogs, and boomed, "Do you know what I am? I am an Invisible Export."

At this moment he was called away and fined £16:8:4 for smuggling cigars. Hugo heard of him later, in London, and learned that during the War he had been a staff-officer.

The forty-one cases were passed through the Customs on payment of £2341 (the officer in charge accepted gold-dust for payment rather doubtfully; he said he would have preferred a cheque), and the triumphal journey to London was resumed.

The Southern Railway, as a rule, runs a swift and punctual service of non-stop expresses in connection with packet-boats and liners, between London and the various southern ports. On this occasion, however, they put on their usual film-star special. This consisted of the largest engine on the railway, seven cream-white Pullman cars, called respectively Greta, Marlene, Felida, Anna May Wong, Norma, Claudette, and Pola, four enormous luggage-wagons, and a miscellany of second- and third-class carriages somewhere at the back. Any station on the route which guaranteed the sale of two hundred platform-tickets was entitled to a one-minute halt of the train, with guaranteed personal appearance of the Divinity at the window. Four hundred tickets entitled a station to a two-minute halt, and six hundred or more to a brief speech on "Your marvellous green fields."

So magnetic was the personality of Felida, so galvanic the preliminary activities of Mr. Dowley, so irresistible the lure of Famous Domesticity to the English heart, that the Happy Couple had a record run from Southampton to London. There were seven halts of one minute, eleven of two minutes, nine speeches on the green fields, while at Surbiton the

crowd was so immense and the cheering so loud that
it was some minutes before Hugo disentangled from
the uproar the hoarse and insistent whisper of Mr.
Dowley in his ear, "Kiss her, you great stiff."

After a moment's hesitation Hugo turned to his
soft and gentle spouse, enfolded her warm body in his
arms, and dabbed an uncertain kiss upon the top of
her left ear. The applause was terrific. Nothing like it
had been heard in Surbiton since Roland de Wilton
had kissed La Tigrita de los Andes (little Maisie
Stubbs that was) a month earlier on the selfsame
train. Women, even the toughest and most experienced in these matters, were openly sobbing.
Children, modern children, found it not so easy as
they had imagined to choke down their emotions and
sneer, while men, of course, were fainting and being
trampled underfoot on almost every platform. Even
the station-master sniffed once or twice.

The superb organization of the Metropolitan
Police prevented any serious loss of life in, or around,
Waterloo Station, and by dint of keeping all other
traffic off Westminster Bridge and out of Parliament
Square, Great George Street, Horse Guards' Parade,
The Mall, St. James's Street, Bennet Street, and
Arlington Street, the happy couple were enabled to
reach the Ritz Hotel safely that evening.

Hugo, worn out with the excitement, and the
novelty of his surroundings, and the succession of new
sights, people, and experiences, went straight to the
luxurious bachelor suite which Mr. Dowley indicated
to him, had a bath and went to bed. The last thing
he heard before he dropped off was the high, tin

voice of Felida saying, "Well, Mr. Evening News, I should say it is fine to be home again."

Madame la Duchesse d'Argentat et de Dôme was fired that evening with six months' salary. As Mr. Dowley shrewdly observed, a chaperone for a married couple would look devilish fishy.

CHAPTER V

A cup of real English tea (brewed from real English tea-leaves that had been borne by long, dusty, slow-meandering, camel-caravan from the valleys of the Kwen-Lun through Semipalatinsk and Akhurolinsk and the desolate country of the Uralsk Cossacks and north to Nijni-Novgorod and the coasts of the brackish, amber sea, and thence embarked on ships called the *Clara Zetkin*, or the *Rosa Luxemburg* or the *Vladimir Ilyitch Ulianov*, to the port of London—in fact, a cup of typical English tea) was brought to Hugo's room at eight o'clock on the following morning. Hugo was asleep. Another cup was brought at eight-thirty, and another at nine. But still Hugo slept. He had been completely exhausted by the excitements of the day before.

At half-past nine Mr. Dowley burst into his room and shook him violently by the shoulder.

"Get up," he bawled; "whatger think you're doing, lying all day in bed?"

Hugo turned over on his back and blinked.

"Eh?" he said mildly.

"Get up," shrieked the publicity expert. "They've been waiting for hours to see you."

"Who? The reporters?"

"The reporters my foot. The Public, you bat-eyed chump," and Arthur Ed. hauled the bed-clothes off and began to hustle Hugo into his shirt before he had taken off his pyjama jacket.

"But I want a bath," protested the latter.

"Bath!" sneered Artie. "Oh yeah! And I suppose you want the Crown Jewels as well, and the Guggenheim copper holdings, and the Standard Oil Company of New Jersey. Hey! Skip into these," and he held out Hugo's trousers.

Hugo, sleepy, unshaven, and unwashed, dressed mechanically and allowed himself to be rushed into the big sitting-room overlooking Piccadilly.

There was a small knot of people assembled there. In the centre, of course, was Felida. She was seated at the large table in the middle of the room. Her left hand was being manicured by a beautiful dark girl who looked as if she had just come from robbing her dying grandmother and was just off to kick her dying grandfather, so hard and brilliant and venomous was her beauty. The toes of Felida's right foot were being polished up and touched with the flame of eternal fires by a platinum blonde with the carriage of a Greek caryatid and the genteel accent of a lady who would like everyone to think that her father had been a clergyman, and that her brothers had all been educated at a public school, but she never could remember at which. Three handsome and respectful gentlemen in morning-coats, knife-edged trousers, button-holes, and patent-leather shoes, were laughing merrily at Felida's quips, and gazing regretfully at Felida's beauty, regretfully because the inflexible and unswerving motto of each was "business is business." And, while it clearly may be part of the business routine from time to time to make love to embryonic stars, in order to prevent the functionaries of rival film companies sneaking in and pinching first-class potential material, or to dukes' daughters who are toying with the idea of "going on the films," it is just as clearly a waste of time trying any funny stuff with those lovely ladies who have reached the top of the tree. With those, there is no advantage, financial or professional, either to be gained or lost. For the three gentleman were Directors of the All-British Colossophone Speakiegraph Co., Ltd., which was affiliated by exchange of shares, interlocking of capital, pooling of theatres, and all the usual ties of sentiment and finance, to the Pan-American Colosso-phone Speakiegraph, Inc., to which Felida was under contract. It was the business of the All-British Com-pany to produce seventeen exceptionally bad and cheap films every year in England in order to allow two hundred and forty-six exceptionally bad and ex-pensive films to be imported every year into England from Hollywood. This is called the Quota System. As it was a waste of professional time, therefore, to goggle meaningly at Felida, the three dark gentlemen had to content themselves—if such a word as contentment can be used—with glancing at her gloomily from time to time, and making three separate and mental notes to follow up the dark manicurist and the platinum blonde at the earliest possible moment, with three separate prayers that the two damsels might not be already bespoke by those infernal stockbrokers.

CHAP. V HOW LIKE AN ANGEL 87

The group was completed by a secretary, a young man with steel-rimmed glasses and a pale face, who was sorting out great piles of letters in a corner.

The three Directors turned to Hugo with interest when he came in. After all, he was a famous screen star too. They shook hands with him cordially, asked how America suited him, whether he chewed gum yet, did he know Babe Ruth, had he heard the one about the American and the Aberdonian, what about Elstree now eh? and wasn't his career all a bloody great romance, what?

Felida looked up sharply at the word "bloody." Kennington was calling. It touched-off one of her best lines, "Say, boys, it's great to be home again."

Mr. Dowley, who had been dancing impatiently in the background during these civilities, twitched Hugo by the sleeve. "Come on," he exclaimed, "come on, come on."

"Where to?" asked Hugo.

"To the window, of course," and the little man dragged him across the room. Greatly puzzled, Hugo made no resistance and, on reaching the window, he looked out. Instantly a roar of ten thousand voices struck the vaults of heaven, and Hugo ducked and jerked his head in again.

"Lean out, you fat goop," shrieked Arthur Ed., "and smile. D'ye hear? Smile."

Hugo leant out again, and again the roar thundered skywards. He looked down. Piccadilly was white with faces from the foot of Jones' Quadriga at Hyde Park Corner to the outskirts of Leicester Square, round, white faces, against a background of

shadow, like pearls embroidered on a cloak for a
Borgia, or the first scattering of snowflakes on a
dark field. Hugo suddenly felt a warm glow in his
breast. This was his Public. At any rate it was
practically his Public. There came over him a gust
of affection towards them all, the dear, good fellows,
the nice, straight girls, right-thinking men and women
all. They had come to see him, to cheer him. What
a wonderful thing the heart of a People is! How
exactly it remains in the right place! How un-
erringly it spots a winner! He smiled and bowed and
waved.

"Do some acrobatics on the railing," screamed
Arthur Ed., shoving him out on to the two-foot
balcony, and slamming the window down behind
him.

Hugo shook the little railing. It seemed only
moderately firm. He glanced down. The drop seemed
enormous. He shook the railing again. The risk of its
collapse was considerable. On the other hand there
was his Public, silent now, expectant, anxious. He
must not disappoint them, and, in any case, they would
very materially break the fall. They were so tightly
jammed that the ones underneath could not possibly
get out of the way. Slowly Hugo swung himself into
a long-arm balance. Provided the railing did not
collapse (and how was Hugo to know that all railings
on the Piccadilly side of the Ritz have been strengthened by Messrs. Dorman Long, the great steel
contractors, against this very eventuality?), he was
completely at his ease. A young man, in the glory of
his youth and the pink of condition, who has learnt

from the orang-outang how to swing from tree to tree, from the chimp how to follow the overhead railways in the tree-tops, and from a German Protestant pastor how to perform on parallel bars, thinks very little of a long-arm balance on a hotel balcony.

The crowd was delirious. Great waves of Oohs! and Aahs! and Ohs! rolled murmurously backwards and forwards along Piccadilly, as feat succeeded feat, and each was ecstatically applauded. Even the faces immediately beneath the window, which would have to bear the brunt of slipping foot or faulty metal, had lost their first early look of faint apprehension. All that mighty heart, the Public, was throbbing with the one emotion, Adoration.

Often and often film stars had displayed a few facile tricks from those same windows, but who had ever balanced himself by holding on to the rail with his teeth? Which of them had leapt from one balcony to the next, turning a back-somersault in the air as he went? Which of them had swung round and round in a complete, whizzing circle, grasping the rail with one hand only? It was epic, as the evening papers said that morning, repeatedly, it was epic in the truest and most literal sense of the word.

At last Hugo began to tire, and, after a particularly daring feat of balancing on his forehead, he looked over his shoulder and saw that the window behind him was open. With a final bow, wave, and smile to the dear folk below, he turned and re-entered the sitting-room. An awed silence met him. Mr. Arthur Dowley stared at him as a first-year fag at a public-school used to stare at the captain of the Cricket

G

Eleven in the days before Proust and James Joyce
queered the pitch, as Watson must have stared at
Holmes, as Bunny at A. J. Raffles.

The dark beauty and the platinum-blonde beauty
were packing away the apparatus of their craft in
neat, suede, diamond-initialled, silver-handled
attaché-cases, yawning the while, for they were tired,
and no wonder. Things were slack on the Stock Exchange in these hard days of slump and crisis, except
in the Gilt-Edged, and both their gentlemen friends—
for the gloomy forebodings of the three handsome
Directors were only too lamentably accurate—being
the one in Industrials and the other in Mines and
Oils, had far too much time on their hands, and that
was the truth, so it was.

The steel-rimmed secretary continued to sort out
letters.

Felida, La Caliente, World's Adored, was lying
face downwards on a sofa in her room, kicking her
lovely legs in the air, tearing a set of fifty-guinea
undies to shreds, and screaming at the pitch of
her voice. It was one thing for Arthur to pinch the
bastard, quite another for the bastard to pinch her
Public.

Down in Piccadilly, normal life was being gradually resumed. The myriad faces came down to their
normal angle on myriad cricked necks; pedestrians
began to circulate; motor-cars to nose their way along
the street; newsboys to sell newspapers describing
Hugo's literally epic acrobatics; and in Sackville
Street the ever-vigilant police had seized an aged
miscreant whose monkey and barrel-organ were de-

lighting a handful of urchins, and haled him off to Vine Street on the two charges of causing a crowd to collect, and obstructing His Majesty's highroad against the free circulation of His Majesty's Lieges.

London was normal again.

CHAPTER VI

At eleven o'clock that morning, after Hugo had at last been allowed to have a bath and a shave, the publicity machine began to work at full blast. Six gigantic Daimlers, cream-coloured with pale-blue wheels, each bearing as a mascot a gold statuette of Felida in her famous rôle of Madame Pompadour, drew up silently at the Ritz. A chauffeur and footman, dressed in the sort of uniform that Hollywood imagines is worn by the officers of the Royal Hungarian Light Cavalry, sat in the front of each. Felida, by this time fully restored to her usual sunny good-humour, sat with Hugo in the fourth motor. The first three were full of film dignitaries, the last two of private detectives. None of Mr. Dowley's industriously circulated tales had gone off with quite such a bang in the English Press as the one about the squad of Chicago Killers who had come over to kidnap Felida and hold her to ransom in exchange for Mr. Capone's freedom. This story had thrilled London's corps of amateur detectives to such a pitch of fever that it was taking a very grave risk for even the most respectable citizen to carry a heavy weight in the right-hand pocket of his jacket. The moment one of the half-million amateur sleuths spotted the sag, a jostling and a hustling was certain to follow until it was proved that the weight was not a gun designed to project bullets at the loving bosoms of Michael and his Felida. Not if London could help it was a hair of Felida's golden head going to be touched.

The procession went first to Kennington, of course, and there Felida wept tears of emotion at the sight of the dear old home. Her family no longer lived there, for she had transferred them, after her rise to fame and wealth, to a neat little bungalow at Southend-on-Sea. Southend was a much more genteel neighbourhood than Kennington, and, besides, it was so much pleasanter and so much less involved in complications to visit one's old home when it was empty than when it was overflowing with grubby and dingy family.

The visit to 613 Foch Street was a vast success. Felida's fame, her beauty, her tears, and her affecting references to the Royal Landlord and his unfailing considerateness, caused a furore of enthusiasm.

From Foch Street the procession drove slowly to Bond Street to do some shopping. From Bond Street they went to the Tower ("After all, we are English," said Mr. Arthur Ed. Dowley); thence to a new Birth Control Clinic in Wimpole Street; thence again to the exhibition of Renaissance Book-binding in a Church Hall behind Theobald's Row. The luncheon hour was fully occupied, not with luncheon, as Hugo had hoped, but with visits to the canteen of a vast Oxford Street Stores and to the Sloane Telephone Exchange. At two o'clock there was a halt of seven minutes for cress sandwiches and lime-juice and soda, a singularly revolting and inadequate meal, Hugo thought, and then the cream-white procession started off again. They visited the headquarters of the Imperial Cochineal Company in its mammoth riverside palace of Carrara marble and aluminium and steel mirrors, probably the finest thing built in England since Torrigiano knocked together the Chapel of Henry VII in Westminster Abbey. They visited the offices of the British Broadcasting Corporation, that magnificent battleship-shaped affair which makes the surrounding stuff of the Adam Brothers look pretty silly, and Felida broadcasted a gracious little message about England and the art of Dame Sybil Thorndike and the really marvellous, too marvellous, reception which the sweet British Public had given her at the Ritz that morning, and added that she knew that her husband, her too marvellous husband—with a delicious little giggle—was just as proud as she was of the wonderful reception she had had. After all, she concluded, there was no place like England.

Hugo, all this time, had to smile and answer questions and admire things and stand on one leg and hang about, growing hungrier and thirstier and crosser. He had only once made a mild suggestion and it had been ruthlessly turned down. After leaving Foch Street he had asked to be allowed to put his head inside the Oval to see the historic ground where the Reverend Eustace had played his immortal innings for the Bermondsey Clergy against the Young Amateurs of Surrey, and where Dr. Grace made 152 against Australia, but Mr. Dowley, who had joined them in their car, was adamant.

"Cricket?" he said. "Cricket? Never heard of it."

"It's what Ronald Colman played in *Raffles*," Felida reminded him.

"Oh, that! I thought it was basket-ball. There's no news value in that old junk," replied Art., totting up a row of figures as he spoke.

"But it's England's National Game," protested Hugo. Art. looked up from his accountancy, gazed at him absently, and then pulled a *Daily Mail* out of his pocket and turned over the pages till he found the paragraph he was looking for.

" 'Cricket,' " he read out. " 'The Mudshire County Cricket Club report a deficit on last year's working of seven hundred and fourteen pounds.' What the hell's the use of deficits to us?" he enquired conclusively, and then expectorated neatly into the silver vase of orchids which decorated the interior of the car.

After the broadcasting was over, the party proceeded to the Serpentine to inspect Mr. Lansbury's Bathing Establishment, paused a minute to admire the sentries outside Buckingham Palace, halted in Parliament Square to set their watches by Big Ben, threw caviare sandwiches and shark's-fin buns to the astonished flamingos in St. James's Park, went back to Bond Street for some more shopping, and finally set the seal on their enduring and unparalleled popularity in London by entering the saloon-bar of the Blue Posts at the corner of Bennet Street and Arlington Street for a half-pint apiece of Messrs. Watney, Combe & Reid's bitter beer. A cheering, laughing crowd took the horses out of the shafts, so to speak, of the fourth Daimler in the procession, and manhandled it gloriously up the slope from the Blue Posts to the Ritz.

Felida at once retired to rest, and Mr. Dowley, the indefatigable, went off to give interviews to the reporters who were massed in the lounge. Hugo was left alone with the steel-rimmed secretary, who was still sorting letters into huge piles.

Hugo watched him in silence for a time and then asked him what the letters were, and who they were from, and who was going to answer them.

"It's the fan-mail," replied the secretary without looking up. "The eighteen piles on that side are Mrs. Seeley's, and those twelve are yours."

Hugo started. "Mine?" he exclaimed.

The secretary nodded.

"But do I have to answer them?" enquired Hugo.

The young man paused long enough to say with a grin, "You can't kid me you never saw a fan-mail before, Mr. Seeley," and then went on with his deft and nimble task.

"Forgive my disturbing you," went on Hugo, "but in view of the fact that women are more devoted cinema-fans—if that is the expression"—the secretary guffawed—"than men, how comes it that Mrs. Seeley has eighteen piles of fan-letters, whereas I, apparently, have only twelve?"

The secretary looked up suspiciously, but seeing no obvious guile upon the great film actor's innocent face, he winked enormously and turned up one of Felida's heaps. The top seven sheets were genuine letters, the remainder were pieces of blank paper.

"Tact," he said with gusto, "Tact. That is what gets us secretaries up from thirty bob a week to a couple of quid."

"What is your name?" asked Hugo.

The young man was surprised. "Do you know you're the first man or woman connected with the films that I've ever had anything to do with, that has ever asked me that? As a matter of fact, it's Cokayne. Tom Cokayne. Usually called Dope."

Hugo asked, "Do you like this job?"

"Do I hell?" replied Mr. Dope. "I was to have been a Diplomat—you know—sell state-secrets to Armament Firms and be seduced by Polish countesses and so on. But what with one thing and another—Guv'nor broke, had to leave Eton, no 'Varsity, no languages, no job, economic slump, and here I am." His thin fingers fluttered with weird dexterity among the envelopes.

"It doesn't lead to much, does it?"

"It's jolly well going to," replied Mr. Cokayne with vigour.

"What sort of thing?" asked Hugo.

"Money," was the laconic reply.

"Oh" said Hugo blankly, and the conversation dropped.

That evening, after three ice-wafers and a sardine savoury, Hugo was dragged out to Mr. Coward's latest Giant Revue. Felida made a short speech from the box on arriving, another during the interval, and a third at the end, and Hugo autographed three hundred and seventeen programmes. After the performance they drove in their Daimler for

sixty-six yards to the door of Chez Savonarola, a
club.

Here an immovably wedged phalanx of beautiful ladies and middle-aged and elderly gentlemen
swayed backwards and forwards, heel and toe, to the
music of all the tunes which had just been played in
Mr. Coward's revue. When the music stopped, they
broke away, as boxers break away from a clinch at
the warning cry of a Corri, a Douglas, or a B. J.
Angle, and rushed to the small tables which were
jammed up against each other round the room, and
loud calls of "More Bollinger '19," "Another Pom-
mery '21," or "Enuzzer Pol Roger eef you pliz,"
rose above the din. Waiters scampered to and fro, for
it was nearly twelve o'clock, and the hour once sacred
to Cinderella is now devoted in places as fortunate
as Chez Savonarola to the cause of what is rather
comically called Temperance. Pubs on the north side
of Oxford Street close at ten o'clock for the sale of
alcoholic liquors, on the south side at eleven, and
Chez Savonarola closes at twelve.

"A lime-juice and soda," said Felida.

"And a bottle of whisky," added Mr. Dowley.

"I should like some champagne," said Hugo
tentatively.

"You can't have it," said Mr. Dowley. "Haven't I
sent out to every paper, news-agency, and topical
screen-news that you're a teetotal non-smoker, so
as to keep fit for screen-work?"

"A little champagne wouldn't do me any harm,"
pleaded Hugo.

"Oh yes it would. It would be all over England in

a week that you get as drunk as an owl every night. United Screenophone of Movietone City would see to that. Dirty bastards. They've never forgiven me for letting loose those lizards in front of Big Bat Morgan last year, and then spreading the yarn that he pretended not to see them. Bat Morgan was Screenophone's backwoods ace. He was born in Harlem, New York City, but he found that if he wore a red shirt in Harlem he was pinched as a Bolshy, but if he wore a red shirt in Movietone City everyone thought he was in the North-West Mounted Police. He cleaned up a packet before I let those lizards loose. But that killed him. Yes, sir, killed him dead. So it's no booze for you, laddie. Fill it up, boy, fill it up," he added to the whisky-pouring waiter.

Felida, entranced, was dancing with a Duke.

Hugo sipped his disgusting drink sulkily. He had never tasted champagne and he was anxious to begin. Monsieur René's accounts of it, its taste and effects, had been distinctly attractive.

That there were definite drawbacks to this life of fame and splendour, Hugo was already beginning to discover. Hardly more than thirty-six hours had elapsed since his first plunge into notoriety at Southampton and he was already feeling jaded. And there were another twenty-seven days to go, before his time would be up. Unless the credit side of the account was very materially strengthened in a very short time, the balance-sheet would become grotesque. So far, the only gratifying feature was that he was a centre of attraction, a cynosure for gogglers. Everybody stared at him all the time. But he had almost grown accustomed to it already, and once the novelty of it had completely worn off, the position would be desperate indeed.

While he was reflecting thus lugubriously, he was aware that a man was standing at a table and addressing him:

"Hullo, Mike," he was saying, "and how's yourself after all these years?"

Hugo looked up and saw a pleasant-faced man of about forty, with a healthy, ruddy countenance, and a long, soft moustache and broad shoulders.

The smile on the stranger's face diminished a little, and he went on, disappointedly, "Don't say you're so grand that you've forgotten who I am."

"No, no, of course not," cried Hugo, springing up and shaking the other's hand warmly. "I'm delighted to see you, my dear chap. How are you? Well, flourishing, prosperous?"

He was babbling, and he knew it, but it seemed to go down well. The stranger beamed. "Come over to our table," he said; "you'll find some old friends there."

Hugo shot a stealthy glance at Mr. Dowley and saw that the Publicity Manager was engrossed in a conversation with a lady of dazzling allure who was hardly dressed at all in a gown of shimmering silver. Hugo got up stealthily and followed his old friend with alacrity to a table that was covered with Bollinger '21.

"Well done, Gerald," shouted a pretty girl from the end of the table, and there was a buzz of excitement as the famous actor approached. Gerald did the honours.

"Miss Betty Pugge," he jerked a thumb at the pretty girl, "you know Squibs, and old Juggins. Juggins was at Oriel, you remember. Lord Arthur Wostonley. Lady Arthur. My elderly sister you've met before, and that's Babette de Warrington—did you ever meet Babette?—and of course you know Mother. Pull in a bit, Squibs, and let's draw up." He pushed Hugo into a chair between his mother, a white-haired lady of bright and serene comeliness, unlined by years or cares, and Miss de Warrington. The latter was tall and powerfully built and had a dark expressive face, rather like an intelligent horse that, without much difficulty and with no cruelty, could be trained to distinguish between a capital B and a capital O on a music-hall stage.

The whole party talked simultaneously at Hugo.

"No good offering you a glass of wine, Mike," shouted Gerald. "I see from the gossip-writers this morning that you've gone off the booze."

"For the sake of your Art," added Miss Betty Pugge with a rather forward smirk.

"Bit of a change from the old days," roared Squibs.

"Was he pretty hot stuff then?" enquired Miss de Warrington.

"Hot stuff!" exclaimed Squibs, Juggins, and Gerald simultaneously. "He was never sober for weeks on end," added Squibs.

"Oh, what a shame to tease you," said Gerald's mother. "I'm sure you're dying for a glass of champagne." And she poured one out.

Hugo drank it, coughed, and blinked. Monsieur René had understated the case. Champagne was good. The table burst into a roar.

"Marvellous!" cried Babette. "You really looked as if you'd never tasted it before."

"The man's a superb artist," said Lord Arthur in an aside to Gerald's sister.

Hugo drank another glass and coughed and blinked again. Again there was a rocket of laughter. Other tables gazed enviously. A woman of about five-and-forty, with skirts a trifle shorter than the fashion, and a hard handsome face, and a magnificent pearl necklace, came across and tapped Hugo on the shoulder.

"Tea to-morrow, Michael," she cried gaily. "Any time after three."

"Who was that?" asked Hugo after she had moved on, and the party shrieked with laughter.

"He'll be telling us he doesn't know us next," gasped Betty Pugge between sobs.

"As a matter of fact I don't know any of you from Adam or Eve," replied Hugo boldly, but this was voted to be too richly comic to be borne. Ribs were getting sore and make-up was showing ominous signs of cracking.

Hugo would have liked to dance, but he did not know how to dance any dances except the minuet, quadrille, Sir Roger de Coverley, and a quaint old Thuringian folk-dance. He was compelled, therefore, to pretend a strained muscle. For as an actor, apparently, he was a particularly brilliant dancer. He also would have liked to sit and watch the gay throng, for it was, of course, a completely new experience in

his life. But he was kept busy answering dozens of
questions, half of which were demands for information about life in Hollywood, and the other half began
with the words, "Do you remember that time?" In
ordinary circumstances he would have been overwhelmed with shame and confusion at the position
in which he found himself. But five glasses of that
admirable yellow wine somehow gave him a self-
confidence the very existence of which was a surprise
to him. How wise was that poetically minded Greek
gentleman who said "Wine is a spying-glass upon
men." Hugo was looking into a powerful spying-
glass and seeing himself at the other end a jolly, red-
faced, rather assertive chap, with a flow of conversation and a lot of assurance. It was the wine which
showed him how to deal with both types of conversa-
tional opening. Any sort of rot that he liked to invent
about Hollywood was received with a mixture of
earnestness and a desperate determination not to be
surprised. It did not matter in the least what he said,
provided it was sufficently extravagant. He told them
how La Fascinadora had bought the entire Schloss
Vogelsberg vineyard in the Saar valley because someone told her that the Vogelsberg wine was the most
nourishing food for pet pumas, and she was thinking
at that time of getting a pet puma, and how she had
got a mechanical monkey from Geneva instead and
had given away the title-deeds of the Schloss Vogelsberg vineyard to a taxi-driver who said her hips were
neater than the Dietrich's. He told them about the
German producer who had come to Hollywood to
produce the *Iliad*, and how with German thorough-

ness he had first raised a hill to correspond exactly
with the hill of Hissarlik, and then had built seven
cities upon the hill, of wood, mud, brick, stone,
stone, stone, and bright Pentelican marble, destroy-
ing each in turn except the last, which was to be
Priam's pyre; and how when all was ready, when
Achilles and Diomedes and Hector of the glancing
helm had been cast, and ten thousand auxiliaries had
been enlisted in the two armies, and a love-scene
written in for Odysseus, and Hecuba transformed
into a comic mother-in-law, and the rape of Cas-
sandra by Ajax, son of Oileus, delicately suggested,
and the wooden horse converted into a sort of mediaeval armoured car, the Head Man of the Corporation which was producing the film suddenly heard
of what was going on and stopped it. He was a
Spanish Jew from Salonika and he wasn't going to
make himself ridiculous by sponsoring a film which
appeared to indicate that there existed anywhere a
nation which the Greeks could defeat in battle—
Venizelos or no Venizelos. So the whole thing was
cancelled, Hugo told them, and the city of bright
Pentelican marble was sold at a knock-down price
to Speakiegraph, Inc., for their new series of "Adventures of Sam Squirrel."

The company nodded wisely to all this nonsense,
and resolutely tried not to be impressed. The young
man called Squibs even had a shot at a yawn, but it
was rather a failure.

The other type of question, beginning with the
words, "Do you remember?" was even easier to deal
with. Hugo assumed an expression of puritanical

innocence and said firmly, "No, I do not remember," each time. Squeals of delight, thumps on the back, admiring ejaculations of "You old dog, you!" greeted each denial.

It was a lovely party. Hugo was enjoying every instant, when a small dark shadow fell across the table. "Time to go home, Mr. Seeley," said the smooth voice of Art. Ed. "A heavy day before us to-morrow." The Publicity Manager's voice was smooth but his dark eyes were burning with an angry fire.

Amid vast expressions of heartiness and goodwill, and a dozen invitations to this, that, and the next thing, Hugo was towed out of the club.

"You've been drinking," said Mr. Dowley severely, as soon as the door of the Daimler was shut. Felida had gone on with her Duke to Chez Ronsard, a dance-club, that conferred honour upon the memory of the French poet by possessing the most famous band of negro saxophonists in London, and they were alone in the back of the car.

"So have you," retorted Hugo vigorously, if a little thickly.

"That is quite different," replied the Manager. "You're under contract not to drink."

"Quite right," said Hugo nodding repeatedly with warm approval. "Sanctity of contracts. Most important. A contract, old boy," he went on, the kindly face of Uncle Hans swimming about in front of his eyes in a sort of blue haze, "is the agreement of two or more persons, by which something is to be given or done upon one side, for a valuable con-sideration either present or future upon the other.

H

Quid pro quo, Art., *quid pro quo*," and he sighed senti-
mentally.

"You're drunk," said Mr. Dowley.

Hugo drew himself up grandly. "I may be drunk,
or I may not be drunk. That is a matter to be decided
by a Mixed Arbitral Tribunal of Maritime Ashesh—
Assesh—of Maritime Assessors. Now you say it," he
added, relapsing into his corner.

"I won't," replied Art. Ed. shortly.

"You won't because you can't," replied the film
actor, leaning out of the window to blow a kiss to an
elderly lady in an ermine cloak who was walking
down Piccadilly on the arm of a distinguished-
looking man in a top-hat. "But what I want to make
clear, to make perfectly, perfectly clear, is that you
are being exceedingly impertinent. You are only a
paid employé of mine, whereas I am a star of the
very first magnitude, earning millions and millions
and millions and millions——" At this point Hugo
fell asleep.

Mr. Dowley had him carried in by the back-door of
the Ritz and sent upstairs in the crockery lift. If any
of those sneaking journalists had seen him, all that
temperate-living, iron-training, keen-eyed, clean-
limbed propaganda would have gone west in a single
headline. Mr. Dowley was worried. After putting
Hugo to bed, he sat down with a bottle of whisky and
a cigar to consider the situation.

The European tour was to last twenty-eight days,
and this was only the second day and that goddam
stiff was soused already. It was true that only the
first ten days and the last three were important, for

they were the only ones to be spent in England. The
remainder were to be spent in Paris and Rome and—
and—well, anyway, in some goddam dago country
or other; Mr. Dowley, for all his extensive travels,
had never been strong on geography, and he divided
the world into two divisions. One contained his own
sort, the white man, and the other contained all the
rest. It was a goddam nuisance having to go further
than Paris, but Felida had to be photographed with
that Mussolini, if only for the South American film-
rights, and Mike had to do a long-arm balance on the
top of that Coliseum, and everyone back in Beverly
would ask had they seen that goddam aquarium at
Naples. So they'd got to go. But the point was, and
Art. Ed. saw it very clearly—for if Art. was weak on
geography he was strong on the proprieties—this
Smith goop could get as drunk as a Senator among
dagoes and hunkies and bohunks and wops, but in
England, no. It wouldn't do. Art. would have to
stick like a brother to that young man for ten days.
No more champagne, no more Chez Savonarola's.
A good lock on his bedroom door, and snuff the
bedside rushlight at eleven sharp. That was the pro-
gramme.

Art. finished the bottle and then went to bed.

Next morning Hugo awoke, not exactly with a
headache, but with what would have been a headache if the champagne had been less good, or if it
had been preceded, as is the custom in civilized
society, by little mixtures of gin and the sticky dregs
of French and Italian vineyards and drops of ab-

sinthe and Jamaica rum, or succeeded by dark, rust-brown, draughts of brandy that was bottled in the year of the battle of Wagram or the birth of the King of Rome.

His head was muzzy and his throat dry, and his memory of last night only conjured up a hazy vision of some dashed decent fellows called something or other. All the rest was a blank.

In the sitting-room he found Dope Cokayne, the steel-rimmed secretary. The latter looked up as he came in.

"Hullo," he cried. "Been out on the bend? You look a trifle albino about the goggles. 'Bloodshot and evening star,' as Tennyson has it."

"I—er—I had some champagne," said Hugo.

Mr. Cokayne glanced sharply at him, and then pulled a large note-book out of his pocket and turned over the leaves. "Well, well, well," he observed blandly, "and here we have an article on 'Why I am an Abstainer,' and another on 'Soft-drinks for Screen Stars.'"

"Oh, shut up," said Hugo irritably.

"Certainly," said the affable secretary. "I would have suggested that you step down the road for a pick-me-up, but the word has gone round that you're confined to barracks."

"What are you talking about?" Hugo stared at him.

The secretary opened the door of the sitting-room and jerked his thumb towards two heavily-built young men in flannel trousers and rough jackets who were sitting on hard chairs with expressions on their faces that made Hugo think of somewhat alert oxen.

"Keepers," said Mr. Cokayne succinctly. "Yours," and he shut the door again.

"But I don't understand——" began Hugo.

"Young Omar Khayyám has been busy," replied Mr. Cokayne. "The Pride of Asterabad, the Rose of Shiraz——"

"Do tell me what you are talking about," pleaded Hugo. His muzziness was almost becoming a near-headache.

"Arthur Ed. bounced in here at crack of dawn," said the secretary. "Posted the sentries and said you weren't to get any letters. And as he pays me, I've got to fall in and salute. Not but what—a classical expression much favoured by the late Henry James—not but what the thing couldn't be rigged."

"For God's sake, explain what you mean in plain English," said Hugo wearily.

"I will," replied Mr. Cokayne with great briskness, "I'm paid to suppress your letters. Do you see? But I'll sell 'em back to you. Half a crown a time for a chap's letter, and a quid for a cutie's. What about it? Unless, of course, you happen to be—er—" Mr. Cokayne coughed with a wealth of diplomatic suggestion. "—as you might say, a chap's chap and not a cutie's chap. In which case, of course, the price would be the other way round."

"I don't know what you are hinting at," said Hugo.

"Then that's all right," said Dope cheerily. "But I had to make sure, hadn't I? There are so many—er—well, what shall we call them—knocking about these days that, upon my soul, you never know where you are. Is that a bargain, old egg?"

"It would be," replied Hugo sadly, "but I haven't got any money."

"Oh, if you've got no money," replied the secretary, "then it's off, and I'm on the other side. There is such a thing as loyalty to one's employer, after all," and he resumed his task with an air of considerable nobility. After a minute or two, he looked up and said:

"You haven't even got a fiver?"

Hugo shook his head.

"Hell," said Mr. Cokayne. "That leaves me no option but fidelity to the hand that feeds me. And there's not much cash in fidelity."

That day was a busy day, and so was the next. Life for Hugo was one long teetotal round of duty without any relaxations. At eleven o'clock each evening he was chivied into his room at the Ritz and the door locked behind him. At eight o'clock each morning he was jerked out of bed and hustled into a cold bath. He protested loudly against this bath, but Arthur Ed. explained to him that he had every reason to believe that the *Evening Banner* had introduced a Special Correspondent, an Earl's daughter, into the hotel in the disguise of a chamber-maid, and if she discovered that Michael Seeley wallowed in a sybaritic, luxurious, enervating hot bath every morning, there would be the devil and all to pay. He might think himself jolly lucky, Arthur hinted, that the bath wasn't specially refrigerated so that the photographers might get shots of him breaking the ice in a bathing-slip.

As for the daily routine, Hugo was beginning to

realize that Uncle Eustace had understated the size
of London town. It seemed to contain a perfectly
fabulous number of Clinics, Baby Centres, and
Hospitals; to give an infinite number of Charity
matinées; to drink uncountable cups of tea upon
lawns at Ranelagh, Roehampton, and Hurlingham;
to possess an unbelievable number of old ladies who
had acted with Sir Henry Irving and could still be
persuaded to play from time to time that infernal old
nurse in *Romeo and Juliet*. All these had to be visited,
and at each Hugo had to watch, lynx-eyed, for the
prearranged signal from Mr. Dowley and, on picking
it up, steal a surreptitious kiss from his deliciously
confused wife amid the applause of the various kinds
of inmates. Hugo's kissing was definitely on the up-
grade since his maiden trip at Surbiton station. It
mingled shyness, tenderness, and a sort of dashed-if-
I-can-help-it-I-love-her-so spontaneity that entranced
all beholders. Indeed, there was a great deal of sincerity about Hugo's shyness and tenderness towards
Felida. Her radiant beauty was like a lighthouse in a
nasty fog. And he definitely was in a nasty fog. The
prospect of seeing London in such charming, experienced, and sociable company as the film-troupe
had somewhat reconciled him to the high-handed
method in which he had been enlisted in its ranks,
but such pleasure as he had experienced at first was
rapidly wearing thin. It was true that he was getting
a vast amount of attention. It was true that he had
no cares or responsibilites. But on the other side of
the balance-sheet, he was completely a prisoner; he
was completely a teetotaller; all his belongings had

been taken from him; and he was signed and sealed
by a solemn contract to continue in this same fearful
mode of life for another twenty-three days, and
threatened with legal pains and pains by pistol-shot
if he broke the contract. Already after five days, his
nerve was beginning to go. How could he possibly
stand another twenty-three? It was a fierce prospect,
and there was only one bright spot in it, and that
was Felida's beauty. She was like the evening-star to
a man whom a mischance has placed at the bottom
of a deep, dark, frog-infested, newt-ridden well.

From the back of a box at a charity matinée it was
a thousand times better to watch the golden tendrils
of hair playing on Felida's neck in the gentle zephyrs
of an electric fan, than to crane awkwardly forward
to see the Guardsman-like accuracy with which the
twenty-four something-or-other girls gyrated and
kicked and bounced upon the stage.

On the lawns at Ranelagh twelve inches of Felida's
foot and ankle were worth a yard or anyone else's
leg. The delicious, outward curve of her eyelashes
was more entrancing than any operating theatre
within a mile of Cavendish Square, and the dimple
on the inside of her elbow was vastly more alluring
than any parade of non-commissioned officers of the
Women Police.

Uncle Eustace would have thrilled with a glow of
Imperial pride if he could have seen his adopted
nephew at Felida's feet.

"The boy's an Englishman," he would have
roared, "an Englishman through and through. I
was just like that myself at his age. Ah! Sir Galahad,

Sir Galahad," and he would have prayed earnestly that night for God's Pity upon all poor foreigners.

It was an exquisite sensation for Hugo to come straight from a world of coppery-brown creatures of an inferior race—"a race of concubines, my dear fellow, a race of concubines," Hugo seemed to hear M. Forgeron's gentle voice as he dismissed in a phrase the feminine portion of Malaya—to this queenly vision of pink and white and gold, born to command, born to conquer and to trample. The whole of every day, from ten o'clock in the morning until eleven o'clock at night, he spent with her, and many times each day he kissed her. True it was a business kiss, and only imprinted upon the signal, and at the chosen moment, of a citizen of Northern Persia. But a kiss is a kiss, and when it is dusted, butterfly-wise, on the lips of a pink and white and golden goddess, even in the way of business, it is worth a great deal more than any amount of rough stuff with the coppery-browns of this world. At least, so Hugo thought during those first wearing, exhausting days of life in London. The mantle of Uncle Eustace was athwart his shoulders, and Felida was upon a pedestal of aquamarine and ivory and chalcedony and pearl.

But after four days of the company of Beauty, of gazing and kissing and opening doors, and smiling devotedly and domestically whenever the faintest vestige of a camera-man hove above the horizon, Hugo felt a slight change come creeping across his feelings. It is impossible to determine what was the primal cause of the change, whether it was a normal reaction from an extreme point of view, or whether it was a visit to the Rubens Exhibition at Burlington House, or whether it was a soirée at a Ladies' Club given to the film-actors by a number of Lady Novelists. Whatever the cause, on the fifth day of stardom the pedestal began to wane in stature and in brightness. The vision before Hugo's eyes of the honest, jolly countenance of the Reverend Eustace Smith began to grow dim and blurred and to give way before the black, pointed beard and dark roguish eyes of M. Forgeron, child of the sunny vineyard, and of the pale grey mountains, and of the olive-woods, and of the shimmering, dusty plains of the South.

"After all," argued Hugo to himself that afternoon, as he handed a cup of tea to a Duchess on the lawn at Hurlingham, "why should Beauty alone be put on a pedestal? Why not Brains also? Or Sterling Worth of Character? or Extreme Wealth? or Extreme Old Age?" And, if it came to that, why should any of them? Looked at dispassionately the thing was absurd. Felida was a pretty girl, an exceedingly pretty girl. Indeed, definitely a regular rasper. But nothing more. Neither brain nor sterling worth of character. Wealth, perhaps, but certainly not extreme old age. Very well. He threw a macaroon absent-mindedly at the elderly unmarried daughter of an octogenarian marquis. While she was still gasping with delight, he had vanished a thousand miles deep into his meditations.

Felida was beautiful. But what of it? A curved cheek should be stroked, not celebrated in a couple of litanical verses. The first inch above the top of a silk stocking, the good Reverend René had once said, was worth the entire Epistle to the Thessalonians, Parts One and Two, and no one in their senses would allow any of this devotional, pedestal stuff to come between him and a kiss in that little hollow just above the collar-bone.

Pedestals be damned, and to hell with Uncle Eustace, thought Hugo, at five minutes past eleven that night, as he put on his orange-silk dressing-gown over his black-and-scarlet hussar pyjamas, and swung himself in one pantherine bound from his balcony to Felida's.

Her window was open and a light was shining inside. Hugo tapped gently. Nothing happened. He tapped again, louder, and whispered, "Felida."

"Come in, darling," the actress whispered back and the light went out.

Hugo stepped lightly over the sill. The room was full of heavy intoxicating perfumes that brought back the memory of nights in the moist tropical jungle with the Hunter's Moon blazing in the wilderness of the sky, and the air drowsy with the honey-sweet scents of the earth. Hugo took a deep breath, and the blood rushed to his temples and beat the little hammer-pulses violently. From the darkness came a faint rustle of silk and a whispered, "Darling."

He moved softly forwards towards the whisper, peering into the shadows. So powerfully were the scents, and the night, and the glamour of exquisite romantic moments working upon his excited imagination that he half believed he could see a white shimmer, like a far-off cloud, or a glimpse of pale

Madonna lilies, or a starlit drift of snow, in the corner of the room. But he could see nothing and he guided himself by the gentle sound of breathing.

Suddenly he stopped and the breathing stopped. For there came, very distinctly in that silence, the sharp sound of another tap on the window. Then Felida said in a hoarse whisper that began with a sort of gasp, "Who's there?"

"It's me, darling," was the whispered reply in a deep voice.

"Then who the hell?" cried Felida, switching on the light, and the three protagonists in the triangle blinked at each other in the sudden glare. The newcomer was the middle-aged Duke who had danced with such verve at Chez Savonarola and Chez Ronsard. He was wearing a dinner-jacket and top-hat, and there was a broad smear of grime across his shirt-front. Felida was sitting on the edge of her bed. She was wearing a very small black crêpe-de-chine chemise, and very long black silk stockings, and a pair of scarlet, high-heeled slippers. She, alone of the three, was completely at her ease. She was puzzled, it is true, and angry, but not in the least embarrassed. The Duke, on the other hand, stood and feebly goggled at Hugo. His knees sagged and his collar seemed uncomfortable, and he was perspiring freely. He had no eyes for the entrancing vision on the edge of the bed, a fact that Felida, who was nothing if not observant of the ways of lovers, instantly spotted.

Hugo, for his part, went through a remarkable number of different emotions in a very short space of time. Surprise at the unexpected entry of a senior

member of the British aristocracy, indignation at the
intrusion, black despair at the realization that the
whispered welcome had not been for him, delight
at the smear across the infernal fellow's shirt, entrancement at Felida's delicious appearance, fear of
Felida's tongue, and a sense of vast superiority over
this damned fellow who was so obviously quaking
with terror, all ran in and out of Hugo's head.

"What the hell!" barked Felida, opening the
engagement briskly. The Duke embarked upon a
desperate story.

"I say, Mrs. Seeley, I say, Seeley," he blurted out,
"I'm most damnably sorry. I really am most damnably
sorry. Can't think how I made such a stupid mistake. Wrong window. To tell you the truth it was
the wrong window. I thought it was my window,
do you see, and it turns out to be your window,
and so you see I made a mistake and it wasn't my
window at all, do you see, if you see what I mean."
He pulled out a silk handkerchief and mopped his
brow.

"Cheese!" replied Felida, using her favourite expression. But the Duke was not concerned with her
at the moment. It was the injured husband, or at any
rate almost-injured husband, that he was anxious
about. For the Duke, although the representative of a
very old and very distinguished family, was not so
totally devoid of brains as might have been supposed,
and he was fully alive to the huge importance that
his appearance as a co-respondent would lend to any
scheme for advertising La Caliente in the journals
of the world. Nor were these the sort of people who

could be bought off with a small annuity. They were already vastly rich, and a ducal co-respondent would make them vastly richer. The essential thing was to smooth down the husband, and as quickly as possible.

The Duke continued his smoothing.

"The windows are so confoundedly alike, you see, if you follow me," he went on, gaining a little confidence.

Hugo suddenly became affable. The game was in his hands.

"My dear Duke," he said cordially, "I quite understand. The sort of mistake that anyone might make quite naturally."

An immense wave of relief surged over the Duke's face. He had bluffed the fellow, after all. For a moment he had been doubtful. The dashed thing seemed to hang in the balance. But it was all right. He had won through.

"There remains nothing for me to do," he observed with a return of all his self-possession and courtesy, "but to apologize once more and take my departure."

"Hey!" cried Felida. The Duke stopped and shuffled awkwardly. There was a pause.

Then "You clear out," cried Felida to Hugo.

"No—I say—er—I mean," began the Duke miserably.

Hugo was beginning to enjoy himself.

"Do you wish to speak to the Duke, my precious?" he asked with a husbandly concern which deserved more than the blistering flash of blue lightning that it got.

"I'm afraid I'm in rather a hurry," said the Duke, edging towards the door.

Felida swallowed hard. The circumstances were new to her.

"Are you going?" she said in a tone that implied that if he did go, she would sock him one on the base of the skull with a length of gas-piping.

"Mustn't keep you good folks up all night," replied the Duke, taking a big risk. "Would you escort me as far as the corridor, my dear Seeley?" he went on.

Felida hesitated, her slim fingers quivering over a heavy inkpot of silver and dark Styrian jade. Never, since the first kiss from the junior partner behind the addressograph, had a man treated her like this. Why, the Duke had not so much as glanced at her. On the other hand, a brawl was desperately bad publicity, especially with an English peer.

With a deep sigh, she drew back her hand from the inkpot, smiled sweetly, and murmured, "Good-night, Duke. See you again sometime."

Without a single backward glance, the Duke almost ran out of the room. Hugo convoyed him as far as the sentries in the corridor, and then went back. Felida had not moved, except that she had lit a cigarette.

"Well?" she said, looking at him thoughtfully under her etched eyebrows.

Hugo coughed. "Perhaps you are wondering," he said, "just what it is all about."

"No," replied Felida.

"In that case," went on Hugo diffidently, "perhaps you would like me to explain."

"No," said Felida.

"You see," said Hugo, "I was a bit bored." This statement was received in silence.

"And I felt that, after all, we are married, so to speak, as you might say, and that sort of thing."

Hugo felt that he was on the wrong lines. This sort of stuff was carrying him nowhere. Changing his style, he threw himself on the ground at Felida's feet and poured out an eloquent flood of ardent wooing. He used all M. Forgeron's adjectives and phrases. He whispered and pleaded and vibrated. Seldom, if ever, had Felida been besieged so beautifully and so romantically. Poetry and loveliness and imagery lapped on the cool night air like water on a beach. The whole bright room softened, and the electric light silvered, and the scent of July roses and honeysuckle eddied among the perfumes of Arabia. It was like an enchanted cave of Merlin, or a dark forest of Hans Andersen—the handsome lover in hussar-pyjamas kneeling at the feet of the gold and white and silken Princess.

At last Hugo paused and laid his burning cheek upon the black silk knees, and it was the turn of the Princess.

She shook her head. "Boy," she said, "I'm a good girl. I never slept with a man in all my life except when it was important to my career as an artist. I've never gone off the rails for the fun of going off the rails. That would be downright wicked, and I'm not going to do it."

"But, Felida——" Hugo began. She interrupted at once.

"No, sir. I'm not a loose woman, and I'm not going to be turned into a loose woman." She rose and walked in as stately a fashion as her costume would permit to the door and held it open. "I've never been so insulted in my life," she went on. "Treated as if I was a common woman. Not even Michael has ever descended to making improper advances to me, treacherous bastard of a husband though he is. Try to remember, young man, for the rest of our trip in Europe, that you are acting as my husband, and no more monkey-business. Do you get me?"

"Not quite," murmured Hugo, who was quite dazed.

"Then do you get this?" the golden Aphrodite replied, swinging a fearful clip with the palm of her hand on to Hugo's left ear.

The next moment Hugo found himself, with his head buzzing like a telegraph-wire, out in the corridor. Mr. Dope Cokayne was standing in front of him, head on one side, looking excessively knowing.

CHAPTER VII

IT was with some diffidence that Hugo entered the big sitting-room next morning after breakfast. He was a little uncertain about the reception he was likely to get from Felida. He need not have worried. No one paid any attention to him except Mr. Cokayne, who was sitting on a window-sill in a carefree attitude, whistling. He nodded jauntily to Hugo and winked.

Mr. Dowley, Felida, and one of the three Directors were deep in conversation with a stranger. At least, Mr. Dowley and the Director were doing all the conversation. Felida was listening and the stranger only interjected an occasional monosyllable, or a noncommittal sound that might have been either approval, disapproval, or interrogation. The stranger was a smallish, thin man with a thin, brown, alert face, and eyes of unwavering blue that rested on the faces of each of the others in turn, scrutinizing, appraising, estimating. His clean-shaven lips were small and tightly shut, and his sharp nose was like an enquiring beak. His arms were folded across his chest, and he nodded from time to time.

"There's the proposition," Mr. Dowley was saying. "Choose your own day. Any time between twelve and two, and a thousand pounds."

The thin man nodded again and gazed unwinkingly at the bridge of Mr. Dowley's dark nose.

"You can do it, I suppose?" demanded Arthur Ed.

"Oh, I can do it," said the stranger in a quiet, easy voice. "I could make it the Serpentine if we got a really calm day."

"No, no, it might not come off in the Serpentine. We don't want a failure."

"No harm done," observed the stranger.

"Ridicule, my dear sir, ridicule," said the Director. "If it stuck in a tree, and had to be fetched down by the fire brigade everybody would laugh. We can't afford that. No, no, we must have a large margin."

"It's all one to me," said the man with a shrug. He addressed Felida. "You'll send the duplicate kit round, Madam."

Arthur Ed. answered for Felida. "It's all ready, Captain. It can be delivered at your flat whenever you like."

"What's wrong with to-day?" asked the captain. "Couldn't be better. Glass high. Dead calm."

"My dear chap," protested Mr. Dowley, "I haven't got any ballyhoo out yet. Give us a chance. To-morrow's the very earliest. I can get the racket going by then."

"All right," replied the captain indifferently. "You let me know when you're ready and I'll let you know when I am. Let's look at the kit," he added.

Mr. Dowley lugged out a pile of cardboard-boxes from a corner and began to open them. Out of the first he produced two identical pairs of pale-green leather breeches, laced at the knee with silver laces and ready to be supported with a broad white silk sash with neat green tassels to match.

"Good God!" exclaimed the captain, shaken for the first time out of his tranquillity, and going a little pale under his tan.

"Aren't they sweet?" murmured Felida.

"No," replied the captain.

From another box Arthur Ed. took two identical leather jackets, of a soft Vermeer yellow, with ermine collar and cuffs, and fastened up the front with silver "zippers."

From the third, a pair of white silk blouses with F. C. embroidered in diamonds near the left shoulder. From a fourth two pale-green leather helmets with white satin ear-flaps; from a fifth two pale-green pairs of goggles; from a sixth two pairs of white canvas leggings, and from a seventh one pair of pale-green gauntlets with fringes of seed pearls, and from an eighth one pair of pale-green shoes.

"There you are, captain," said Arthur Ed. proudly. "You'll have to run across to get fitted for the gloves and shoes yourself. All the rest's here."

The captain regarded the revolting collection of garments with a humorous look of resignation. "I shall earn my thousand quid," he observed. "All the nancy-boys in town will be after me." He turned and noticed Hugo for the first time.

"This, I suppose, is the gentleman," he said with a slight bow.

The Director waved a couple of suave white hands. "Mr. Michael Seeley, Captain O'Sullivan. The captain is kindly going to help us in a little publicity venture, Mr. Seeley, from which we hope great things."

Hugo bowed politely.

"In connection with your forthcoming production, Mr. Seeley," went on the Director. "I refer, of course, to the Death-Watch Vampire."

It was the first Hugo had heard of this rather alarming creature, but he bowed again as if he was perfectly *au courant* with affairs.

Captain O'Sullivan, in the meantime, was standing in front of Hugo, gazing at him with the same steady dispassionate calm which appeared to be habitual with him. "If you jump when I say jump," he remarked at last, "you can't go wrong. Always provided that it opens," he added drily.

Hugo blinked.

"And it's seven to four on these modern ones opening," went on the captain. "I remember the days when it was eleven to two against."

"I'll take seven to four in quids, Paddy," exclaimed Mr. Cokayne cheerfully from the window.

"You won't get 'em," was the imperturbable reply. The dark Director scowled at the secretary.

"If that's all," said Captain O'Sullivan, "I'll be getting along. You aren't sick by the way, are you, Mr. Seeley?"

"Sick?" said Hugo puzzled. "No, thank you. I'm in the best of health."

"I mean in an aeroplane."

"I've never——" began Hugo, but Arthur Ed. clipped in vigorously, "Mr. Seeley is never sick in a plane."

"That's all right," said Captain O'Sullivan, nodding. "So long, all," and he went out.

"What—er—I mean, what is it all about?" asked Hugo. The Director stared at him.

"Haven't you been told?" he asked in surprise.

"Why, sure I told you, Mr. Seeley," exclaimed Mr. Dowley.

"Told me what?"

"There now. Gosh darn me if I haven't been so busy that I forgot to tell Mr. Seeley about it." He laughed a little nervously, Hugo thought, and then he pulled out a toothpick and starting a Herculanean excavation with a rather ostentatious assumption of carelessness.

"It's simply part of our September publicity appropriation," explained the Director, and he too spoke with an offhandedness that was painfully overdone. "Almost routine as you might say. That's all."

There was an awkward pause and then Hugo asked, "Do I come into it?"

Felida took up the running swiftly. "Only as an incidental. It's my show. You're only walking on."

Hugo breathed a sigh of relief. He had been afraid for a moment that the constraint in their manner meant that they were planning to thrust him into some particularly glaring limelight. So long as he was allowed to lurk about in the background in a walking-on part, things would not be so bad. The more Felida bossed the show, the better for all of them. And she did not seem to show any resentment at the unfortunate incidents of the previous night. He smiled genially at the party. "I don't mind being a super. What do I have to do?"

"Well, it's like this," said Arthur Ed. "Felida's going to take an aeroplane——"

"Those are my flying-clothes," said Felida, purring over the pale-green breeches with the sound of a steel saw that has lost a few teeth.

"And she's going to fly it one day during the rush-hour, when everyone is out in the streets."

"I see," said Hugo. "And if I may say so, Felida——"

"Miss Caliente to you," snapped his wife. "Who do you think you are? A scenarist, eh?"

"Sorry," said Hugo. "I was only going to congratulate you on your courage."

"And it's going to be on a very still day," went on the Director smoothly, "so that she can make smoke-rings from the exhaust, one above the other, if you see what I mean. Do you follow me?"

"Yes, I follow." said Hugo brightly. "You mean one smoke-ring above the other."

"That's it. That's the idea. I thought you'd tumble to it," cried Arthur Ed., rubbing his hands together enthusiastically. "There's nothing like smoke-rings to attract attention."

"How clever of Felida to be able to do it," exclaimed Hugo, filled with an immense admiration for the practical gifts of this wisp of a girl.

"Oh, well," said Arthur Ed., "Felida won't actually do the flying, of course. That would be just a waste of time and energy. She makes the speech to the crowd from the top of the car down at Hendon, and smiles and kisses a few babies and shows off her legs in those pants, and then she goes into the hangar, and this captain gink comes out with the plane, wearing the other green pants and goggles. And everyone thinks it's Felida. Do you get me?"

"And it's the captain who makes the smoke-rings?"

"That's it."

"One above the other?"

"You've said it. One above the other."

"And I give him a kiss when he comes down, I suppose," said Hugo with a gay laugh.

"Not exactly," said Mr. Dowley, with a sudden return to his nervous manner. "You see, you jump down with a parachute through the smoke-rings into the Welsh Harp."

The room buzzed and roared round Hugo. He felt faint and giddy. Drops of perspiration rolled down on to his eyelids. He clutched at the table and gaped from one face to another.

"There, there," said the Director soothingly. "There'll be a boat to pick you up, won't there, Mr. Dowley?"

"Several boats."

"Several boats," went on the Director. "There's really not the slightest chance of any mishap. You'll be just as safe as if you were sitting in your armchair by the fire."

"Safer," averred Art.

"Safer, in fact," said the Director a little un-certainly.

"I won't do it," gasped Hugo. "I can't do it. I refuse."

"Oh no," said Art. "You're under contract."

"It will probably take place to-morrow," said the Director, glancing at his watch. "Perhaps you would get on with the newspaper story, Mr. Dowley. The sooner it goes out the better," and he picked up his beautiful silk hat, kissed Felida's fingers, bowed to Hugo, ignored Mr. Cokayne, and went out.

Hugo sat down on the sofa and buried his face in his hands.

"Hey, you!" cried Mr. Dowley to the secretary, "take this down."

"Mr. Cokayne to you, please, Artie," replied the secretary pleasantly, pulling out a note-book.

"Film-king's perilous death-leap," dictated Mr. Dowley with gusto.

Hugo shuddered.

"Takes life in hands," went on the heavy, glutinous voice. "Will 'chute spread?"

Hugo groaned. He longed for the quiet lagoons of Kalataheira, and the days when he was young, and the glow of far-seen volcanoes and the gentle voices of his three dear uncles. Why, oh why, had he ever left that enchanted isle, to come and dwell among maniacs who wanted to throw him out of aeroplanes into reservoirs? If he had known that men like Mr. Dowley existed, no power on earth would have got him aboard the rescuing yacht, not even a vision of Felida in chemise and stockings. Even Uncle René would have hesitated, Hugo felt, at pursuing the vision if he knew that the route lay via a lot of smoke-rings and that large sheet of water known as the Welsh Harp. What a vast deal, Hugo reflected miserably, the world must have changed since the days when the three missionaries had last visited civilization! Talking-films and aeroplanes would stagger Uncle Hans all right. Uncle René had no conception of the development in the manufacture of artificial silk. Uncle Eustace would never believe that a Cambridgeshire man called Hobbs had already made more centuries than the Doctor himself. Yes, the world was a very different sort of place from what he had expected. And to-morrow he had to jump from an aeroplane—

The lubricatory voice rolled on, "Mr. Seeley has been warned of the dangers of this leap . . . experts are quoting seven to one as a reasonable chance against . . . 'what Felida and I can do,' said Mr. Seeley to me with his D'Artagnan smile . . . the spirit of England . . . Empire . . . Eton . . . sun never sets . . . heritage . . . Rupert of Hentzau . . . I trust Felida . . . Old Contemptibles . . . Eton——" the phrases oiled themselves round the room.

Hugo felt sick. He was in the maw of some fearful machine that had scooped him off a liner near the thirtieth degree of longitude, and would not let him go until it had hoisted him a mile or two into the heavens and then dropped him into a pond.

He looked round wildly. The door was open. Mr. Dowley's rounded back was towards him. Felida, inexpressibly saucy in the pale-green leather breeches, was preening herself in a distant mirror. Dope Cokayne lay deep in an armchair with his feet on the mantelpiece, taking down the dictation. Nobody was paying the slightest attention to him.

Hugo got up and crept stealthily towards the door.

He slipped through into the ante-room. Still there was no sound. He grabbed a hat and stick at random, shoved an embroidered hand-bag into his pocket on the chance that it contained some money, opened the outer door and made a bolt for it. But he had forgotten the sentries.

Within twenty seconds he had been collared, low and expertly, by the two men. They were a couple of Rugby Football Internationals who were earning a precarious income by taking posts as chuckers-out or chuckers-in, quite impartially. But, fortunately, they were nice young gentlemen (for it is a notorious fact that if you play football with an egg-shaped ball under a code of rules that allows you to punch your adversary under the jaw, you are automatically a gentleman; whereas if you play with a round ball, and do not punch your adversary under the jaw, you are automatically a cad. Hugo, of course, was well acquainted with this somewhat peculiar standard of gentility, as the Reverend Eustace had invariably worn steel tips to his football-boots in the days when he was leading the English pack, and he had explained the whole system to him. Monsieur René and Herr Schmidt, on the other hand, had left their native shores for ever a long time before the Teutonic frenzy for Soccer had made Austria predominant in the one game and the Gallic frenzy for breaking the rules of Rugger had made France universally shunned in the other).

The two young gentlemen in the passage, then, were extremely civil. One of them went even so far as to refrain from kicking the prostrate Hugo smartly in the ribs, a playful little custom that had several times brought him into sharp conflict with narrow-minded referees, while the other stopped sitting on Hugo's head in quite a short time. They smoothed his hair a little, and, playing their comparatively unusual role of chuckers-in to perfection, decanted him back into the sitting-room.

No one even looked at him as he tottered in, pale, dishevelled, panting, and humiliated. By this time Art. Ed. was speaking on the telephone. "Yes, sixteen long ermine," he was saying, "and four waist-length jackets of the same costly fur. Twenty-one chinchilla mantles, each more luxurious and expensive than the rest. Thirty-eight black foxes nestling round mink capes. What? What? No, I never said anything about old foxes wrestling round the minx. Whatcha hell do you take me for? Hey, you! Get this. Making a total of sixty-one fur coats, coatees, cloaks, and mantles, all supreme examples of the fur-merchants' art."

He rang off and went on with his dictation to Mr. Cokayne. Hugo, sitting in an appalled daze on the sofa, heard the words, coming dimly through a haze of horror, "orchidaceous dame . . . sultry-hipped . . . swivel-hipped . . . soft lush blonderie . . . curve-conscious lady of the lureful lips and alabastrine neck . . . winsome fragrance . . . like Helen of—of——" Mr. Dowley broke off for a moment and wrinkled his brow in puzzlement.

"Hey, Dope," he cried at length. "What was the name of that hot-ziggety-dam show that Charles B. Cochran put on, about a cutie called Helen of some location or other?"

"*Helen of Huddersfield?*" suggested Mr. Cokayne, with a demoniac gleam in his dark eyes.

"Say, boy," replied Mr. Dowley admiringly, "you just know everything," and he went on with his dictation, "like Helen of Huddersfield she has known what it is to watch her ship of matrimony dissolve like a house of cards about her ears, her shell-pink ears," he added after a moment's thought, "but she bravely shot another arrow into the air on the chance of making another home-run. And Miss Caliente, World's Adored, has succeeded. For her love-arrow ensnared Mr. Michael Seeley, and lassoed him properly so that now the fair shooter and the handsome shootee are literally a pair of veritable turtle-doves."

"No such word as shootee," said Mr. Cokayne briefly.

"Aw! What the hell," replied Art. "Whooper— whoopee. Shooter—shootee. I know these things. Multigraph a hundred copies——"

"And get them to the Press," Mr. Cokayne completed the sentence for him.

"Any more from you——" began Mr. Dowley crossly.

"And I'm fired. I know," Mr. Cokayne chipped in again. "You just try it."

"What do you mean?" asked the manager, starting a little.

"Oh, just this and that," replied the secretary in an off-hand way. "Shall I get on with my typing now?"

All this Hugo listened to in a dream. Somehow the

weird expressions, and the phrases, and the words, which he had never once heard Uncle Eustace use, added to the unearthly feeling of nightmare in which he was groping.

"If this is civilization and progress and culture," he thought with a groan, "give me savagery in Kala-taheira. At least there were no madmen there. And here everyone is obviously stark, staring mad."

At half-past twelve that morning a young gentle-man called the Marquess of Kilkenny arrived to take Hugo out to lunch at a London Club. It was the first he had heard of the Marquess of Kilkenny, and the first he had heard of the lunch-party at the Club, but he was delighted at the prospect of getting out unescorted. His hopes of making an escape were, however, quickly damped. For Mr. Dowley, while handing him into his astrakhan fur-coat—it was mid-summer but Art. insisted upon astrakhan—and giving him his gold-tipped malacca—they were going to drive to the Club in a Daimler but Art. insisted upon a gold-tipped malacca—said casually, "No funny stuff, now. Sir Kilkenny is one of our squad. Packing your gas-piping, Sir Kilkenny?" he went on, turning to the young peer.

"Yes, sir, and the stuffed eel-skin," replied the Marquess deferentially. Poor Marquess! He had to be deferential, for he depended entirely for his income on such work as this. His grandfather, the sixth mar-quess, had been under the impression that gold could profitably be extracted from a mine that lay three hundred miles from the sea in the hinterland of

British Guiana, and his impression had turned out to be incorrect. The seventh marquess, inheriting a much diminished patrimony, had put his entire shirt on a scheme for raising the Tobermory galleon, that fabled treasure-ship of the Spanish Armada, by building a concrete dam across the bay and pumping out the water. The managing director of the scheme was a dark and subtle Caledonian who emigrated with the funds of the Company to Ecuador, a country which is not very particular about the enforcement of extradition treaties, especially when a rich man is involved. A poor man might be in some danger of eviction, but a rich one is perfectly safe, at least until he has spent all his money in Ecuador. So the Armada Salvage Company was left with no assets except three brass culverins which the Caledonian had alleged that he himself had fished up in no time from the sandy depths of Tobermory Bay, and which subsequently turned out to have been made in Birmingham for export to the Touaregs and other loyal tribes of Morocco for the purpose of firing salutes in honour of the late Marshal Lyautey.

The present holder of the marquisate, then, was left with nothing at all except an education at Harrow and sixteen cocktail-shakers. But the latter were useless without the alcohol, and the former was useless with or without alcohol, and so the young man set to work to earn a living. It is greatly to his credit that during the three years that had elapsed between his father's death and his meeting with Hugo, Lord Kilkenny had declined offers of employment at Cannes, Juan-les-Pins, Antibes, Nice, Monte Carlo, Hyères, and San

Remo, with all expenses paid and a weekly honorarium, in return for comparatively small services, from
no fewer than sixty-seven wealthy dowagers. But his
lordship rejected this life of languorous ease and preferred to earn a living in the manner of the Duchess
of Plaza-Toro, who sang that she presented any lady—

> Whose conduct is shady
> Or smacking of doubtful propriety ;
> When Virtue would quash her
> I take and whitewash her
> And launch her in first-rate society.

And when Mr. Dowley instructed Dope Cokayne
to produce a young man who would conduct Mr.
Michael Seeley to such an exclusively masculine
institution as Wace's Club, Dope went straight to
Lord Kilkenny. In consequence, at 12.45 on that
bright midsummer day Hugo found himself bowling
down St. James's Street with his new acquaintance,
and was compelled to admit to himself that he was
looking forward to the experience of actually entering
that world-famous institution—a London Club. For,
of course, Hugo knew all about them. Many and
many a time he had listened to Uncle Eustace trying
to explain to Uncle René that no gentleman ever
uttered a lady's name in the smoke-room of a Club
("Then of what else do you speak?" had always been
Uncle René's bewildered counter), that no gentleman ever uttered a syllable in the Club library,
and that the most terrible crime that an Englishman
could commit—worse than sneering at the Union
Jack, worse than matricide, worse even than lifting
a hand to strike a woman or a foot to kick a horse—

was the unforgivable offence of offering money to a Club servant. "Why, it would be like—it would be like"—said Uncle Eustace on one occasion, groping round in his mind for a crime of parallel enormity— "it would be like a Club servant divulging the address of a member to a third party."

"Would the servant not divulge the address," asked Uncle René, "if the third party wished to inform the member that his wife had eloped with another member?"

"The occasion would not arise," Eustace had replied with quiet dignity. "If a member of a Club wished to elope with a fellow-member's wife, a most improbable contingency, he would first of all resign his membership."

"Ah!" René had mused, shaking his head. "Truly the two races are very different. I once—in my student days I need hardly add—belonged to a Club in the Boul' Miche to which members were forbidden to bring their mistresses unless they were the wives of other members."

There are three main groups of Clubs in the West End of London (and this is the first occasion in the long and illustrious record of British literature that a statement of that kind has not been attended by a witty and highly original reference to All Gaul). The names in each group of Clubs are almost identical with each other, and the utmost confusion is caused by this singular arrangement.

There is, firstly, the Academic Group, consisting of the Senior Leeds University, and the Junior Ditto;

the Senior Sheffield University, and the Junior
Ditto. That makes four. But is that all? By no means.
There is the Senior Leeds and Sheffield, and the
Junior Leeds and Sheffield. There is the Old University Club, and the Combined Universities Club,
and the University Club, and the Union of Universities Club. In the same way, in the second group, the
belligerent group, the changes are rung between the
Infantry and the Marines, and occasionally, as in
the Senior and Junior Mounted Services, between the
Cavalry and the Marines. All this is very confusing
for a stranger who wishes to master this queer phase
of Life in England. Nothing annoys the proud, be-
medalled hall-porter, in his little glass porter-hutch
at the Hellenic Annexe of the Classical University,
half so much as the shy and tentative enquiry,
"Are these the premises of the Junior Mechanized
Hussars?"

And the third group is made up of Clubs that have
survived from the Regency days. Wace's, Black's,
River's, Esmond's, they all breathe a faint atmosphere of the curricle and the tiger, the Brighton road,
the building of Regent Street, the stucco frontage of
Nash's Carlton House Terrace, the Corinthian, the
link-boy, Bath's Royal Crescent, the Castle Inn at
Marlborough, and the portly figure of the First Gentleman of Europe. There is a scent of old snuff about the
rooms, and a rattle of ghostly dice can almost be
heard, and a whisper of ghostly voices repeating over
and over again, "Boney ought to be shot. Boney
ought to be shot," and Lord Steyne drives past in his
carriage, and Mohun and the Duke are fighting their

duel in Hyde Park, and Bully Macartney is lurking
in the shadows. They are a relic of a dying oligarchy
which once stood alone against Europe, confident in
itself as human beings have never been confident
since that golden age, and secure in the knowledge
that the armed forces of a united Europe could never
prevail against them, for the simple reason that the
fellows weren't gentlemen. It was to one of these
historic survivals that Lord Kilkenny was taking
Hugo for lunch, and Hugo gazed round him with
eager interest. Everything was almost exactly as he
had pictured it. At the door the porter sat in his
glass hutch, checking off the names of the members
as they came in, his chest resplendent with medals
that included Sir Garnet Wolseley's campaign in
Ashantee, the epic march of Bobs Bahadur from
Cabul to Candahar, and even the invasion of Abys-
sinia by Lord Napier of Magdala. (In the Reverend
Eustace's day, of course, the medals had been the
Mutiny, Crimea, Hugh Gough's victory at Chillian-
walla, and the early affairs in the Khyber.) While
Hugo was admiring this functionary, another, apparently about six years of age and dressed entirely in
round brass buttons, took his hat and stick, and tried
gallantly but ineffectually to help him out of his
astrakhan coat. Then his lordship, nodding here and
there to acquaintances and receiving answering nods
from some and a cold, frog-like stare from seven
lieutenant-generals, who were agreeing that Gandhi
ought to be shot, led the way into the dining-room.
    Conversation at the luncheon-table was a little
awkward, for his lordship naturally assumed that

Hugo had been at Eton at about the same time that he himself had been at Harrow, and enquired after a prodigious number of supposedly mutual acquaintances. After Hugo had sulkily denied all knowledge of any of them, young Kilkenny tactfully changed the subject with the mental note that success certainly made some people into crashing snobs, and he added the second mental note that, after all, anything could be expected of an Old Etonian.

In the smoking-room afterwards an unfortunate incident took place. For young Kilkenny met a youthful acquaintance and casually observed to him that he had seen his sister in the Row that morning. Hugo winced and flushed up to the roots of his hair. He was plunged into an agony of fluster and apprehension. To be the guest of a man who could commit this blackest of solecisms was bad enough. But to have to stand by and watch two young men of high social position fighting with bare fists in the smoking-room of a West-End Club, was a terrible situation to be in! For of course a fight was inevitable. Young Kilkenny knew the way of the world quite well enough to understand what he had done. For some reason or other, he had flung this hideous insult at the other with the utmost deliberation and a complete consciousness of its implications and its consequences. If it had happened in his own Club Hugo would have known how to behave. Uncle Eustace had seen to that. "My Lord," he would have begun with an emphatic dignity, "such an action is unworthy of your rank and station. I must ask you to tender your apologies to this gentleman," and, with the final addition, after an impressive pause, of the word "immediately," the matter would have been regularized. But as a guest, he knew that he had no status, and that he had neither the right nor the duty to interfere. He backed, therefore, into a corner like a timid hare, and waited for the storm to burst.

Nothing happened. The youth, instead of squaring up to Kilkenny, simply nodded and replied, "She was riding with Daphne Pembleham. Dashed good figure for jodpores Daphne's got, hasn't she?"

"Yes," replied the Marquess, "and you can't say that about all of them."

"You cannot," agreed the other warmly.

Hugo, hardly able to believe his ears, came blinking out of his corner. Truly the world was a very strange place. But he had little time for reflection, for already his host and jailer was looking at his watch and exclaiming, "Come on, Seeley. Time we were getting back. Mr. Dowley will be furious if we're late, and I can't run the risk of that."

They went out, the Marquess being ostentatiously cut by the lieutenant-generals, now eleven in number —who were damned if they knew what the world was coming to, what with damned fellows bringing actor cads into Wace's, damn their eyes.

CHAPTER VIII

WHEN Hugo returned to the Ritz after his compulsory visit to Wace's, he was justified in imagining that he was finished with London club-life, at least for the day. His gloom and general sulkiness were increased, therefore, by Mr. Cokayne's first words of greeting as he was tactfully edged into the sitting-room by the Rugby-players.

"The Parnassus at eight. Black tie. Speech."

"What are you talking about?" asked Hugo wearily.

"Your engagements. Message from Oily Artie. You've got to dine and make a speech at the Ladies' Parnassus Club to-night. Subject—Domestic Happiness. Is it compatible with a Career?"

"I won't," said Hugo doggedly.

"Just as you like," said Dope pleasantly. "Only I think I would if I were you."

"Why? Mr. Dowley can't force me to make a speech if I don't want to."

Mr. Cokayne tapped his nose. "I'm not thinking of the Joy of Shiraz. You needn't be afraid of him. I can arrange that for you—on terms, of course. No, it's the ladies of the Parnassus Club that you've got to be afraid of."

"Afraid of the ladies . . ." faltered Hugo, his spirits falling even lower than before.

"You bet your life," replied Dope cheerfully. "You don't know what a Ladies' Club is like."

"Nonsense," replied Hugo with some spirit. "I know all about Clubs. I've just been lunching at Wace's."

"Poor child," replied Dope sympathetically. "Do you really believe that a Ladies' Club is like an ordinary club? Why, the members are demons in feminine shape. Mind you, I have nothing against the feminine shape. *Au contraire.* But when the said shape is occupied by a fiend of hell, then the result is a club-woman, and I start padding for the emergency-exit. If they get the notion into their heads that they want you to make a speech, the wisest thing you can do is to make a speech. But of course you must do just as you like. But don't say you weren't warned." And he started pounding away on his typewriter.

Hugo, painfully reminded of the brief conversation between the two young aristocrat cads on the subject of the fitness for jodpores of Miss Pembleham's figure and legs, was profoundly distressed at the general tone of Mr. Cokayne's statement, and even more profoundly alarmed at the prospect of meeting these fiends of hell in feminine shape and making a speech to them.

At last he said timidly, "I say, Mr. Cokayne——"

"Call me Dope," interrupted the secretary.

"Well—er—Dope, what shall I say in my speech?"

"Oh, don't you worry about that," answered Cokayne. "I'm composing the speech for you now.

Just listen to this. 'One glance into the deep, lustrous eyes of my adored Felida is worth more to me than all the careers in the world.' What about that? Hot. Eh?"

Hugo sprang up. "But I can't say that," he exclaimed.

"Why not?" enquired Dope in surprise. "Grand stuff. Make a horse cry. What more do you want?"

"But it's—it's sloppy," pleaded Hugo, "and it's untrue as well."

"Come, come, Mr. Seeley," said the secretary sternly. "None of your unchivalrous stuff here, if you please. If you don't adore Mrs. Seeley, you ought to. Far be it from me to come between man and wife—at least"—he coughed self-consciously—"when I say far, I mean fairly far, and of course the circumstances would have to be exceptional. But I have the strictest instructions from Artie that any tendency towards marital infidelity on your part—I am speaking, of course, solely about your behaviour in public—is to be severely dealt with. In private you can do what you like. But in public you worship the ground her dainty little feet walk upon, and don't you jolly well forget it, and you'll be saying so in those very words to-night at the Parnassus. And if you don't believe me just take a look at your speech and see for yourself," and he shoved a sheet of typescript across to Hugo.

"Dope," said Hugo earnestly, "what did you mean just now when you said that I needn't be afraid of Mr. Dowley and that you could fix it for me?"

Mr. Cokayne looked at him narrowly. "I was forgetting," he said. "You haven't got any money, have you?"

"I've got fifty packing-cases full of gold-dust and ambergris and pearls," replied Hugo with a sigh, "but they've confiscated them."

"What do you suppose they're worth?" enquired Mr. Cokayne, with a dark gleam in his eye.

"I haven't been able to get the market quotation for the pearls and ambergris," replied Hugo bitterly. "I've been too busy playing this tomfool farce of pretending to be this damfool Michael Seeley. But with gold at a hundred and thirty-three shillings an ounce, the gold-dust is worth £82,340 and a few shillings."

Cokayne looked at him without even so much as a blink.   "So you're not Michael Seeley, are you?" he asked slowly.

"No."

"Then if it is not an awkward question," went on Mr. Cokayne, "who the devil are you?"

Hugo had a sudden wild impulse to tell the whole story to the young secretary. Single-handed against Mr. Dowley's inexorable machine, Hugo was helpless. But with an ally of Mr. Cokayne's calibre and of his avowed lack of any sort of scruple, Hugo's chances of escape would be greatly increased. With a great rush of words he acted on the impulse, and poured out the whole story from the very beginning. Mr. Cokayne listened imperturbably. He did not betray either the astonishment or the elation which he felt. That the story was true he did not doubt for a moment. It was so ludicrously improbable that it was obviously true. No one would try to invent a

story like that. Nor indeed was the real Michael
Seeley the man to invent any story at all. Imagination was not Michael's strong point. Nor was the real
Michael Seeley the man to tell a cock-and-bull yarn
with the acting sufficiently skilful, sincere, and powerful to carry conviction. Acting was not Michael's
strong point either. Having mentally accepted the
story, Mr. Cokayne's active mind at once began to
explore the problem of how best to exploit the situation for his own financial betterment. There were a
good many different ways in which hard cash could
be extracted from the position, and it was important
to select the one which promised to be the most
lucrative. Caution was necessary, and a lot of hard
thinking. Mr. Cokayne decided to temporize.

"Not a word to a soul about this," he said at the
end of the story. "You're in a tough place—er—
Smith, and I'm the man to get you out of it. But I
must think the matter over very carefully before I
decide on a course of action."

"Be as quick as you can," pleaded Hugo. "I'm
getting desperate."

"Leave it to me," replied Dope with a demoniac wink.

The Literary Section of the Parnassus Club was a
truly formidable affair. Almost all the older members
of it appeared to be six feet in height, equipped with
hawk noses, and covered with jewellery. The younger
ones were smaller, but somehow they seemed to be
equally formidable with their excess of make-up,
their marked lack of clothing, and the knack, which
they all appeared to possess, of lowering the tempera-

ture of a room several degrees with a single glance. One and all they glanced at Hugo with a contemptuous iciness that chilled his bones. The elder, more Amazonian ladies were definitely inclined to be friendly, if indeed it is possible to imagine a cross between Hera, the wife of Zeus, and a sixteenth Duchess, being really friendly to anyone. But the younger ones were obviously hostile and the reason was soon forthcoming. Each of them had written immortal works, called novels, which had been rejected by the scenario department of the Colossophone Speakiegraph Film Corporation which retained the services of Mr. and Mrs. Seeley at such a stupendous cost, and each of the young and talented authors felt that somehow or other they ought to retaliate by emphasizing their contempt for the art of the cinema, and for the personalities, characters, and intellectual equipment of all who were connected with the scenario departments of the big film companies. It was rather unfair, partly because even Mr. Seeley himself had no sort of influence over the scenario director, and partly because the central theme of each of these highly successful, but nevertheless rejected, novels had been an elaborate description of the first seduction of each of the young authoresses, and the British Board of Film Censors is so absurdly small-minded. In fact it is not overstating the case to say that the unfortunate Hugo was being made the target for silent abuse that ought to have been levelled at those Government officials who draw the tenuous line between the decorous and libidinous in the world of celluloid.

Dinner, which consisted of clear soup, fried fillets of plaice, chicken rissoles and boiled potatoes, and fruit salad, washed down with a glass of sweet white wine, was over all too soon from the oratorical, not nearly soon enough from the gastronomical, point of view, and the speeches began.

Hugo clutched desperately at his typescript and rolled it and unrolled it nervously. From time to time he nerved himself to look at it, but the phrases which leapt to his eyes were of such a revoltingly sloppy mawkishness that he could not bear to read more than a line or two at a time. "The winsome fragrance of my wee Felida," was one that especially nauseated him, and another was "my bonnie little woman." Suddenly a wave of revolt swept over him, and he tore the document into fragments, and, when he was called upon to speak, began in confident, ringing tones, "Domestic happiness depends upon the woman who knows that Woman's place is in the kitchen." This challenging start was received with polite incredulity by the Amazons, with frank derision by the young novelists, and with sneers by the overtired and overworked waitresses.

Noting, with his quick sensitiveness, the somewhat unfortunate welcome which his epigram had received, Hugo promptly threw Uncle Hans Schmidt overboard, and added, "I should have said that Domestic Happiness depends entirely upon the man who knows that Woman's place is on a pedestal."

This time the reception was a considerable improvement, although the younger ladies yawned and fidgeted. The senior members lay back in their

chairs and purred gently, while the waitresses forgot
their tiredness and their long day's work, and were
thrilled into an eager attention. This was the stuff to
which they had been accustomed by the novelettes
and the serials. Although few of them had actually
been in the position of gazing down from a pedestal
upon mankind, nevertheless they felt instinctively
that the novelettes, the serials, and now this charming
young man were in the right of it. Hugo began to
gain a little confidence, and he was developing his
theme along the well-worn lines of Uncle Eustace's
famous lectures, when there was a scraping of chairs
and a murmur of voices and the young novelists rose
to their dainty feet and filed out, with their faces
drawn into an expression of blank boredom. Hugo,
disconcerted, missed the thread of what he was saying, flushed, and began to stammer. Then suddenly
he lost his temper. A wild rage surged up to his forehead and he struck the table a terrific blow with his
fist and bawled out, "Damn you all, a Woman's
place is in bed." The waitresses screamed, the Amazons got up majestically and the meeting dispersed
in hasty and embarrassed confusion, and the officials
of the Club rushed off to nobble the Press before
any news of the lamentable episode could reach Fleet
Street.

CHAPTER IX

NEXT morning there was a strong wind blowing, and a conference was called in the sitting-room the moment that Captain O'Sullivan reported for duty. The Irish flying-man was more laconic than ever, but from time to time Hugo fancied that he detected a swift wink being exchanged between the Captain and Mr. Cokayne. Mr. Dowley opened the discussion and a magnum of Roederer simultaneously. "Well, Captain," he said as the cork hit the ceiling, "what about it for to-day?"

"I won't do it," exclaimed Hugo violently. No one paid the slightest attention to him, except Felida, who glanced up from the pile of press-cuttings through which she was laboriously ploughing, and swept him from head to foot with a slow, contemptuous glance. It was the identical glance with which she had rejected the proposals of old Duke Maltravers-Darcy in the super-film *Oh! Honey-Sweetie*, and it had subsequently been imitated by stenographers, barmaids, and other maidens in the outlying suburbs of London and in the gayer of our provincial cities, when called upon to defend their honour against—to quote from *Oh! Honey-Sweetie*—the fate that is worse than death. The only effect it had upon Hugo was to make him crosser than ever. And the curious thing about his crossness was that for the first time it was directed against a new target. It was only a vague, semi-subconscious feeling, and Hugo found it difficult to believe that it really could be existent at all. It was almost impossible to realize that he was just a little bit vexed, not so much with the fantastic crew of lunatics who had kidnapped him and were compelling him to go through strange and terrifying antics, but with his three devoted uncles who had instructed him how to comport himself towards women. For if ever a pupil had followed the precepts of his teachers, it was Hugo in his endeavours to placate Felida. He had worshipped her, and she had ignored him. He had tried to restore her to her rightful place among the pots and pans, and she had cursed him in good, set terms, in good, set, Kennington terms. And when he had tried to make love to her, she had clipped him across the ear and thrown him out. It was all exceedingly puzzling, and Hugo began to wonder whether his uncles had not let him down rather seriously. At the end of all his patient devotion to the three separate Theories of Life, the only result was the famous Duke-Maltravers-Darcy stare of contempt. Hugo tried desperately hard to put these disloyal thoughts out of his head, but the more he considered Felida's behaviour, the more persistently did the disloyal thoughts come back.

But there was no time for further reflections, for the conversation in the room was proceeding as if he did not exist.

"It could be done to-day," said the Irish captain.

"But more dangerous. I'd need two hundred more."

"Dollars?" asked Dowley with a hopeful note in his voice that Dope Cokayne instantly detected.

"Pounds," said Dope swiftly, and this was one of the occasions when Hugo thought he saw a flash of understanding pass between the secretary and the airman.

"Who asked you to butt in?" said Mr. Dowley savagely.

"Looking after your interests," replied Cokayne with the utmost smoothness. "The Captain asked three, but I beat him down to two."

"That's it," O'Sullivan said, nodding darkly. "Two hundred."

"Pounds," said Cokayne again.

Mr. Dowley became peevish. "I don't see why it should cost so much more on a windy day," he exclaimed.

"More danger," said the Captain. "Parachute mayn't work."

"Hi!" exclaimed Hugo plaintively.

"And I might miss the Welsh Harp," went on the imperturbable O'Sullivan, "and he might get hurt."

"That won't harm you," pleaded Arthur Ed.

"Harm my reputation."

"That's it," Mr. Cokayne corroborated officiously. "Harm his reputation. Your reputation's worth an infinite amount to you, isn't it, Captain?"

"More than that," replied the Captain.

"Will you stop butting in," shouted Mr. Dowley at the secretary. "Another word from you and you're fired. Get me?"

"Yes, I've got you," was the affable answer, with the unexpected and sinister addition of the single word "properly."

"I tell you what we'll do," Mr. Dowley said. "We'll put it off till to-morrow, and we'll do it to-morrow whatever the weather. If it's fine, you get the original sum. If it's bad, you get an extra two hundred."

"Pounds," said the Captain and Mr. Cokayne simultaneously.

"Yes," replied Mr. Dowley crossly.

"Memorandum please," said the Captain.

"All ready," said Cokayne, producing duplicate memoranda of agreement with suspicious alacrity and distributing them. The documents were signed and exchanged. Captain O'Sullivan gallantly kissed Felida's hand and was rewarded by the dazzling smile which was such a feature of *Broadway Bonanza* and which brought Felida a hundred and seventy-one proposals in four days, some honourable, some dishonourable, and some just ambiguous.

As the Captain reached the door he paused, gazed at his toes for a moment, and then looked up and said, "Insurance, hey?"

"What do you mean?" snapped Arthur Ed. He was getting rather tired of this laconic young man who seemed to be so sordidly voracious about money.

"How do I stand if he does get killed?"

"Hi!" said Hugo plaintively.

"We'll cover that," said Cokayne. "I know a company that will take the risk."

"Dammit all," shouted Hugo, "I'm taking the risk."

Mr. Dowley gazed at him thoughtfully.

"I wonder," he said, in a tone of profound meditation. "I wonder how it would hit us. Felida," he went on, turning to the beauty, "how would you figure out as a widow?"

"You mean," said Cokayne sardonically, "how would it figure out if she was a widow?"

"Yes, that's it," replied the Publicity Manager, too immersed in his far-flung speculations to be angry with the secretary for divining his schemes at the first shot. "What would the reactions be? Gold coffin of course. Felida in black. We'd get some black orchids. Funeral by airplane. How would it run? 'First Air Mortician-Cortège takes Sorrow as Freight.' That might be a wow. What say, Dope?"

"Grand stuff, Art.," replied Dope. "Get O'Sullivan as pilot. 'Sorrowing airman loyal from Crash to Crematorium.' "

Mr. Dowley smacked his leg. "Oh boy, it's a sneezer."

Captain O'Sullivan chipped in smoothly. "What about my reputation?"

"Aw hell, make it a thousand."

"Ten."

"Ten!" Arthur Ed. screamed.

"Ten or nothing."

"Then it's nothing."

"Till to-morrow then," and O'Sullivan went out.

"I suppose it wouldn't have done," murmured Mr. Dowley meditatively. "After all, he's still got a three-years contract to run, and the Directors might have made a fuss if we'd knocked him down now." He sighed, and shook his head. "It's a pity to let it go. 'First film-star to be killed in parachute-accident over London, England.' But, then we can't have everything, can we, Mr. Seeley?"

"No, thank heavens," said Hugo faintly.

The expensive high wind having made aeroplaning impossible for that day, Mr. Dowley, like a good strategist, fell back upon a second plan which he had up his sleeve, and sat down to the telephone. In half an hour he had arranged for the blissful young couple to visit three of the most famous gardens in Surrey, at a total cost, excluding the normal standing charges for Daimlers and Rolls-Royces, of thirty guineas to the owner of each of the gardens, and ten guineas to each of eighteen illustrated papers. Hugo was hustled into a beautiful pair of white serge trousers, a dark blue coat, a pair of those singularly repulsive shoes of black and white which are called "Co-respondents" (quite wrongly called, incidentally, for co-respondents at least get and give some fun, and these shoes do neither), a straw hat cummerbunded with a Zingari ribbon the wrong way up, a Free Forester tie, and a handkerchief trimmed with the M.C.C. colours. This was Felida's notion of the costume for her beau-ideal of an English gentleman. She had got it firmly into her head in the old days in the neighbourhood of the Oval, that all gentlemen wear plenty of cricketing-colours, and later in life she had been supported in this notion by the appearance of Mr. Ronald Colman in the film *Raffles*. For everyone will remember how Mr. Colman played the part of the immortal A.J. in that film, and how, off the cricket field, he wore lots of blazers and scarves and ties (and, incidentally, on the cricket field how he wore tight linen trousers, and a snake-buckled belt, and a small cap, button-surmounted, on the top of his head, and how he took a swift, mincing patter up to the wicket and bowled slow, right-handed, round-arm, long-hops to leg).

The visits to the three famous gardens turned out to be extremely similar. There was the same walled garden, rich with Doyenne de Comice pears and plums and peaches and wasps. There was the rock garden. There was the gardener's boy panting over the lawn-mower, and resting on his handles, so to speak, the moment that the visiting procession had turned a corner and was out of sight. There was the same sort of ancient head-gardener who called a laburnum tree a Piptanthus, and a guelder-rose a Viburnum Yunnanensis. And above all, there were the three hostesses who each began by saying, coyly, wittily, and daringly, "Well, I mustn't be a second Ruth Draper, you know, but all the same you *should* have seen this border last week." One of them added, "And I wish you could come again next week when that border over there will be at its best." The second added, "There really isn't anything out at all now." The third summoned a small dog off a bed of begonias with a shrill yelp that made the yelp of the dog itself sound like a rather mellow contralto crooning a Tyrolean love-song. And when the dog had duly come to heel, the hostess giggled and said, "There, exactly like Ruth Draper after all."

All these delicate allusions fell rather flat, however, because Hugo had never heard of the divine lady (how could he, poor fellow, marooned in Kalataheira?), and Felida's only knowledge of her was acquired from a newspaper-cutting which said, "La Caliente's voice is eight times as harsh as Miss Draper's is soft." It was, consequently, a slight social gaffe to mention Miss Draper in her presence.

But Hugo's day was spoilt for him by the strong wind which bowed the tall delphiniums, and shook the hollyhocks, and rustled the shiny, dark green leaves of the magnolias. For that same wind, if it did not abate, would on the morrow be blowing a parachute hither and thither over London like a wisp of thistledown, and the parachute would have a human freight attached to it.

The reactions of the London Press to Mr. Dowley's hazardous experiment in aeronautical publicity were various, interesting, and characteristic. One group of journals, controlled by an extremely vivacious magnate, discovered that Michael Seeley had had a Canadian grandmother and was very pleased with the discovery. For it served to point an illuminating moral on the necessity of welding our already close-knit Empire into an even-closer-knit Empire. The importance of making a single economic unit of the Commonwealth was stressed, and it was pertinently revealed that Mr. Bonar Law, that clear-thinking statesman, would never have dreamt of handing over our entire economic freedom to Finland or Latvia as the corrupt and miserable Government had recently done. This group of journals persistently rendered the word "aeroplane" as "airplane."

Another group of journals, controlled by a somewhat richer but somewhat less vivacious magnate, saw with the utmost clarity that if Miss Caliente could drop her husband into the Welsh Harp, a hostile fleet of aeroplanes could reduce London to matchwood exactly one hour and forty minutes before a declaration of war, and that the only counter to such an attack was the instant construction of fifty thousand bombing aeroplanes. As a result of this powerful article, which was signed by the magnate himself, the ordinary shares of all the aeroplane-manufacturing companies jumped eight to ten points, and the rise was correspondingly reflected in the shares of those firms which make machine-guns, bombs, anti-aircraft guns, gas-masks, poison-gas, coffins, marble headstones, and artificial wreaths.

A Liberal penny explained that the League's Convention for the Standardization of Parachutes had not been ratified by Britain, San Salvador, or Honduras, and said that this disgraceful state of affairs was due to the reactionary forces in the Tory party. In the course of this exceptionally powerful article, the word "lip-service" was used no fewer than eleven times.

A ponderous penny die-hard pointed out that anything was possible now that a Rebel Junta was terrorizing loyal Ireland and a Red Junta, subsidized with Red Moscow Gold, was in control of the London County Council; while the Socialist penny protested loudly against the pollution of the People's water by a Capitalist stunt, and *The Times* said nothing about it at all.

Although the wind had somewhat abated during the night, it was still blowing a nice fresh breeze when Hugo peered wanly down into Piccadilly. It was the sort of wind that would have made the ladies in earlier days clutch from time to time at a billowing skirt. Indeed Hugo had been led by Uncle Eustace to expect that this would happen. "A lady who is a lady," Uncle Eustace had often remarked, "wears a skirt which would touch the dust or the mud, according to the meteorological conditions of the season, if she did not raise it slightly by gathering it in her hand. In these circumstances a gentleman who is a gentleman concentrates his gaze upon her delightful three-cornered, be-feathered hat, upon her fur boa, upon her muff, upon her parasol, upon anything, indeed, rather than that inch or two of her person which she has been compelled by the unhygienic state of our thoroughfares to reveal for a moment."

But then neither Uncle Eustace nor Hugo had known about the brief-lived fashion of the extremely short skirt. Since that charming, but alas! fleeting fashion, no one has attached the slightest importance either to leg-concealing or leg-gazing. Wind-blown skirts are no longer clutched, because wind-blown skirts are no longer noticed.

But on that breezy morning there was plenty of hat-clutching, and Hugo was appalled to see a young man in beautiful spats and gardenia go whizzing across the street in pursuit of a topper.

Nor was Hugo's courage in any way fortified by the almost hilarious entry of young Mr. Cokayne into his bedroom.

"Fine breezy day," exclaimed that young man, rubbing his hands. "Extra two hundred yellow-boys for Timsy O'Sullivan. Twenty per cent rake-off for yours truly Dope Cokayne, esquire, gent, of the county of Beds."

"You don't seem to think of me," said Hugo bitterly.

"Oh yes I do," replied Cokayne. "Day and night I think of ways of getting your gold-dust out of little Artie, the Dream-Child of Teheran, and sharing out, fifty-fifty."

Uncle René's years of business training had not been wasted. Hugo retorted sharply. "Fifty-fifty, huh? Five-ninety-five. Usual commission."

"Make it ten, Micky," said Dope.

"Seven and a half."

"Done. Payable in advance."

"In arrears."

"All right. We'll shake on that."

"No, we won't," replied Hugo firmly, his mind leaping from the business acumen of Uncle René to the methodical caution of Uncle Hans. "You'll draw up a deed of partnership and we'll sign it and get it witnessed and stamped at the Rathaus——"

"At the rat-house?" exclaimed Cokayne in surprise. "I never heard the House of Commons called that before."

"Sorry," said Hugo, "I was thinking of something else. I should have said Somerset House."

"All right," replied Dope in a rather depressed voice. This chap was not such a mug as he looked. It was more than ever obvious that he wasn't Michael Seeley. Michael was a good fellow and all that, but he was a perfect ass when it came to talking business or looking after money. Whether this chap's name really was Hugo Bechstein Smith or not, he was certainly no product of Eton and Oriel. Cokayne's spirits drooped until he remembered that even a seven-and-a-half per cent of eighty odd thousand pounds was a very tidy little sum, quite apart from anything that might be realized on the pearls and the ambergris. And there were other possibilities of profit which had to be considered. Mr. Cokayne's spirits revived prodigiously on these reflections.

The next few hours were a perfect nightmare for Hugo. Felida, in her pale-green breeches and her yellow leather jacket and her pale-green flying-helmet, was utterly entranced with herself. She skipped about the suite in the hotel examining herself from every angle in the numerous mirrors with which the room was equipped, and gurgling with delight. At least she was making sounds which to her represented a gurgle of delight. To those who heard it, and were sufficiently men-of-the-world to make the comparison, it resembled nothing so nearly as the cry of an Arizona coyote which is afflicted with a sharp quinsy.

Captain Timsy O'Sullivan, thin, brown, sardonic, leant against the wall and reflected how frightful Felida looked, and how still more frightful he himself would look in the duplicate costume, and yet how pleasant a cheque for £1200 would look even if Mr. Cokayne had to get his twenty per cent rake-off. And Mr. Cokayne was also delighted with the out-look, for twenty per cent of twelve hundred is two hundred and forty. The Marquess of Kilkenny was there, hovering round Mr. Dowley for the opportunity of suggesting to him that if he had any idea of having a nice little flutter in Kaffirs, the stock-broking firm of which his friends the Viscount Whipsnade and the Earl of Clontaghty were partners, was an admirable one to deal with. And young Kilkenny had inside information that there was a packet to be cleaned up in Kaffirs, but whether the packet was to be cleaned up by the buyers or by the sellers was a matter upon which he had been instructed to preserve a discreet silence.

But Mr. Dowley was too busy, and far too shrewd, to be blandished into a discussion of high finance. He went across the room to Hugo and began at once to talk business. It was clearly one of Ed.'s Napoleonic days.

"No funny business, Seeley," he said snappily. "Keep calm and everything will be O.K. We start in two hours five minutes."

"Is that the Press Association?" asked Cokayne into a telephone. "Cokayne here. We start in two hours five minutes. Hold the line."

"You go in the first car," went on Arthur Ed.

"The daring young couple will be in the first car in the procession," said Cokayne. "Hold the line."

"And you've nothing more to do till we fish you out of the water, and then you make a speech."

"Mr. Seeley has been persuaded to broadcast a short speech on 'What I saw over London,' after he has descended. Hold the line."

"But what shall I say?" faltered Hugo.

"Hey, Dope," barked the manager. "Have you got that speech?"

The secretary nodded and pushed across some typescript.

"But I can't read a speech from a typescript," Hugo protested.

"Why in heck not?" demanded Mr. Dowley.

"Well, when am I supposed to have typed it? When I'm coming down in the parachute? Or when I'm swimming round and round this damned lake?" Hugo spoke with some bitterness, and, he felt, with some justifiable bitterness.

There was a fearful silence. Mr. Dowley looked at Dope in consternation and Dope looked at Mr. Dowley. There was a short laugh from Timsy O'Sullivan, and then Felida looked bewitchingly over her pale-green suède shoulder and croaked, "Say, Cap, don't I just look a cutie?"

"No," replied the Captain.

Felida pouted enchantingly and went to another mirror.

"Hey, Dope," cried Art. Ed., coming to the surface. "Where do we go from here?"

Cokayne pondered deeply. Then he said, "The poor fish will have to learn it by heart on the way to Hendon."

"Aw nerts," replied Mr. Dowley with more emphasis than elegance. "And him bowing to the folks all along the route. Can't be done."

"Then we must alter the hour of the broadcast."

"Get the Radio folks on the wire," shouted the manager.

"Ring off, P.A.," said Cokayne. "Call you later. Hullo. Get the B.B.C., quick."

After a moment he went on, "Hey, B.B.C.? Give me Sir James Frith. What? Mr. Michael Seeley's manager." He was interrupted by a shrill scream from Felida. "Miss Felida Caliente's manager, you big stiff," she cried. "Cut out that Seeley stuff. I'm the Big Shot here."

Then followed a long parley on the telephone. So far from persuading Sir James Frith to run round to the Ritz to adjust the programme of the day's broadcasting, Cokayne could not even get in touch with Sir James' secretary. A courteous official explained that if Miss Caliente's manager cared to write and ask for an appointment, he was quite sure that he would be able to see the Assistant of the Deputy-Assistant Director of External Relations, say on the following Tuesday fortnight for a few minutes, or at any rate that gentleman's secretary. Alternatively a junior official of the Programmes Department would be calling in at the Ritz within a few minutes, to explain the alterations which the Director of Policy would like made in the script of Mr. Seeley's talk, and it was more than likely that that functionary would be able to explain or adjust any little difficulty that might have arisen. Hardly had the telephone con-

versation finished when the Junior Sub-Assistant
Director of Programmes was announced. He was a
small, pale man of about twenty-five or twenty-six,
with sloping shoulders and a narrow chest. But his
manner was as self-assured as if he had been a cross
between the late Rudolph Valentino and the presumably late Phœbus Apollo.

He wore a black felt hat with a very wide brim,
a black cloak lined with scarlet silk and fastened at
the throat with a silver buckle, and he carried a tall
ebony cane, silver-topped, in one hand and a rolled-
up bundle of paper in the other. This singular youth
bowed with an old-world grace to Felida, slightly
less floridly to Hugo, and nodded casually to Mr.
Dowley. O'Sullivan glanced at him and then at
Felida, and then, gazing abstractedly at the ceiling,
observed, "Is it at a fancy-ball in the Hoxton Baths
that we are?"

"Permit me to do myself the honour of introducing
myself," said the youth, taking a jade snuff-box out
of his waistcoat-pocket and tapping it neatly with a
long forefinger-nail. "My name is de Montmorency
Wigg." He took a little snuff, bowed again to Felida,
and unrolled the paper.

"The Director of Policy," he went on, "has asked
me to communicate to you, Mr. Seeley, one or two
changes he would like you to make in your 'talk' of
this morning." He coughed with supreme delicacy,
and began to read from the typescript. "The Director
wishes you to add, after the words 'in the far distance
the House of Commons,' the words 'in which the
National Government is so splendidly saving the

country.' After 'House of Lords,' he wishes you to say, 'that sole bulwark of our constitution against Communism.' Then the expression 'the Needle, once belonging to glamorous Cleopatra,' is to be deleted."

This aroused Felida from her apathy. "Say, mister, don't you allow glamour on the Radio?"

"Certainly not," replied Mr. de Montmorency Wigg. "And still less any reference to Cleopatra, Madame de Pompadour, Ninon de l'Enclos, Rabelais, Lenin, de Valera, or Dean Swift. It is one of our most rigid rules."

He returned to his papers. "Where was I? Ah yes. The reference to the effect of sunlight upon Portland Stone must come out. It is too like an advertisement, and the cement and paint-manufacturers might make a fuss. Let me see—the description of Whitehall can stand, except, of course, that for 'the majestic pile of the India Office,' we have put in, 'the majestic pile of the Office of the Board of Education.' We have to be very careful what we say about India in these days, and there's a standing order that in every talk in which it is proposed to mention India, the Board of Education shall be substituted for it. It is a little confusing for new listeners, especially if the talk happens to be about 'Life in Travancore' or 'The Caste System in British India,' or 'What I saw in Kashmir,' but they soon get into the habit of understanding what we mean. Let me see now, where was I? Ah yes. You can't mention the brewery in Pimlico. The temperance people wouldn't stand it for a moment, and the temperance people are particularly active with their postcards and their questions in the House. No, no, my dear sir, that would never do."

"Then why not change it to the derelict brewery across the river?" suggested Cokayne. "The idea of a brewery going derelict ought to please them no end."

"Ingenious, my dear sir, ingenious but very dangerous. The brewers would not like it, and so of course the Conservative back-benchers wouldn't like it. No. We've altered the brewery into the Shell-Mex building. Everybody likes petrol."

"Those, I think, are all the amendments. Now for the additions," he went on. "The Director of Policy would greatly appreciate a friendly reference to Lord Trenchard and his new police-college. In fact, I have myself drafted a little paragraph on the lines of 'this crime-free metropolis . . . thanks to Lord T. . . . can almost see the foundations of the great new college . . . public-school spirit.' "

Captain O'Sullivan laughed drily, and Mr. Wigg looked shocked.

"Then again, we feel," he went on, with a cold glance at the interrupter, "that a complimentary allusion to the British Fascisti . . ."

"The B.F.'s," murmured O'Sullivan, as in a dream.

"The British United Fascisti," amended Mr. Wigg severely, "a complimentary allusion to that movement would not be out of place. Something about the majestic outline of the Duke of York's School in the King's Road, Chelsea, the Headquarters of this splendid and virile movement, which stands, as everybody knows, for the maintenance of Law and Order and the freedom of the citizen."

"But I don't know what Fascism is," protested Hugo.

Again Mr. Wigg looked profoundly shocked. "Whatever your private views on the subject may be," he said in an acid tone, at the same time half-raising his arm in front of him and hastily dropping it as he realized what he was doing, "it is understood that you will make no derogatory references to it in your talk."

"Hey," said Mr. Dowley suddenly. He had been listening with some perplexity to Mr. Wigg's strange talk, and he felt that it was high time for him to assert himself. But Mr. Wigg did not even glance in his direction. Instead he went on reading from his manuscript.

"The Lieutenant-General——" he continued in his flat, even voice.

"The what?" enquired Hugo.

"The Director of Practical Politics," replied Mr. Wigg patiently, "is a Lieutenant-General."

"I thought he was an Air Vice-Marshal," said Captain O'Sullivan, coming unexpectedly out of his brown study.

"You are confusing him with the Deputy Directors of Practical Politics." Mr. Wigg pretended to stifle an incipient yawn with an exquisitely manicured hand. "The Deputy Directors are a retired Air Vice-Marshal and a retired Engineer Rear-Admiral. But the Director himself is a retired Lieutenant-General."

Arthur Ed., who for all his Napoleonic stuff was distinctly lacking in the military qualities, was so abashed by this galaxy of martial splendour that he allowed the representative of so much Glory to continue speaking.

"The Lieutenant-General," went on Mr. Wigg, "deprecates the emphasis which you propose to lay upon certain religious edifices, notably St. Paul's and the City Churches, and he wishes Woolwich Arsenal to be substituted for St. Katherine Coleman, the site of the Chemical Factory at Silvertown for St. Margaret Pattens, and the Naval College at Greenwich for St. Magnus the Martyr. And now, sir," he wound up, handing two documents to Hugo, "here is the text of your talk, for which the Director wishes to thank you and of which he cordially approves, and here is a statement which you will please sign."

The statement was a printed form.

Hugo read it. It ran as follows:

To the Director-General,
Broadcasting House.

DEAR SIR JAMES,

I wish to tell you—entirely voluntarily, of course,—that the talk which I broadcasted to-day was not in any way altered or amended by the British Broadcasting Corporation, and there was no kind of censorship of what I wished to say.

Yours truly,

"But—but—but——" Hugo started to object.

"Oh, sign it, sign it," shouted Mr. Dowley, getting impatient again. "We can't wait here all day." Hugo shrugged his shoulders. After all, what did it matter? The whole world was quite crazy, anyway, and one

M

bit of lunacy more or less was of small moment. He
signed the paper, and then Mr. Dowley began to
explain to Mr. Wigg, with a wealth of vivacity and a
multiplicity of gesture, the difficulty about the typescript of the talk.

Mr. Wigg settled the whole thing with a calm dis-
dain.

"Perfectly simple, my dear sir," he said. "One of
our men will do the actual broadcast in Broadcasting
House. It will be connected by land wire to the
microphone at Hendon. Mr. Seeley will just open and
shut his mouth as if he was talking, and there you
are. I will arrange it for you at once. And now I must
return." Mr. Wigg bowed, flung a streak of scarlet
silk over his shoulder, took up his enormous hat, and
sauntered out as if he had been the heir to all the
Spains.

"Wind's dropped," observed Captain O'Sullivan.

Mr. Dowley wheeled on him in a flash. "Gimme
back that extra two hundred," he barked.

"Not on your life," replied the Captain coolly.
"The agreement says 'windy morning,' and it was a
windy morning."

"I am afraid that is the case," purred Mr. Cokayne.
"I distinctly remember putting that in the agreement."

Napoleon Dowley continued the wheel. "You're
sacked," he shouted.

"Oh yeah?" replied Dope, winking at Hugo.

Napoleon climbed down. "Well, I mean, you will
be if you don't take care."

"I'm going to take more than care," was the cryptic
response.

But Hugo did not listen to any more of the snappy exchanges of the two men. The sudden fall of the wind was the only thing that mattered. He might yet escape with his life, or at the worst a broken leg or two. He might even get off with only a wetting and a severe fright. And once this nightmare was over, Mr. Dowley would probably give him a rest for a day or two, and Hugo felt confident that Mr. Cokayne would work himself to the bone during that day or two, to get him out of the clutches of Felida's travelling circus. After all, seven and a half per cent of fifty boxes of pearls, ambergris, gold dust, ivory, turquoises, and topazes would pan out very nicely. And Mr. Cokayne was not the man to let it go past him if human ingenuity could prevent it.

The dropping of the wind was to Hugo what the change of the wind had been to Dunois the Bastard when he and the Maid were playing the desperate game at Orléans, and the fortune of France was the stake. It was a sign that the luck might change, and that the world was not entirely controlled by the sort of people who arranged for total strangers to be thrown out of aeroplanes into lakes.

The procession to Hendon was, of course, an enormous success. There is no city in the world that enjoys a procession more than London, although it has fewer to enjoy than New York. But there is this difference. New York's processions are almost all composed of people in ordinary civilian dress. Morning-coats, frock-coats, toppers, striped trousers, lavender socks, these make up the usual New York procession. In London, on the other hand, although there are fewer of these delightful spectacles, they make up for it by being almost always in fancy dress. When the Mall is occupied by large limousine-cars containing the loveliest and noblest (or at any rate the best-vouched-for) of our Feminine Youth, you will notice that each of the young ladies wears a wonderful plume of feathers for the first and probably the only time in her life. When there is a Levee you will notice that the Mall is filled with elderly gentlemen in cocked hats, and scarlet coats, decked out with gold braid, and parti-coloured ribbons, and rows of medals, and wearing tightish trousers, and quaint little spurs. These elderly gentlemen are, in the main, the survivors of desperate encounters on the Maidan, of terrific chukkas by far-off cantonments, of fierce border shikarris, of battles long ago at Ooticamund, and Darjeeling, and Poona, and they correspond in the Public Service with the First Grade Clerks of the Offices of Education, Agriculture and Fisheries, Health, and so on. But they have, all their lives, grasped the fundamental importance of Fancy Dress to the citizens of London. And they are rewarded for their knowledge of psychology. For those Public Servants who have not grasped this eternal truth, have to creep about by themselves, apologetically, wearing bowler hats and carrying small bags, and are called Clerks, and earn the C.B.E. and sometimes the M.V.O. third, fourth, or fifth class, whereas the other wears gold braid, and cocked hat, and the ribbons of the Bath, of Michael and George, of the Order of Distinguished Service, and is called a Major-General. Such is the power of Fancy Dress.

Then there is the Lord Mayor's Show, so beloved by the Londoner. There is the opening of Parliament, when the young gentlemen of the sidewalks worship the Peeresses from afar, and the young ladies of the sidewalks swoon, not because of the crowds and the heat, but because of the extreme personal beauty of the Heralds, Rouge Croix Pursuivant, and Portcullis, and Bluemantle, and Windsor, and Clarenceux, and Norroy King-at-Arms. There are the Beefeaters, and the Judges in their wigs. There is the majestic march of the Guard as it blocks all the traffic by striding along, quite absurdly and quite unnecessarily, eight or ten abreast in the middle of the road on its way to duty, wearing those highly comical hats which the cognoscenti call bearskins and the illiterate busbies. London will cut dead the Town Clerk of Gospel Oak, even though that official may have faithfully served the borough for forty years, and applaud vociferously the Gentleman Usher to the Sword of State. A great scientist will pass unnoticed, where the Clerk of the Cheque and Adjutant of the Gentlemen-at-Arms will be hailed with delirious excitement. And all because the one is dressed in plain clothes, and the other in fancy dress.

As a consequence of this strange fancy of the cockney populace, the procession of the film stars to Hendon was a colossal success. For Felida looked incredibly alluring in her pale-green breeches and jerkin, and Hugo had been compelled to dress up as Henry VIII, not because he looked like Henry VIII, or had ever acted the part of Henry VIII, but because Mr. Dowley felt that it would be a graceful gesture if he paid a small compliment to the British Film Industry, as personified in the stately figure of Mr. Charles Laughton. And as, by a characteristic stroke of genius, Mr. Dowley had arranged for the devoted couple to make the journey to Hendon in a Daimler car the body of which was constructed entirely of glass, the London populace was given the greatest thrill that it had had since the Emir of Wallachistan had visited Buckingham Palace a week before. During this journey Hugo kissed Felida two hundred and sixteen times, to the delirious entrancement of the onlookers. During the two hundred and sixteen, Felida managed to smother two hundred and fourteen yawns, and Hugo found himself almost cursing his three uncles.

At last they reached the aerodrome. A crowd, variously estimated by the reporters as fifty thousand, a hundred and ten thousand, 'well on for a quarter of a million,' 'upwards of half a million,' and 'a veritable myriad,' was waiting. An aeroplane, painted pale green and gold to represent Felida's costume and hair, was lying snugly in front of a hangar. Near the hangar was a platform covered with red baize and adorned with a microphone. Mayors, aldermen, and councillors, be-chained and be-furred, stood in a phalanx, and hundreds of cameras were poised on hundreds of tripods.

The sun shone brightly. The Welsh Harp was a sheet of blue. Hugo thought that it looked very wet.

CHAPTER X

"Jump," shouted Captain O'Sullivan, "and may the Holy Saints keep you."

Hugo gulped twice, shut his eyes, and jumped. There was a sickening moment of downward rushing and then a strong pull on his back and shoulders, and he knew that the parachute had opened. The terrible rushing stopped and Hugo began to sway gently from side to side. After a minute of this rocking movement, he ventured to open his eyes and there, spread out below him, was the great city. Suddenly Hugo felt a wave of exhilaration. All fear left him. The roar of Timsy O'Sullivan's aeroplane died away from his ears, and he was alone, twenty thousand feet up in the heavens, like the Almighty God Himself. The silence of the eternal cosmos enveloped him. The earth was as quiet as the sun. Hugo drifted slowly, slowly down like the gentle, unhasting snowflakes of the Russian winter.

Hugo smiled a little as he pictured himself as a god from Olympus, paying a casual visit to see how the mortal midgets were behaving. Below him was the greatest city of the mortal midgets, their proudest achievement in the art of dwelling together in pleasant community. Once they had crouched in caves, and on tall poles over the waters of lakes, and in huts in forests. Now they made superb cities like this London.

Hugo stared down at the superb city which lay so far beneath him in the summer sun. Far away to the east a great pall of black smoke hung low on the jumbled mass of tall chimneys and the gaunt, grim arms of giant cranes, and the tangle of warehouses and the ten thousand miles of squalid, yellow-brick, dingy hovels. No summer sun could force a way through that fog of smoke, and the silver gleam of the river was lost as it plunged into the cauldron. Across the river, southwards, Hugo could see the pleasant hills of Surrey and the green fields where soon the crops would be ripening and the rolling line of down-land with the dark mass of the grand-stand at Epsom. Between the river and the green fields, separating the two creations of God, lay another part of the vast achievement of mankind, the streets and houses, the factories, the tenements, the railway embankments, the locomotive sheds, the cuttings and sidings and bridges and viaducts, of South London. Hugo could see all this part more clearly than the east, for the cloud of smoke was slightly less dense in the south, and he could distinguish the majestic out-line of one of London's two Palaces. There are older Palaces, perhaps, in Rome and more historical Palaces in the royal outskirts of Paris. The Escurial of Madrid, and the Schönbrunn of the Hapsburgs, and the Kremlin, and the Alhambra, all may be bigger, and the Palaces of Venice may have a quality of beauty of their own, but London can hold its head

high among the nations so long as the southern shore
of the Thames is adorned by the Crystal, and the
northern by the Alexandra, Palaces.

The river itself was at low tide, and the sun al-
chemized the yellow mud-banks into patches of old
gold, dotted here and there with tiny black specks
where coal-barges lay marooned, waiting for the
return of the tide. Along the northern bank ran the
thin white ribbon of the Embankment, but the south
was a maze of industrial works, jetties and wharves,
and machinery and chimneys. Here and there the
spanning bridges shot their straight black lines across
the silvery water and the gilded mud. Round one
bridge Hugo could see a swarm of ants busying themselves with its destruction. Already there was a great
gap in the masonry and barges were moored to the
piers, waiting for their loads of condemned granite
like sinister jackals waiting for the death of a noble
animal.

This was the bridge, Hugo remembered, which had
been built as a memorial for that victory which
Uncle Eustace and Uncle Hans never mentioned in
front of Uncle René. It was now being torn down as a
memorial to a victory which a Socialist party had
won at a municipal election. A strange development of the practice of commemorating great hap-
penings. But then, and Hugo smiled, this time a little
wryly, the destruction of Waterloo Bridge was a perfect example of the system of thought and action
which had poised him "betwixt Heaven and Charing
Cross" on a fine summer's morning. To throw harm-
less citizens out of aeroplanes was really the same sort

of thing as choosing London's most beautiful bridge for demolition and leaving all the other monstrosities to stand. There was as much sense in the one as in the other.

A light puff of wind swung the parachute round so that Hugo faced towards the south-west and the west. On this side, London, the supreme creation of the community-dwellers, looked like an octopus. Long, white, concrete arms stretched out, snakily, twisting, curving, like the adornments of the head of Medusa, and each was lined, on each side, with a never-ending row of small houses. Between the snakes were meadows and farm-land and the sad survivors of apple-orchards. But the ribbons of houses brought the joys of community-dwelling and the thrills of suburbia into the rustic scene. It was neither town nor country, thought Hugo, just before another puff whirled him round again so that his eyes were caught by a spark of fire which the sun struck out of a Cross. It was the Cross on the Dome of St. Paul's, and he gazed, swinging to and fro, at that mighty out-pouring of Genius. Uncle Eustace had often told him about the Great Fire, the Great Architect, and the Great King, and how the blind, selfish, money-grubbing merchants of London would not allow Sir Christopher Wren and the Second King Charles to rebuild the town into the latest of all the Wonders of the World. The magnificent broad streets which Wren would have built, where were they? Hugo peered down at the tiny alley-ways in which the most business-like, most commercially-efficient, most self-consciously intelligent, financial society in the world spends hours and hours every day sitting in motor-cars in traffic-blocks, and marvelled. There, fifteen thousand feet below him, the acutest brains of the swift age of Progress were jammed, one against the other, interminably, in narrow, stone-lined, tarry, airless trenches which were called streets, their ears assailed with a never-ending clatter of steel machines, and their lungs absorbing the deadly fumes of carbon monoxide.

But Wren and his King were visionaries. They understood nothing of ground-rents and freeholds and the value of real estate, and so their plans for broad streets were rightly discarded, and London gained wealth and picturesqueness by a single stroke of financial common sense. The increased site-values produced the former, and the labyrinth of alleys, and *culs-de-sac*, and twisty lanes, produced the latter.

As Hugo sank lower and lower, like a wandering morsel of thistledown, the individual glories of London's architecture became more distinct. The dark red Gothic majesty of the St. Pancras Hotel was silhouetted against the hills of Hampstead and domi-nated the surrounding loveliness of yellow-brick and pigeon-coloured slate and railway sheds, just as its twin, the offices of the Prudential Assurance Com-pany, dominated the fairy-like fret-work of inter-secting viaducts, iron-bridges, and tramlines, further to the east. A handful of little black dots was visible near Chancery Lane, busily tearing down the useless, unprogressive, fourteenth-century hall of Clifford's Inn, with its windows that were made when the archers were letting fly their arrows at Creçy, "so

wholly together and so thick that it seemed snow,"
and the Black Prince was winning his spurs. Hugo
could see the stones go tumbling down, just as Robert
Clifford, who once owned them, went tumbling down
on the field of Bannockburn in 1314. Soon his Inn
would be as dead as Robert Clifford, but his memory
would be perpetuated in the block of residential flats
which, in a month or two, would soar grandly into
the sky where once was only an out-of-date hotch-
potch of old stones.

Beyond Clifford's Inn the broad white pavement
shone bravely in the sun. That splendid breadth was
the gift of the City Corporation to the poor pedestrian, for the Corporation made it broad by pulling
down the ancient porch of St. Ethelburga's Church
and the only fifteenth-century, pre-Fire, shops in the
whole of the purlieus of the City, a notable and
generous act in these days when the pedestrian is too
often overlooked in the dispensation of any gift but
Death.

Lower and lower sank the parachute. Charing
Cross Station lay like a giant Zeppelin-hangar
exactly athwart the line between the Cathedral of
St. Paul and the Abbey-church of Westminster,
Cannon Street Station brooded, a great black slug,
against the silvery Monument and the fantastic out-
lines of the Norman Tower. And everywhere there
was concrete evidence of the activity of the citizenry,
of their prosperity, and of their tireless determination
to improve and improve and improve their Imperial
City until it rivalled the glories of Imperial Rome.
Vast white masses of offices were rising on every side,

from which the ever-increasing trade of the country might be directed, and superb hotels and blocks of flats in which the ever-prospering business-men might spend their leisure hours.

Hugo could distinguish the handsome new building in St. James's Square all decked out in smart pinkish-red brick, and ornamented with some tasteful scroll-work and symbolical figures in yellow stone—such a pleasing contrast to the dull severity of its Queen Anne neighbours. And only a few yards away there was the new office-building in Carlton Gardens, shimmering in all the whiteness of its Portland stone, shining like a good deed in a naughty world of stucco. "There is a symbol of this brave new world," thought Hugo, swinging lazily in a gentle breeze a few thousand feet up, "a great, strong, stone building, founded upon a rock, and standing up there in a wilderness of painted stucco. A symbol of Commerce amid Uselessness," cried Hugo in a loud voice. "A symbol of Strength amid mere Art. Strong naked stone amid dingy paint. Down with Uselessness. Down with Art. And down with Paint. And down with me," he added a few minutes later as he fell gently, gracefully, but none the less uncomfortably, into the Welsh Harp. Captain O'Sullivan was a man of his word.

CHAPTER XI

THE Publicity results of the parachuting adventure surpassed Mr. Dowley's wildest hopes. The newspapers, always excepting *The Times*, were full of enthusiasm for what was generally described as a typical bit of British pluck. "Our womanhood is universally admitted to be the pluckiest in the world," was also a common theme. The cinematograph-pictures were shown at all the one thousand and forty-six theatres that were under the control of, or affiliated to, the Pan-American Colossophone-Speakiegraph Corporation, Inc., and a new song entitled *Shooting the Chute with my Cutie* was specially composed by a distinguished song-writer. Nor was Mr. Dowley in any way cast down by the abrupt refusal of Mr. Arnold Bax to make a Symphony out of it, or even a Sonata which could be played on the electrical harmoniums which had recently been installed in the thousand and forty-six theatres.

And, crowning proof of success, on the very afternoon of the venture, rival film companies began to make tentative enquiries of Mr. Dowley on the tricky question of whether he could arrange for the temporary release of the two stars from their contracts. The Productions Manager of the Super-Stella Corporation, for instance, hinted that a very considerable sum of money would be forthcoming if Mr. Seeley were allowed to play Sir Walter Raleigh to Miss Caliente's Elizabeth in their new historical film *The Virgin Queen*.

The Imperial and Universal Company, on the other hand, suggested that the young couple would be an ideal pair of leads for their tremendous new historico-dramatic film *Elizabeth and Drake*, Miss Caliente of course playing the Queen, and Mr. Seeley the famous General Drake who won the battle of Blenheim by playing bowls on the playing-fields of Harrow. Of course, the Productions Manager of Imperial and Universal explained, the scenario was not quite completed, but he could promise Mr. Dowley that whatever else was changed the character of Elizabeth would probably remain, and he could rest assured that whether or not she married General Drake she would certainly marry somebody, either Essex, Sussex, Lancashire, Leicestershire, Northamptonshire, or whatever the names of those famous peers of the realm might be, and Mr. Seeley would play that part.

By seven o'clock on the evening of that eventful day, Felida had been offered the rôle of Queen Elizabeth by no fewer than six separate companies, and Hugo had been twice offered Raleigh, and Drake, Essex, Philip of Spain, and Richard Cœur de Lion once each. The offer of Richard was subsequently withdrawn by an apologetic secretary who said that the Productions Manager was ill and that there had happened to be no one in the building at the time who knew exactly whom Queen Elizabeth had married. The ridiculous mistake had now been discovered, the secretary said, and the part for Mr. Seeley was not Richard Cœur de Lion at all, but, of course, Oliver Cromwell.

Hugo, lying exhausted after the day's exertions, on a divan in the sitting-room of the suite, was greatly puzzled by the similarity of the parts which he was being invited to play.

"Why are they all doing the same film?" he asked Cokayne.

The secretary, who was sitting in a corner by himself, was pondering so deeply over something or other that Hugo had to repeat the question twice before he got an answer.

"Because of the colossal success of *Elizabeth the Great*," said Cokayne at length.

"What was that?"

"Oh don't be a fool," began Cokayne impatiently, and then he added, "Sorry. I keep on forgetting that you're not Mick Seeley. *Elizabeth the Great* was a film that the Beverly Hills people did a few months ago. They cleaned up a packet over it."

"But do you mean to say that six other films about the same person are going to be made?"

"Of course," replied Cokayne. "If one film about Elizabeth is a success, seven films about her will be seven successes. Stands to reason."

"But why do they want me to play Oliver Cromwell. He had nothing to do with Elizabeth."

"Well, why shouldn't he?"

"Why shouldn't he what?" Hugo's head was beginning to ache.

"Why shouldn't he have something to do with Elizabeth?"

"Because he lived about fifty years later," replied Hugo in some triumph.

"If Historical Productions Limited want him to live fifty years earlier, you'll find that he jolly well did live fifty years earlier."

Cokayne resumed his meditations and Hugo lay back. His mind could not grapple with such intricacies.

At last the secretary jumped up and went to the door, opened it, peeped out, shut it and came back to Hugo.

"Listen," he said in a whisper. "I've worked out a dodge for getting you away. It'll cost money though."

"You know I haven't got——" Hugo began, but the other interrupted.

"It can be paid in arrears, after we get hold of your doubloons."

"But how——"

"Hush! I've got a scheme for that too. Not a word. All you've got to do is to watch me like a cat and follow any cue I give you. See?"

"I can't see that there's anything to see," replied Hugo.

There was a sound of footsteps in the corridor and Cokayne skipped nimbly across the room to his desk. "Follow my cues," he hissed, and started to pound on his machine.

N

Mr. Dowley came in, rubbing his hands together briskly. He was feeling very pleased with himself. And he had every reason to be pleased with himself. For he had just been speaking on the long-distance telephone to no less a personage than the President himself of the Speakiegraph Corporation, sitting in the Presidential office in Hollywood, California. The President had described in almost glowing phrases, and occasionally even in something approaching grammar, his pleasure in Mr. Dowley's work, and he had added, as a concrete expression of that pleasure, a substantial increase in salary and a private recommendation to Mr. Dowley to buy gold-shares for a rise. No wonder the little gentleman was pleased. The President had also emphatically refused to consider the temporary release of the two stars from their contracts, as they would be required, as soon as the Publicity Tour of Europe was over, to return to Hollywood to take the leading parts in a new colossal production entitled, provisionally, *The Great Armada*. Miss Caliente would play Queen Elizabeth and Mr. Seeley the "guy who threw his tuxedo into the puddle for the old girl to step on."

Arthur Ed., therefore, beamed genially upon Hugo, and even upon Mr. Cokayne, as he danced a few neat little steps round the table, pointing his shiny, patent-leather, suède-topped, fat, short feet in the most elegant fashion. He looked rather like an Eastern Mr. Pickwick, if such a remarkable vision can be conjured up in the imagination. Nor did he frown severely upon Mr. Cokayne when that young gentleman remarked, "Artie, I've got an idea."

"A little less of the Artie, if you please," he replied
benignly, skipping nimbly over a footstool and bowing to an imaginary audience, with a podgy be-
diamonded hand on his massive gold watch-chain,
"but go ahead. Shoot the works."

"It's another publicity stunt for Micky," said
Cokayne, and Hugo shrank back. "Did you hear
what young Fatface was saying about Kaffirs?" went
on Dope. Mr. Dowley, the President's advice about
gold still ringing, even if somewhat nasally, in his
ears, instantly was all attention.

"Who's young Fatface?" he asked, by way of a
cautious opening.

"Young Kilkenny, of course, He got a red-hot tip
to deal in Kaffirs."

"Buy or Sell?" put in Hugo sharply, forgetting his
momentary apprehensions and feeling a sudden re-
vival of the business instincts which Uncle René and
Uncle Hans had so soundly encouraged.

"That, of course, is the point," said Dope.

"Half-witted ass," retorted Hugo with asperity.
"It's always the point." The other two stared at him
in amazement. This was a Hugo that they had not
seen.

"Go on, Dope," said Mr. Dowley at length.
"What's the big idea?"

"You see the price of gold at this moment,"
Cokayne lowered his voice to a whisper. "Record
high price. Micky has got boxes and boxes filled with
gold-dust. Let's organize a procession of tanks and
armoured cars and take the gold-dust down to
the Bank of England and sell it over the counter.

Record sale by private individual. Film star's stupendous——"

But he was not allowed to continue. With a loud
whoop Mr. Dowley jumped clean over the sofa,
seized the telephone, and started shouting excitedly,
"Hey! Get me the British Army. I want the British
Army. Get the Commander-in-Chief on the line. Tell
him to come round to the Ritz. I'll make it worth his
while. No. The Army. Army. Guys with guns."

"Half a minute, hold on," said Cokayne, also
leaping the sofa, and tearing the telephone out of Mr.
Dowley's reluctant grip. "Keep calm."

"How in heck can I keep calm with such a wow
of a scheme on?" enquired the Publicity Director
plaintively.

"We've got to get a story out first. How we've got
this gold, and Micky is such a patriot that he wants
to let the old country have it in her hour of need——"

"Or sore travail," amended Mr. Dowley, almost
mechanically.

"All right. Sore travail," Dope conceded the point
and proceeded. "We're in a jam. How to get the
stuff to the Bank? Rumours of hold-up. International
crooks. Will the War Office help? You get the idea?"

"Oh boy," said Mr. Dowley almost reverently.
"Your salary is raised, here and now, by fifty—well,
by fifteen per cent."

"You said fifty."

"No, no, no, fifteen. I said fifteen."

Cokayne looked at him sardonically. "All right.
Fifteen. You'll regret it. Anyway, the first move is to
get the stuff round here. Where is it?"

"In a furniture repository near Victoria Station."

"Give me the ticket," said Cokayne, casually. "I'll go and fetch it."

Arthur Ed. winked. "Like hell you will. I'll go myself."

"We'll both go."

"What about me?" asked Hugo with some warmth. "After all, it's my stuff."

"It's in my custody until your contract's up," replied Mr. Dowley.

"Then we'll all three go," suggested the secretary. "I'll ring up and say we're coming to-morrow morning."

"And get on with the news-story," ordered the Director. "I'll go round to the War Department. Who's head man there?"

"Ask for the Secretary," said Dope.

"And no funny business while I'm away," were Mr. Dowley's parting words.

The moment he had gone, Cokayne began to whisper urgently into Hugo's ear.

For many years before the invention of the internal combustion engine and the ingenious experiments of the Brothers Wright had brought back the long-disused art of Daedalus to the world of men, it was the custom of the harried and hustled lower orders of journalism to refer to the Army as the Cinderella of the Fighting Forces. It was not an especially striking metaphor, nor an especially accurate one. But to poor men striving to get a newspaper to press on an inadequate education and an even more inadequate salary, the phrase had served. The Army had never liked it, and even the creation of the Royal Air Force and the consequent passing-on of the title (with the consequent, also, regularization of the position, for, after all, there were three sisters in the original tale), had only slightly diminished the ingrained sense of inferiority which a comparison, sustained over a long period of years, to a lady who wore glass slippers, had engendered in the manly breasts of Britain's land forces.

The arrival of the super-film had, if anything, increased the feeling of annoyance. The Army had lent itself to various war films, but the public soon grew tired of the spectacle of men going over the top. One section of the populace coughed modestly and said, "That is just what we did," and the other section, vastly the larger section, sneered openly and retorted, "We don't believe you," and alternatively, "If that is what you did, we don't think much of it."

On the other hand the new Cinderella flung herself with enthusiasm into the new game. It afforded a splendid opportunity for her to justify her sensational rise to fame and fortune. The original Cinderella had only to gain the affection of a Prince in order to rise in the world; but the Air Force had to win the approbation of a fickle public which was conservatively startled at the sight of British troops dressed in blue uniforms and carrying shaving-brushes in their Sunday hats. So the Air Force, from Air-Super-Marshal or whatever it is, down to Leading Air-Craftsman, strongly applauded the arrival and development of the super-film.

But it was the Navy which came off best. There are few spectacles more thrilling than the spectacle of two battleships pounding each other with mammoth artillery, and if it is so contrived in the studios that the British battleship wins in the end, ten million film fans can be thrown into an ecstasy of patriotic joy.

And thus it was that, at the moment when Mr. Cokayne had his inspiration, the British Army was moping in its lair on account of the recent naval activities in the celluloid world. Mr. Dowley, therefore, was welcomed with metaphorically open arms by the War Office, not perhaps so much for himself as for his proposals.

The War Office was enchanted with the notion. The majestic building began to hum with activity for the first time for several years. Dust began to rise from the files and to dance gently in the sunbeams; a staff-colonel was actually seen to hurry down a corridor, and in the general confusion a telegram was discovered for the first time, announcing the outbreak of hostilities on the North-West Frontier of India, despatched from Peshawur, and dated four years earlier.

Orders began to whizz round the building, and the signing and countersigning and the "passed to you, please, for information and necessary action, if any," grew to alarming proportions. One set of orders instructed all concerned to discover the whereabouts of the Tank Corps, if any, and to mobilize it at once for gold-escort duty. A second set instructed all concerned to obtain a list of the fighting units, if any, which had taken part in the hostilities on the North-West Frontier in May 1930, and to arrange for a medal to be struck and awarded to all the staff-officers who had taken part in the punitive expedition which, presumably, had been despatched to quell the Afridis, or Waziris, or Wahabis, or Riffs, or whichever tribe was discovered by the Intelligence and Geography Sections of the War Office to have caused the schemozzle. A strange by-product of the suggestion of Mr. Cokayne and the activities of Mr. Dowley came out of the first set of orders. For owing to the exceptionally bad writing of a staff-officer, to whom the file had been passed for information, the words "gold-escort" became so lamentably distorted that a whole battalion of the latest whippet-tanks arrived on the Gold Coast before anyone, except themselves, knew that they had been despatched to that insalubrious seaside resort. And such is the intricacy of the mechanism of a modern war-machine that, as the unfortunate battalion had gone to the Gold Coast unofficially, as it were, it was impossible to bring it back. There existed no contrivance for the moving of units from places in which those units ought not to be, and it was only by disbanding that particular battalion and re-enlisting the personnel as recruits for the Central India Light Horse that it was possible to bring those who had survived the coast-fevers back to England. The whippet tanks, of course, had to be left behind, and are now used by the more enterprising of the local residents as hot-houses in which to force early cucumbers.

By a strange chance an official was found in this

hasty but always dignified search through the War Office, who not only knew where the various units of the Tank Corps had been stationed during the early part of the year, but had actually met a man that very morning, a civilian with rather well-developed powers of observation, who had seen some tanks in a meadow just off the Kingston By-Pass road. They had halted there, the civilian said, because the officers wanted to practise their horsemanship and there was a riding-school handy.

It was the work of a moment, or at any rate let us say of six hours, to despatch a message to this battalion ordering it to repair for duty at the Ritz Hotel at 11 A.M. on the following morning. A squadron of Rolls-Royce armoured cars was also mobilized, and two squadrons of a famous cavalry regiment that had recently been mechanized. It was this cavalry regiment, incidentally, that had extracted from the Army Council the concession that all ranks should be allowed to retain their spurs in memory of earlier, happier, and less useful days. It is fortunate that the tax-payer was never told how many motor-bicycle tyres were irreparably punctured during the first years of their mechanization by the rowellings of gallant riders who could not remember what kind of steed they were mounted upon.

Punctually at 11 A.M. on the following morning, sixteen large tanks, twelve Rolls-Royce armoured cars, twenty-four whippet tanks, innumerable motor-bicycles, two-seater Austins, and motor machine-guns drew up on Piccadilly. The leading tank halted across the mouth of Bond Street, and the rear motor

machine-gun exactly jammed the junction of Sloane
Street and Knightsbridge, so that in ten minutes the
above-ground traffic of the West End of the Metropolis had been brought to a complete standstill.

The packing-cases containing the precious gold-
dust were loaded into the armoured cars. The populace cheered. Felida kissed the A.P.M., an elderly
gentleman of dignified carriage and extreme military
distinction who had served in no fewer than eight
campaigns without seeing a shot fired in anger, or
even in a fit of petulance. A group of young Fascists,
who had not read their morning newspapers and so
had missed Dope Cokayne's brilliant news-story, got
the notion into their heads that another General
Strike had been declared and that the Constitution
was in danger of being trampled under the heel of
Moscow, and they added to the general excitement
by mobbing and attempting to lynch an elderly Jew
who was being wheeled past in a bath-chair. Their
loud, polyglot, but somewhat muddle-headed cries
of "Heil El Duce" and "Viva Das Führer" rang
shrilly from Dover Street to the corner of Curzon
Street, and the scents of long-unwashen black blouses
mingled with the ordinary perfumes of Piccadilly.
There was a second fracas in Arlington Street when
an urchin cocked a disrespectful snook at a leading
officer of the Fascisti (his official title was that
beautiful old English one of Commendatore of the
Ponder's End Maniple of the East London Legion)
and shrieked at him, "Garn, old B.F."

The Commendatore, flushing to where the roots of
his hair had been, many years before, appealed for

protection to a passing constable, and the urchin was promptly seized for causing a public commotion. In the furore, however, which was caused at that moment by the appearance of La Caliente on the top step of the Arlington Street entrance of the Ritz, the urchin contrived to wriggle out of the clutches of the Law and thus escaped the severe penalties which so many magistrates inflict, and rightly inflict, upon those who cock snooks at the theory and practice of Fascismo. During the scrimmage round the elderly Jew only three women were kicked at all severely by the sorely-tried, patient, young followers of the bald Commendatore.

Felida was conducted to an armoured car. The officers, non-commissioned officers, and men of the Royal Tank Corps were enchanted at the close proximity of the famous beauty, and each right hand flew instinctively to each jolly little beret—the quaint headgear which the Tank Corps shares with the pillion-carrying motor-bicyclist, the Basque, the hiker, the Frenchman, and the small child—and each right heel clicked sharply against each left.

The usual routine which every portion of troops has to go through when it is on the point of doing something or other, was carried out. Each vehicle reported itself all present and correct to its commander; each vehicle-commander passed on the glad tidings to each leader of a pair; each pair-leader repeated the news to each leader of four, and so on, until at last the commander of the entire column was able to assure himself that every officer, man, and vehicle was not only correct but present as well. And it speaks a great deal for the efficiency and organization of the Corps, that the order to move off was given actually within fifty minutes of the scheduled time.

There was a slight hitch in Piccadilly Circus, for the leading tank was controlled by a young gentleman who had never been in London before. He had only just returned from many years' service in the heavy sands of Mesopotamia and was working out the route by means of a large map, and he had never heard of the roundabout system of traffic control. Quite naturally, therefore, he steered straight across the Circus, leaving Eros on his left-hand side. The next seven vehicles followed their leader. The officer in charge of the eighth, however, was a keen supporter of the Good Road-Manners League, and nothing in the world could make him disregard an official road-instruction. He broke off from the leaders, wheeled majestically round to the left of Eros, leaving it of course on his right, and arrived in front of the Piccadilly Tube Station to find that a major excavation for the purpose of examining a gas-main was in progress in the road, and that the eight leading tanks had been halted on the near side of the narrow gap by the slow advance of one of those horse-drays, usually the property of a railway company, which amble so lugubriously about London's busiest thoroughfares at the busiest times of the day. The expert in Good Road-Manners, seeing that the eight leading tanks were held up, decided that it was his duty to push on ahead and thus prevent the whole column from being delayed. Unfortunately, as soon as the ancient railway nag had groaned and tugged itself out of the way, the young man who had made the original mistake decided that it was his duty to regain his place at the head of the column, and he crammed on all sail, so to speak, to catch up. In this manœuvre he was so successful that the leaders of the two rapidly converging columns met simultaneously at the mouth of the gap and became locked in an inextricable embrace. Within half an hour, however, the gold-convoy was again on the move, at the trifling cost of one lamp-post totally demolished and the temporary loss of the leading tank, which could only be extricated from the death-grapple by being allowed to topple over sideways into the excavations of the Gas, Light and Coke Company. Luckily its fall missed the gas-pipes, and the bursting of the water-main was a minor catastrophe in comparison with the damage that might have been done by the bursting of a gas-main. In fact it was almost a blessing in disguise, for a huge volume of water rushed down the Haymarket and across Waterloo Place, and cascaded down the Waterloo Steps and into the Lake in St. James's Park, which was sadly in need of replenishment owing to the exceptional dryness of the season. After the flow had been finally stopped, the custodian of the Duke of York's Column said that never in forty years' service had he seen the steps so clean, and the oldest member of the Athenæum said that the rush of water reminded him of nothing so much as the opening of the Caledonian Canal in 1823.

The stately procession of Britain's mechanical might rattled down the Strand and Fleet Street, took

Ludgate Hill in its stride, and at last came to a halt outside the Bank of England. The officials of the Bank were mustered; the Beadle wore a new costume; the air was charged with the magic with which only fame, beauty, and gold can charge an atmosphere.

The boxes were unloaded, opened, checked, weighed, until at last the senior cashier was able to announce that the Bank of England would be delighted to place to the account of Mr. Michael Seeley in any Joint-Stock Bank that he would like to mention, the sum of eighty-one thousand and two hundred pounds sterling.

"Imperial Union, Hackney Marshes branch," hissed Cokayne in Hugo's ear, and the latter repeated the words mechanically.

The formalities were completed; hands were shaken all round; bows were exchanged, and Mr. Dowley shepherded his little party out into the street. There was a brief halt for more photographs, and then, just as Mr. Dowley was handing Felida to the captain of the Tank Corps whose duty it was to hand her to the colonel who was waiting to hand her into the armoured car, Mr. Cokayne grasped Hugo's arm, whispered, "Now," and forced his way into the heart of the dense, tiptoed, all-agog crowd.

A moment later they were swallowed up as if they had never been, and Hugo was free. It had taken most of the British Tank Corps; it had immobilized a good deal of London's traffic for six hours; it had cost a lamp-post and ten million gallons of London water.

But Hugo did not care a straw.

He was free.

CHAPTER XII

THE instant that Cokayne was convinced that the get-away had been successfully brought off, he hailed a taxi and the two young men drove to the Hackney Marshes branch of the Imperial Union Bank. An interview with the manager was demanded by the ebullient secretary, and conceded by that functionary after a short interval.

Mr. Cokayne plunged into business at once. "We want some money," he said.

The manager froze. "Have you any security to offer?" he began icily, and Dope interrupted at once, "Of course we haven't."

The bank official got up. "If you imagine," he said, "that we hand out five-pound or ten-pound notes to total strangers without security——"

Again Dope interrupted. "It isn't a question of five or ten pounds. We want at least ten thousand."

"Ten thousand," exclaimed the manager, his manner changing abruptly to a delightful geniality, "sit down, gentlemen, sit down." He beamed at them.

"We shall certainly want ten thousand to begin with," said Mr. Cokayne, "and we want it at once."

"I doubt if this gentleman can give it to us at

once," said Hugo, recalling Uncle Hans' lectures on the theory and practice of Joint-Stock Banks.

"Why ever not?" demanded Cokayne.

Hugo smiled in a superior way.

"If we haven't enough security to raise a fiver, we are not likely to have enough to raise ten thousand."

"Gentlemen, gentlemen," protested the manager, spreading out his hands in a deprecatory way. "A fiver is a fiver, but ten thousand pounds are ten thousand pounds. You surely do not expect us to regard the two transactions as being in any way parallel."

"But do you mean to say," enquired Hugo incredulously, "that the larger the sum asked for, the less security you require?"

"That is a blunt way of putting it," answered the manager. "But in effect that is the case. You see, no honest man is so foolish as to expect a banker to lend him a fiver, and no crook is so optimistic as to expect a banker to lend him ten thousand. It would be wasting the crook's time for him to try."

"And does that apply to all crooks?" asked Cokayne, with an exquisite blandness, but at the same time raising a sceptical eyelid.

The bank manager almost blushed. "Well, of course," he said with an embarrassed cough, "there are times——" He broke off as a subordinate entered with a slip of paper which he silently handed across the table. The manager looked at it and then stared at the two young men. "Is either of you gentlemen Mr. Seeley?" he asked severely. Something seemed to have gone wrong, and it was with a certain amount of diffidence that Hugo admitted his alleged identity.

"I am informed," proceeded the manager sternly, "that you wish to open an account with us, and that the Bank of England has placed to your credit with us the sum of eighty-one thousand and two hundred pounds sterling."

"Quite right," answered Mr. Cokayne briskly. "We would have explained that before, only you wouldn't give us a chance——"

The manager held up his hand. "Mr. Seeley," he said, and there was a distant austerity in his voice, as of a schoolmaster rebuking one of his urchins, "before you can open an account with us, I must beg you to answer a few questions."

"But when you were going to lend me ten thousand pounds just now," cried Hugo in astonishment, "you said nothing about asking any questions. And now that I'm lending eighty thousand pounds to you——"

"I fear you do not understand the principles of banking," interrupted the official with dignity. "Lending is one thing. Opening an account is another. Now, if you please, Mr. Seeley, I want your address, your occupation, your reasons for wishing to open an account with us, the names of two citizens, both in the telephone-book——"

"The possession of a telephone is the best guarantee of integrity," murmured Cokayne dreamily, and the manager threw him a cold glance.

"Both in the London telephone-book," he repeated with emphasis, "the name of your solicitor and your stockbroker."

"I have no address," said Hugo, a great weariness

o

descending upon him suddenly as he saw that once more he was being enmeshed in the strange workings of Civilization, "nor an occupation, nor a solicitor, nor a stockbroker. I do not know two citizens of this town, and until a week ago I had hardly been aware of the existence of such a thing as a telephone, and I had never set eyes upon the instrument. As for reasons for opening an account——"

"Is your friend crazy?" cried the manager, turning to Cokayne.

"Far from it," replied Cokayne, that diabolic gleam shining for a moment in his eyes. "He is an American, and I am his secretary."

The manager sprang up with an exclamation of delight. As an indifferent master of English prose might have expressed it, "The word 'welcome' was literally written all over his face."

"My dear sir, my dear Mr. Seeley," he cried, "I cannot tell you how delighted I am to meet you. Of course these little formalities are unnecessary. I must apologize for having misunderstood the situation. Please forgive me."

He tore up the questionnaire, threw it into the waste-paper basket, and pressed a bell. A subordinate entered.

"Mr. Jones," said the manager peremptorily, "take ten thousand pounds in notes—bills I believe you call them across the—ah—herring-pond, Mr. Seeley—round to Mr. Seeley's hotel. Is it the Ritz, Mr. Seeley?"

"Yes," answered Hugo automatically.

"We'll take the money with us," Dope chipped in.

"Nine thousand-pound notes, eight hundreds, and the rest in fivers."

"Are you sure it is not too much trouble for you to carry it, gentlemen?" asked the manager with an admirable touch of paternal solicitude. "We could easily send it for you."

But Cokayne was firm, and a few minutes later the two young men were driving in a taxi from the region of the Hackney Marshes to a small and unobtrusive private hotel in the Cromwell Road, called the Universal and West Kensington Hotel.

During the drive Cokayne was busy figuring out seven and a half per cent of eighty-one thousand and two hundred pounds, and Hugo was musing on the extraordinary change that seemed to have come over banking methods since the young days of Uncle Hans.

After dinner Cokayne announced that he was going back to the Ritz for an hour or two. "I must put in an appearance," he explained, "otherwise it will look jolly fishy. I'll tell young Dowley that you bolted and that I bolted after you to bring you back, thereby adding another chapter to the deathless book of English loyalty and devotion to duty. Failing to catch up with you, I returned, tired, disappointed, dusty, thirsty, hungry, but ever loyal, to my beloved employer. And that reminds me, young Smith," he proceeded with great earnestness. "It is most vitally important that you should stay in your room here all to-morrow. I've got to think out a scheme for squaring Arthur Ed. to-morrow, otherwise the air will be so full of writs against you for breach of contract that

you won't be able to see your breakfast on the tray.
So you lie low till I come round. And don't forget that
I'm your best friend. In fact I'm the only friend
you've got."

"I know you are, Dope," said Hugo forlornly.

"Good," replied his best friend briskly. "And now
what about that cheque? I make it six thousand one
hundred pounds."

Hugo sat up indignantly. "Six thousand and fifteen
pounds," he exclaimed.

Mr. Cokayne sighed. "What a damned queer fish
you are, Smith," he said in a plaintive voice. "I don't
seem to be able to swindle you at all. All right. Six
thousand and fifteen."

Hugo wrote out the cheque, and Mr. Cokayne put
it away in his pocket-book, and turned to the door.

"Stop," cried Hugo. "Receipt, please."

This time Mr. Cokayne did not even sigh. With
a gloomy air he made out a receipt and handed it
over. "Don't forget," were his parting words, "you
mustn't leave this room to-morrow, and I'm your
best friend."

"And after to-morrow?" asked Hugo.

"I think I'll have fixed you up all right," was the
slightly enigmatic reply, and Mr. Cokayne went out
with a wink of infinite roguery. In the hall of the hotel
he beckoned to the porter and took him aside.
"Here's a ten-pound note," he said. "Don't send any
newspapers up to my friend to-morrow. Do you
understand? I'll be back to-morrow evening, and
there's another tenner for you if you've played up.
Understand?"

"Yes, sir," replied the porter with the profoundest deference. It was at least a quarter of a century since a tenner had been seen in that small and unassuming hotel in the Cromwell Road.

That night Hugo slept a long, dreamless sleep. It was his first since he had discovered civilization, and he looked forward to many more, now that he was free and rich. He would not have slept quite so soundly if he had been aware of Mr. Cokayne's nefarious plans. For although that young gentleman returned to the Ritz, it was not with the intention of protesting his undying fidelity to the hand that fed him. It was a very different Mr. Cokayne from the typewriter-pounding secretary that swaggered into the hotel sitting-room at half-past nine that evening.

The moment he appeared Mr. Dowley, who had been pacing savagely up and down the room with the telephone to his ear, gave a wild yelp of rage, flung the telephone on to the sofa where it narrowly missed one of Felida's entrancing ankles as she lay at full length on it, and burst into a torrent of invective. It was one of those moving moments in a man's life when the carefully acquired lacquer of education melts in the furnace as though it had never been, and the spirit returns to the mother-land. Mr. Dowley, Hollywood Publicity King, reverted to Arfa-ed-Dovleh, the camel-holder of the bazaars of Tabriz, and seller of news at the street-corners of Ispahan. The quiet air of S.W.1 shook with the jargon of the alley-ways of Kermanshah. *Argot* of Nishapur whistled round the room. The windows rattled under the insinuations of dubious parentage which are so sadly common in the lower quarters of Teheran, and there was a mingling of the dialects of Khurasan and Kurdistan and Azerbaijan that would have keenly aroused the professional interest of the scholars in the Oriental Section of the British Museum.

At last Mr. Dowley paused. For even a Persian must breathe sometimes.

"There's a big boy," observed Mr. Cokayne gently, as he dexterously removed Felida's legs from the sofa, thus converting her recumbency into a sitting position, and sat down where her feet had been.

Felida gasped. Mr. Dowley gaped.

"Do you know what the eminent firm of theatre-ticket-sellers, Messrs. Keith Prowse, say?" proceeded Mr. Cokayne. " 'You want the best seats. We have them.' And so with us. You want Mick Seeley. I have him."

There was a stupefied silence and then Dope went on. "But you can have him back. To-morrow night. It will cost a thousand pounds."

"I'll see you in hell first," shouted Mr. Dowley furiously.

"Oh, I don't think so," replied Cokayne. "And it won't cost you a thousand pounds. Someone else will pay. Listen."

Half an hour later there was intense activity in the office of that famous penny newspaper *The Morning Yelp*.

CHAPTER XIII

MR. COKAYNE, shrewd, swift, far-seeing though he was, made one elementary mistake and that mistake cost him the thousand pounds by the fraction of an inch. Perhaps in a sense it was not his fault. Perhaps it was a justifiable error to underestimate the speed at which Progress has advanced westwards along the Cromwell Road. Perhaps in the back of his mind there lingered a vague notion that civilization gradually tapered off into primitive communities as the intrepid traveller forced his way westwards along that dreary street, until the street became a grass-grown road, and the grass-grown road became a pathway, and the pathway merged imperceptibly into a faint, ill-defined track which, winding hither and thither amid the jungle, reached at last the rough log-cabins and the fearful, peering faces of a lost tribe of forest-dwellers.

At any rate, Mr. Cokayne completely forgot that even a small residential hotel in the far west of the Cromwell Road might have a wireless set in each bedroom. And this piece of forgetfulness cost him the sum of one thousand pounds.

For Hugo, having spent a blissfully happy day in his small but comfortable bedroom, experiencing the

joys of solitude for the first time since he had passed
the thirtieth degree of latitude, at five minutes to
nine o'clock in the evening rang the bell for the
chambermaid and requested her to adjust the wireless instrument in such a way as to enable him to
listen to the news bulletin. The chambermaid, being
a country girl from Shropshire and therefore extremely efficient in the practical affairs of the world,
immediately twiddled various knobs and discs and
switches with such competence that at nine o'clock
precisely Hugo was enabled to hear the elegant voice
of the latter-day muezzin calling the faithful to
worship at the altar of the Livestock prices, the Stock
Exchange dealings, the cricket-scores, and the
winning race-horses of the day.

Hugo leant back in his chair and put his feet on the
mantelpiece. The refined voice went on and on and
on, now touching upon the price of Imperial Cochineal
Ordinaries, now requesting that Mrs. Maria Stiggins
should repair to her sister's home at Paradise Dwellings, Thugs Alley, Leeds, as soon as possible, now
informing a rapt world that the Honourable Miss
Bethesda Fairleigh-Fairleigh-Swifte had won, for the
seventeenth year in succession, the croquet handicap
at Hurlingham, playing off a handicap of owe three
hoops and a bisque. A gentle cloud of peace came
descending slowly upon Hugo. The world was leaving
him alone. The crazy creatures who organized the
system of modern society had forgotten about him,
and were concentrating all their infinitesimal re-
sources of common sense, and all their giant re-
sources of scientific achievement, upon the task of

spreading, throughout the ethereal cosmos, the tidings that the Honourable Miss Bethesda Fairleigh-Fairleigh-Swifte had won a croquet handicap. If it was true, Hugo reflected lazily, that waves of sound go on for ever and ever and ever, in the ultimate reckoning of immortality the Honourable Bethesda will take her place beside Socrates and Galileo and Newton and Copernicus, and the sister who lived in Paradise Dwellings, Leeds, will be no less known than Cleopatra.

Pleasant, easy, half-dozing speculation. Hugo sighed contentedly.

The Oxford accent trickled on: "*The Morning Yelp's* Prize. No one has yet claimed the thousand-pound prize offered this morning by *The Morning Yelp* to the first member of the public who recognizes the famous film star, Mr. Michael Seeley."

Hugo sat up with a start. The voice went on: "You will remember that the conditions of the competition are that Mr. Seeley is to walk about the streets of London, either disguised or not, as he pleases, and the first person who is observant enough, and intelligent enough, to recognize him and challenge him wins the thousand pounds. The challenger must have a copy of *The Morning Yelp* under his arm when he makes the challenge."

Hugo sprang to his feet with a torrent of French and German oaths. (Uncle Eustace's vocabulary was much too refined to be of any satisfaction.)

Hugo saw in a flash what had happened. He understood Dope Cokayne's treachery. And at any moment now the traitor would be arriving, probably with a

squad of tough assistants, to collar him and cart him
off to the Ritz and sell him back to Arthur Ed.
Dowley for a thousand pounds.

Hugo seized his hat and rushed downstairs. He
had formed a very exact appreciation of the strateg-
ical position, for in the hall of the hotel was standing
a group of six men. Cokayne was one of them. The
other five were young, large, and muscular. Their
faces were startlingly red in comparison with
Cokayne's pallor. Three closed motor-cars were
standing at the door.

Hugo turned and whizzed upstairs again. The
posse whizzed after him. The lock and bolt of Hugo's
bedroom were doomed from the start. To five heavy-
weight international forwards, each animated by the
traditional English Spirit of the Chase, and the prospect of a tenner apiece if the quarry was run down,
a Cromwell Road bedroom door was as a sheet of
tissue-paper. The defences were splintered to matchwood in nine and a fifth seconds, and the scrum
went through into the room with a roar of victory.

They were two seconds late, for Hugo was going
down the drain-pipe at a remarkable speed, and
once he reached the pavement he turned towards the
Earl's Court Road and bolted. The heavyweights
rushed to the window, peered out, unanimously
decided not to risk their respective fifteen stones
upon such a flimsy pipe, and dashed for the door
again. But Cokayne was made of sterner stuff. Besides, the international forwards only stood to gain a
tenner apiece. Cokayne, after paying them, would
collect nine hundred and fifty pounds. Without the

slightest hesitation he flung himself at the drain-pipe
and reached the street in time to see which way Hugo
was going.

Then there was a stern chase. Hugo was fitter than
Cokayne, and he was desperate for freedom. On the
other hand, Cokayne was desperate for the nine
hundred and fifty pounds. And the five rugger
players were so fit and fast that they soon overhauled
their commander. Another factor which told heavily
against Hugo was the theory of the local populace
that he was an escaping malefactor, a theory that
was greatly strengthened by Cokayne's incessant cries
of "Stop, thief!" The officers of the local constabu-
lary, of course, were unable to interfere in the pursuit,
as they were too busily occupied in directing the traffic
and pouncing on villains who ignored the coloured
lights at cross-roads. But the civilian population of
Earl's Court threw themselves with gusto into the
hunt, and by the time the Tube station was reached
Hugo was barely a dozen yards in the lead. Glancing
frantically over his shoulder, and at the same moment
swerving to avoid a flower-barrow, he saw that unless
he took some desperate step the game was up. And
then the brilliant, beautiful, lucid idea came into his
mind, very simply, very gently. He had climbed with
the monkeys in the forests of Kalataheira. He would
climb across the house-tops of London. One, at least,
of his primitive accomplishments would come in useful in a world of modern civilization.

Hugo almost laughed as he went up a creeper on
the wall of a small two-story villa, hand over hand,
and dodged behind chimney-pots until he found a

lightning-conductor on the side of a huge block of
flats, and swarmed up that until he reached the roof
and was able to pause for a rest. The crowd, completely baffled, stared up at him just as the crowd
outside the Ritz had stared at him when he per-
formed his acrobatics. But there was a difference. The
other crowd had been adoring, this one was malevol-
ent. Worse still, it was rapidly being organized.
Pickets were being thrown out into the side-streets
to encircle, as far as possible, the building, and Hugo
did not need to use a great deal of brain-work to
guess that the astute Cokayne was already in control
of the mob. The cordon was being rapidly extended,
but Hugo had the advantage of working on interior
lines, and he recalled one of Uncle Hans' lectures on
the strategy of the Austro-Prussian War of 1866. It
was child's play, therefore, for him to retreat to the
corner of the building which was furthest from the
mob and would therefore be the last point to be
reached by the pickets, and to skim down a drain-
pipe into a mews and up another drain-pipe across a
row of garages. The sporting cries of the chauffeurs,
offering to lay odds against the field and imitating
the peculiar squeals of fox-hunters who have seen their
quarry hastening out of a wood unnoticed by the
baffled dogs, attracted the attention of a few of the
pursuers, but Hugo had got too good a start. He
jumped off a roof and dexterously caught a branch
of a laburnum tree in a square-garden; vaulted
the spiked railings which are designed, in London
squares, to ensure that the children of a great sporting
race shall play their cricket and football amid the

motor traffic in the road-way rather than on grass; dived down an alley-way and reached, by way of a cherry tree and a tremendous jump, the haven of a row of roofs that stretched as far as the Fulham Road.

Twilight was beginning to fall and a violet mist was creeping up the river. The stars were picking their way through the thick purple velvet of the sky, and there was a faint glow of sunset over Chiswick. A breath of evening air came freshly up from the sea, and Hugo's tangled hair waved for a moment on his temples. He took a deep breath and stood up on the roof of a house in Redclyffe Gardens and stretched his arms above his head. He was scratched and bruised, his clothes were torn, his face and hands were covered with grime, but he was still free. He had some reason to be pleased with himself. Delicately picking his way southwards among the chimney-pots, he descended cautiously into a dark lane just off the Fulham Road and walked straight into the arms of Mr. Dope Cokayne.

"Mistake to silhouette yourself against the sunset," remarked that young man affably. "I've been watching you for some time."

Hugo's reversion to the primeval methods of the Kalataheiran forests had not yet worn off. The exhilaration of the climbing, the thrill of feeling a branch of a tree in his hands once more, the magnificent swish of the great swing from the corner of one house to another across a fifteen-foot gap, were sending the blood rushing about in his veins. He said nothing, but stared at Cokayne.

"Better come quietly," said the latter. "My strong-arm boys will be here in a moment."

The mere suggestion that he should go quietly and meekly back into slavery, he, who had raced in triumph across the roofs of London, exulting in his strength, was the final insult, and Hugo punched Mr. Cokayne smartly on the lowest waistcoat-button but one and raced for the King's Road.

The pursuit went across the King's Road and on to the Embankment.

Hugo had a lead of a good fifty yards as he turned into Cheyne Walk. But he could not keep up the race for ever, and he made up his mind to take a decisive chance. There was a wide-open, brilliantly-lit window on the ground-floor of a house just in front. Hugo glanced over his shoulder. The pursuit had not yet rounded the corner. He took a tremendous flying leap and went full-pitch through the window without so much as grazing the window-frame, so accurate was his judgment of distance and velocity.

The hunters went thundering past, and a moment or two later the sound of their scurrying feet upon the pavement had died away into a silence.

CHAPTER XIV

THERE was a party that night at Aurora St. Hilaire's, in that ground-floor flat in the Chelsea Embankment. The full moon was up by the time that Hugo made his perfectly timed leap through the window, and it was shining gently on the river and on the moored barges, and the chimneys of the Power Station were outlined against the stars like four giant fingers pointing to heaven, or four modern altars pouring the smoke of sacrifice not to the Olympians, but to the newer God of Electric Power. The ripple of small wavelets against the keels of anchored canoes was mingled with the sound of metal saws on metal, from the factories on the Battersea side. Sometimes a police-launch went swishing up the tide in search of malefactors; sometimes there came the long strange cry of a ship's siren that seems to call upon restless souls to leave their desks and their offices and wander for ever in the search for Lodore or the islands of Atlantis. And at intervals all through the evening, as always on the Embankment when the citron moon is at the full, couples, interlinked, wandered down the side-streets and crossed over and leant upon the parapet, and sooner or later one of each couple would say something about Whistler and the other would say that John Burns had called it Liquid History, and then they would kiss and drift away in an enchanted oblivion.

Aurora St. Hilaire often gave parties. She had many friends and enough money to entertain them, and in consequence she had become the central figure of a small coterie which in turn was amalgamated with a lot of other small coteries into one large amorphous, ever-changing, undefined and undefinable Set.

Miss St. Hilaire was the youngest daughter of the first Baron St. Hilaire, a common, tubby little man, *né* Tuke, who had made a lot of money in manufacturing something or other, rumoured to be corsets, in a northern town that was rumoured to be Accrington. Nobody ever saw him except his three eldest daughters by his first marriage who lived with him at Putney and were thought to have Lancashire accents, and known to have long, sad faces. Aurora, daughter of a second, fashionable, ephemeral marriage, departed at nineteen from the family fold, and now, at three and twenty years of age, was installed on the Chelsea Embankment. Her appearance was of startling splendour. She was strong, and her shoulders were square, and her deportment Ouidaesque. A mass of dark, coppery, tawny hair would alone have been sufficient colouring for any ordinary person. But Aurora had an apple-rosy complexion, all her own, and a shining white neck and green eyes, and when the genius of Miss Elizabeth Arden had added a pair of vermilion lips, there was no parrakeet or macaw in all the southern seas that was fit to be seen in the same forest as Aurora St. Hilaire. In the great days of London, when England's Prince Florizel was roaming the town in search of adventure, the days of the orchid and the hansom cab and the Jersey Lily and the stage-door, Aurora would have been a reigning toast. But Youth knows better nowadays, and Aurora had to be content with a small coterie.

Glance for a moment at the coterie as they sat, or lay, propped in graceful attitudes, and all wearing pyjamas, round the huge studio. There was Lady Honoria Jique, who a year before had created an immense sensation by almost walking on foot across Asia Minor from north to south, from Trebizond to the Gulf of Iskanderun by way of Shebin Karahissar and Sivas and over the Anti-Taurus Mountains and down the ancient valley of the Pyramus. It was only the impossibility of getting a Turkish visa that had prevented her. In consequence of this almost remarkable feat, Lady Honoria had naturally taken her rightful place among Orientals, and she edited from time to time a graceful little quarterly magazine about Things Oriental, called *The Tulip of the Soul*.

Then there was Miss Crystallina Pontefract, who hunted a great deal, and was often photographed for the illustrated weeklies while going through a gate with the Bicester, or finding a gap with the V.W.H. (Cricklade), or enjoying a rest with the Quorn, and, of course, in ever so many of those rather unfortunate groups that are taken towards the end of every Hunt Ball.

Lady Bunty Spriggs was there. Lady Bunty painted

P

portraits upon silk, and was probably going to have a
one-man show in Bond Street as soon as that ludi-
crous Velasquez Exhibition at Burlington House was
got out of the way.

Miss Euphrosyne Caerleon was probably the most
intellectual of the party. She wore her sleek, polished
hair very straight across her forehead, and her
pyjamas were made of American linoleum to a
pattern designed by the latest man in Paris, an albino
engine-driver who had been expelled from the Soviet
Republic of Daghestan, not for any crime, but simply
because it was felt by the more sensitive minds of the
local Ogpu that the extraordinary whiteness of his
eyes was a direct incentive to counter-revolution, and
who was now living in a flat near the Rotonde in
Montparnasse. So original were these pyjamas, that
had they been worn by anyone but Euphrosyne,
there might have been jealousy. Even as it was,
Cyprian Pontefract, Crystallina's brother, had observed almost with petulance, "What a bother you
are, Euphrosyne. You really are most vexing." For
Cyprian's pyjamas were made of gold-beater skin,
designed by a Kentucky miner who had taught himself to read, and had then read a book of poems by
T. S. Eliot, and had subsequently gone mad at the
thought of the time he had wasted. However, he was
allowed to take up pyjama-designing in the asylum.
In ordinary circumstances Cyprian's would have
been the cynosure of the evening. But something
écrasant was only to be expected of Euphrosyne. For
after all, she was the editor of a monthly magazine
published in Paris and printed on crêpe-de-chine, in

English on one side and in mediaeval Provençal on the other, called *Unicorne de Lesbos.*

Cyprian Pontefract was a tall and willowy young man, with black, wavy hair and a sensitive, clean-shaven handsome face. He was salesman in a firm of antique dealers and decorators, and a very successful salesman too. His manner was compact with charm, blending harmoniously the courtly deference of the Old Wykehamist with the debonair *élan* of the Old Etonian, for Cyprian had put in almost a couple of early years at one of the two schools before passing on, abruptly, to the other, and his New College accent was a weapon that the hearts of few bargain-hunting dowagers could resist.

Valentinian Tracy had started his career in about 1925 as a painter, etcher, draughtsman, and, generally speaking, idealist. He starved first in a studio in Exeter, and then in a studio near the British Museum, and after that in a studio near the Chelsea football ground at Stamford Bridge.

After six years of starvation, during which he sold a landscape, fourteen etchings, six bookplates, and a hundred and twenty designs for Christmas cards at eighteenpence a time, and an extra bob a robin, young Valentinian came to the conclusion that the Public did not want his stuff. So he borrowed some money from an old aunt and set up as a photographer instead with extraordinary results. For as he could not understand all the business about focussing and lenses and time-exposures, and never got any results except a smudgy blur, he was forced to depend upon his skill with charcoal and pencil for his results as a photographer, and within six months he was employing a small negro in a crimson velvet suit to do the actual manual labour of squeezing the bulb each time a Beauty Queen smiled dazzlingly into the lens. Once established, Valentinian never looked back.

The third man of the party, reading from left to right, as it were, was young Lord Cholly Plumptonstoke. Lord Cholly had burst into the news a few months before by financing a couple of Senegalese dancers in the World's Long-Distance Ballroom Dancing Championship at Hoxton (called usually a Marathon, in commemoration of the feat of Pheidippides in 490 B.C. when he ran in less than two days from Athens to Sparta, a hundred and fifty miles, to appeal for help against the overwhelming armies of the Barbarians). The Senegalese had failed to stay the course, but feeling that they ought to do something by way of compensation to their patron, had shot the umpire and been duly hanged.

The fourth, and last, man was Evander Spruce, an old youth of about fifty, rosy, round, bespectacled, bland, very sensible to flattery, very impermeable to insult, a patron of the arts, and a member of every Sunday Play-Producing Society.

It was a slow party. Conversation went in fits and starts with heavy pauses in between, and there was not even the fictitious gaiety of alcohol. For none of the nine were drinkers, in any real sense of the word. Mr. Spruce, for example, did not drink because he actively disliked the taste of alcohol; Lord Cholly because he was afraid of his figure; Mr. Pontefract because he was terrified of being considered a "hearty good fellow." Mr. Pontefract had been to a party once where half a dozen guests had suddenly burst into a tumultuous and utterly Rabelaisian marching song of French infantry of Louis Quinze, and he had never been the same man since. The fifteenth Louis to him meant a mode of decoration, a style of furniture, almost an attitude of mind, and it was real physical agony to hear it associated with the suggestion that once there were eighty-four *chasseurs* in the bed of a Marquise.

As for the five girls, they all possessed that instinctively aristocratical habit, which reached its zenith at the court of the Romanovs at Petersburg and Tsarskoe Selo and Yalta in the old days, and which is all too rare in these times of demagogy and blunted perceptions, the habit of drinking just whatever the men of the party were drinking. Later on in the evening, unless a Chronicler of the Follies of the Age happened to drop in for a glass of champagne and a couple of paragraphs, there would be Ovaltine and Horlick's and cocoa and buns, and perhaps a glass of lager beer.

The talk, such as it was, rambled dully from Art Exhibitions to Wimbledon, from sighings for Juan-les-Pins to sighings for Antibes, from feminine fashions to masculine fashions, from the poetry of D. H. Lawrence to the prose of D. H. Lawrence.

The change which was wrought by Hugo's sensational entry was quite astonishing.

Mr. Spruce had just observed languidly that he thought the waists of double-breasted coats were being cut a trifle too high this year, and Mr. Pontefract had remarked that he did not mind the new waist so passionately, but what he did bar was this new *Rêve de Spiquenard* scent that they were using at Magdalen so much this term, when the tousled, ragged, grimy figure came hurtling through the open window, gave one wild glance round, and then went to earth with a headlong plunge behind the divan on which Aurora's magnificent form was reclining.

There was a loud simultaneous gasp, and then a complete silence, broken only by the quick breathing of the fugitive.

The chasing footsteps receded into the distance. Then Aurora suddenly sprang up, and went across to a writing-table, and wrote rapidly on a sheet of paper, and passed it round. This is what she wrote: "It's a stunt of a gossip-writer. It's either Cicerone of the *Lightning*, or Vigilante of the *Thunder*, or Mr. Pepys of the *Meteor*." The note went round to an accompaniment of comprehending nods, gentle whistles, and the hasty production of powder-puffs and lip-sticks from several more than five vanity-cases. A Chronicler of the Follies of the Age had arrived. The party was looking up.

There was another pause. Everyone seemed to be concentrating with tense ferocity. Then Mr. Spruce and Miss Euphrosyne Caerleon spoke simultaneously, and dreamily.

"Nothing can cure the soul but the senses," said Mr. Spruce; and Miss Caerleon said, "Nothing is serious except passion."

"Ah! the Soul!" observed Lady Bunty with sudden

languor. "The soul is born old but grows young. That is the tragedy of life."

"The real tragedy of life," contradicted Cyprian, lighting a rose-tipped cigarette, fragrant with the essence of frankincense, "is getting what one wants." He placed the cigarette in a holder made of flawed turquoise and blew a slow ring.

"Who will have champagne?" asked Aurora, "and who will have absinthe *frappé*?"

"*La sorcière glauque* for me," replied Euphrosyne, somehow conveying an impression that, if people only knew, she had once been Verlaine's mistress. "Simple pleasures are the last refuge of the complex," she added.

"Yes," said Crystallina, "moderation is a fatal thing. Nothing succeeds like excess. That's my motto over the sticks. Give me some sloe-gin, Aurora."

"An English country-gentleman fox-hunting," remarked Mr. Spruce maliciously, "is simply the unspeakable in pursuit of the uneatable."

"Sin," said Lord Cholly triumphantly, as if he had remembered something at long last, "is the only real colour-element left in modern life."

"All thought is immoral," countered Aurora, suppressing a yawn. "Its very essence is destruction."

"When you say, Evander," said Lady Bunty, "that nothing can cure the soul but the senses, it is equally true that nothing can cure the senses except the soul," and there was a murmur of applause at her readiness.

"If all thought is immoral, Aurora," said Cyprian, "all Art is quite useless."

"Nowadays," murmured Euphrosyne, "to be intelligible is to be found out."

"Yes," cried the lady who had almost won immortality by walking from Trebizond to the Gulf of Iskanderun, "and what is more, the man who moralizes is usually a hypocrite, and the woman who moralizes is invariably plain."

There was a ripple of applause at this daring aphorism.   .

Aurora poured out the drinks, sweet champagne and sparkling Burgundy, and little glasses of absinthe, and honey-thick Advocaat of the Netherlands, and beer laced plentifully with Hollands gin.

"Are you still sleeping with Bertie, Honoria?" cried Valentinian above the rising clatter of brilliance.

"No," replied the Orientaliste, "Bertie is not Sheik-conscious. I asked him to let me share him with Fleurette and Angela and Jane, but he said monogamy was good enough for him, so of course we parted."

"I think I shall live with Vissayanjisinghi for a bit," said Euphrosyne thoughtfully. "He has an ivory and sapphire bed that belonged to the Great Mogul. I told him to come back when he had got it modernized by Heal's."

"Very wise," said Cyprian paternally. "These black men are getting slipshod."

"I hear that Amelia is living with the Shelmerdine triplets," remarked Lady Bunty.

"A Trinitarian effect," said Mr. Spruce.

"Amelia is so thorough," said Valentinian. "I

wonder if I could get them to pose for a modern Judgment of Paris."

"I think it's selfish of her," said Cyprian petulantly.

"Wouldn't you like a drink now?" said Aurora suddenly, leaning over the back of the divan.

Hugo extracted himself with some difficulty and a good deal of diffidence and swallowed three tumblers of champagne straight off. This exploit removed any doubts in the minds of the party that he might be other than a gossip-writer. He was running true to gossip-writer form. But having removed the doubts, he proceeded in the next moment to establish once and for all the certainty that he was not a gossip-writer.

"I say," he said fervently, "thank you so much. I was badly in need of that. I am most awfully grateful to you. Really most awfully grateful."

"Good gracious!" cried Mr. Spruce, who, alert-minded as he was, knew just as well as his neighbour that gratitude and gossip-writing do not go together. "Who is this fellow?"

A chorus of indignant twittering arose, and a circle of flashing eyes concentrated their fire upon the stained, dishevelled, and blackened figure.

"It's all right," said Hugo blinking.

"It's not all right, sir," said Euphrosyne formidably. "It is very far from being all right."

"You have made a forcible entry," shrilled Mr. Spruce, "under false pretences."

"Under false pretences?" demanded Hugo, suddenly fortified by the champagne, and becoming desperate.

"You said you were a Society journalist," cried Cyprian angrily. Apparently he had completely wasted that one about the Tragedy of Life.

"Do you mean to tell me," exclaimed Miss Caerleon, "that you haven't put a note down about Vissayanjisinghi?"

"Oh I know about him," replied Hugo brightly, recalling the Reverend Eustace's heroes. "He played cricket for Sussex and invented the leg-glance."

"The leg-glance is as old as the hills, thank God," murmured Lady Bunty archly, and then she pulled herself up with an oath. She had forgotten that the man was an impostor.

Aurora was looking at Hugo steadily with her great green eyes, and there was a faint line across her forehead. He met her gaze once and nervously turned away.

"Well," remarked Mr. Spruce with disgust, "I'm going home. It's been a nice party, I must say. Not even a Bloomsbury novelist, and this cad masquerading as an important journalist. Any of you boys going my way? Val? Cyprian? Cholly?" He went out and came back almost at once. "Botheration!" he said. It's raining in sheets. I'll ring for a cab."

The solitary cab that was drowsing on the rank soon drew up at the door, and the four men, taking all the umbrellas from the umbrella stand to shelter them in their wild dash across the pavement, departed.

The ladies, wrapping their dainty cloaks round their shoulders and rolling their pyjamas up to the knee, set out through the torrent towards the King's

Road, the mud leaping and slapping their thin silk ankles. If they had not been so cross with Aurora, they would have waited for the storm to abate. But they were in no mood for civil exchanges. As for the dirty refugee, Aurora could do what she liked with him, or he with her, for all they cared.

The party, which had begun so slowly and then flared up like a sluggish bonfire upon which paraffin has been flung, flickered out with startling suddenness. One moment the daring epigrams were whizzing from divan to divan, and the reckless avowals of guilty passion and illicit love were dignifying the moral atmosphere; and the next the studio was empty save for the fugitive and the tall red-gold lady.

Aurora stopped gazing thoughtfully at Hugo, and filled him another glass of champagne.

"Well," she said, at last, with a smile, "I think I win, don't I?"

"Win what?" exclaimed Hugo recoiling.

"The thousand-pound prize. You are Michael Seeley, aren't you?"

"No, no, no, I'm not. My name is Smith."

"Would you care to wash your face?" enquired Aurora politely.

"I only want to be left alone," wailed Hugo, falling on his knees in front of Aurora and burying his head in her lap.

"And so you shall be," crooned a soft voice above him.

"I don't want to be a bother to anyone. I don't want to be in the limelight. I don't want to jump out of aeroplanes."

Aurora patted his nice curly hair soothingly.

"I did so want my first visit to England to be a success," went on the unfortunate youth, and the patting stopped.

"Your what?" said the tawny-haired Magnificence.

"My first visit to England."

"What are you talking about?" enquired Aurora politely.

"This is my first visit to England," said Hugo, doggedly.

"But, Mr. Seeley——"

"I am not Mr. Seeley, I tell you. My name is Smith."

"In that case," said Aurora coldly, lifting Hugo's head off her lap and getting up, "I don't see why I shouldn't get that thousand pounds as much as anybody else."

" No, no, no, no, no," screamed Hugo, leaping to his feet and rushing after the girl and again falling on his knees in front of her, "I implore you not to. On my knees I implore you not to."

"If you'll be straight with me."

"But I am being straight with you. I swear I am. My name is Smith. Hugo Bechstein Smith. I'm the victim of an extraordinary coincidence."

"Indeed?" said Aurora drily.

"Yes." Hugo licked his lips nervously and gulped. "You see, it's like this." And he plunged again into the long, rambling, semi-coherent account of his life at Kalataheira, and of his singular adventures since he left Nassau, Bahamas.

Aurora, her pyjamaed legs crossed elegantly, her

coppery head lying back against a cushion so that her shining neck was like the pillar of a Greek temple, her eyes closed, and her interlocked fingers buried in the jungle of hair at the back of her head, listened impassively. At the end she remarked slowly, "It's very difficult to tell if such a thing is possible."

"But I swear to you——" She swept him aside.

"I don't mean that. I mean whether such a transformation is possible. The Michael Seeley I've seen at the cinema is just the ordinary, stupid, romantic-looking booby who can't act for toffee. Like all the rest of them. But if you're acting now, you're the greatest actor in the world. Can a boob become a genius suddenly?"

"Every word I've told you is the truth," said Hugo earnestly.

"If you really were Michael Seeley," replied Aurora, "you wouldn't want this thousand-pound stunt ruined on the first night. And as I've ruined it by recognizing you, naturally you've got to try every dodge you can to persuade me that you're not Michael Seeley."

"But if I was him, why should I come jumping in at your open window?"

"Because a crowd was after you, of course," retorted Aurora, and Hugo was silenced.

"I suppose someone spotted you," she went on. "Well, if it's a choice between someone else and me getting the thousand, I vote for me," and she went towards the telephone.

Hugo had to think quickly. Again he was face to face with that situation to the handling of which his three uncles had devoted so many of their lectures and so much of their anxious thought. He had to impose his will upon a woman, and, in this case, to impose it jolly quickly. The maximum time at his disposal that he could count upon was the three minutes that normally elapse before any London telephone number is connected to any other number, except a wrong one, by the automatic dialling system. This Time Factor, as military historians call it, ruled out Uncle Eustace's method. Sir Galahad himself, with all his shining armour and all the prestige conferred upon him by Lord Tennyson's implied suggestion that he was reincarnated in the person of the Prince Consort, could not have worked so fast as to get a strange girl on to a pedestal and, by sheer worship, persuade her to take her hooks off a thousand yellow-boys that were hers for the telephoning, all inside three minutes. It simply wasn't in the form-book, and Hugo dismissed it even before Aurora's shell-like, coral-pink ear had picked up the dialling-tone.

Uncle René's method was definitely more promising, but here again Time was against him. Hugo's natural diffidence had been, if anything, increased by the rebuff from the cherry lips of Felida, and he had hardly recovered his self-confidence sufficiently to lay siege to a total stranger, even if he had been his normal, or rather Michael Seeley's normal, exquisite, Savile Row self. But in a state of nervous depression, covered with soot and grime, tattered and torn, scratched and bruised, it was ludicrously out of the question. Besides, to judge from the brilliant and extraordinary conversation to which he had listened when hiding behind the divan, this girl had lots of lovers already, including a black man as like as not. What chance had he to join their ranks in a wooing of three minutes? Nothing remained, then, but the practical common sense, the sturdy Nordic downrightness, of Pastor Schmidt. To tie this girl hand and foot with that silk sash that was lying on the chair, if need be to gag her with a handkerchief, and to retreat by the way he had come would be a matter of a few seconds. Aurora had her back to him and was busy manipulating the time-saving and labour-saving dial when Hugo sprang upon her. A moment later he was lying on his face on the floor, a sharp knee grinding his spine, and his left arm twisted in such a way that the least movement would break it, and a moment after that he was released and scrambled to his feet.

Aurora was standing in front of him, hands on hips, and a radiant smile on her face. "Wonderful thing jiu-jitsu," she remarked, and the smile suddenly faded, and she stared at him in perplexity. "That's funny," she murmured.

"I'm sure it is," said Hugo sulkily. He was feeling uncommonly foolish.

"Why didn't you slip the ordinary counter across?" she asked.

"Because I don't know jiu-jitsu, blast you," replied the ungallant and unsuccessful advocate of the Big Stick.

"But I always heard you were an expert in it before you went on to the films. It was the only thing you were an expert in——" She broke off and stared at him. Then she said, "Look here, if your story about the South Sea Islands and all that is true, you ought to be able to speak French," and she went off into fluent French. Something gave way in Hugo's head, some last repression relaxed after that evening of strain and chase and roof-climbing, and he slipped easily, like a motor going into top gear, into the language that a citizen of the neighbourhood of the Fortifications of Paris, beyond the Cimetière de Montparnasse say, or in the region of Pantin, might use to another citizen of the same quarter who had defrauded him of one franc seventy-five. He told Aurora exactly what he thought of her and her friends and her black men and her relations with her mother and father. He then said it all over again in a different way. Then he did it again, this time with the help of metaphor and simile, combing the drains and the gutters for new variations, delving into refuse-heaps and peering under the flaps of gypsy bivouacs and lifting old tin cans and kicking over garbage. It was a beautiful performance and would have been of immense interest to students of the Parisian *argot*, the Parisian habits, and the Parisian life in general, of forty years before. A faint flavour of Boulanger permeated it. The ghost of Gambetta was hovering near, and surely young Dreyfus peeped in through the window to see if Esterhazy was selling any more secrets, and the Coquelins were playing at the Comédie, and Fantin-Latour was quarrelling with Legros, and Steinlen was drawing for *Gil Blas*, and Loti was back from Japan, and the painters lunched at the Rat Mort, and the figures of Metz and Strasburg were sheathed in funerary black in the Place de la Concorde.

Aurora had long ago coiled herself down to a pouffe and, chin on hand, she listened like an Elder of the Scottish Free Church to his Minister, nodding agreement at the more impressive points, raising her brows in admiration at the more daring flights, and lowering her eyes modestly at any especially garbageous piece of vituperation. When Hugo brought his last swinging cadence to a full close, Aurora said quietly, "Bravo, that clinches it."

"Clinches what?" said Hugo after he had recovered his breath.

"You aren't Michael Seeley," the girl replied decisively.

"I'm not. But why does that clinch it?"

"Michael was Eton and Oriel."

"I don't understand."

"He can't speak a word of French."

"But why not?"

"Well, he was at Eton and Oriel."

Hugo was quite baffled by this, but wisely let the matter drop. If the lady was satisfied at last, why pursue the reasons further? Nor was her active mind dallying about with the obvious past. It was already exploring the dubious future.

"What are we going to do now?" she was saying to herself. "Have these people got a legal hold over you? I mean, have you signed a contract?"

"Yes. At the point of a pistol," said Hugo sulkily. "But I've no evidence for that except my word."

"And of course they'll lie like troopers. No. You can't get out that way."

She propped an exquisite chin on the palms of her hands. There was a long silence. Then she said slowly, with a smile that curled up one corner of her mouth, "If I get you out of this, Mr.—er—Smith, what is it worth to you?"

Hugo's business instincts were at once aroused. "Let me see," he said incisively. "If you betray me you get £1000; if you save me, well—let us make it guineas."

"Twelve hundred guineas?"

"Eleven hundred pounds."

"Eleven hundred guineas."

"Done."

Aurora held out her hand and Hugo took it.

"I say," he stammered awkwardly, "I'm awfully sorry I attacked you like that——"

"It was a pleasant change," said Aurora, and she blushed faintly and looked even more adorable than ever.

"A pleasant change from what?" demanded Hugo.

"Oh, I don't know."

"But you do know."

"It wasn't anything really."

"You mean your black lovers don't knock you about."

"I haven't got a black lover."

"Oh no, I beg your pardon," said Hugo. "It was that other girl who was living with a native. . . . Oh!" He recoiled suddenly.

"What is it?"

"I must go away at once."

Aurora laughed. "But why?"

"It's nearly two o'clock in the morning. They wouldn't like it."

"Who wouldn't?"

"Well, I mean, from the way you were all talking . . . I don't mean the epigrams, of course. They were all Oscar Wilde. But you lead such wonderful lives. . . . I mean all your lovers. . . ."

"Silly child. I haven't got a lover. And none of the others have either."

"But the way you talked——"

"Run away home to bed, child."

"But where shall I go?" asked Hugo. "I can't go back to my hotel."

"Why not stay here?"

The young man blushed bright scarlet, and backed nervously into the table on which the drinks were placed, and knocked the whole thing over.

"I—I—couldn't do that," he cried in distress. "It would compromise you hopelessly."

Aurora wrinkled her brows. "Compromise me? Whatever does that mean?"

"It's a thing," said Hugo, recalling one of Uncle Eustace's most famous phrases, "that no gentleman does to a lady."

"But are you a gentleman?" asked Aurora with an enchanting demureness.

"Most certainly," answered Hugo firmly.

Aurora sighed. "The public schools never seem to turn out anything but pansies and gentlemen in these days. It's a hard life for a young girl."

"Pansies?" said Hugo doubtfully. "I never heard that they went in much for horticulture."

Aurora looked at him sharply for a moment and went on, "Listen. I want that money. And I'm not going to run the risk of your going to a hotel and being recognized. So I'll go to a hotel and you can stay here. You'll find a bed through there."

"Splendid idea," cried Hugo. Aurora looked extremely cross. "If you think it's a splendid idea to drive me out into the rain at two o'clock in the morning, then your notion of splendour is not the same as mine."

She looked so tawnily magnificent in her anger, that in Hugo's imagination the dim silhouette of Uncle René began to grow firmer in outline against the now-receding majesty of Uncle Eustace, and he said diffidently, "If you'd like to stay—I wouldn't mind—I promise you I'll behave——"

"Like a gentleman, eh?" cried Aurora in a fury, hitting him on the ear with her open hand and sweeping out of the room. As she was left-handed, the ear which suffered was not the one which had received Felida's buffet.

The world was humming and buzzing in Hugo's head with such a strong drone that he hardly heard the bang of the front-door and the rich contralto of Aurora's voice as she hailed a taxi and ordered the man to drive to Claridge's.

Hugo undressed slowly and put on a suit of lilac silk pyjamas that he found in a wardrobe. He lay awake for a long time wondering what he had done wrong. The rough, homely methods of Uncle Hans had brought him an ignominious overthrow; Uncle Eustace had brought him anger; and Uncle René a fearful blow on the side of the head.

Hugo pressed his throbbing temples, and thought of the slow fall of the rollers upon the coral of Kalataheira.

CHAPTER XV

THERE was a strained atmosphere in the sitting-room of the Ritz when Miss Aurora St. Hilaire was announced. Cokayne was biting his fingers instead of attending to the fan-mail. Felida was languidly repulsing the advances of an Argentinian dancer, and Mr. Dowley was perpetually leaping to the telephone. The entry of the russet magnificence caused a profound sensation. Cokayne automatically sprang to his feet and pulled his waistcoat down. Mr. Dowley dropped the receiver and smiled a beautiful ivory smile, and exclaimed, "You wish a job? I will see what I can fix." The Argentinian glanced over his shoulder, rose from his knees beside the divan, and came forward with the slouching shamble that is so often described, when it is used by a famous person, as pantherine. "You dance, señorita, yes?" he began at once. "Then you shall dance with me?"

Felida, relapsing for one second into little Maudie Maggs of Kennington, pulled off her shoe and threw it as hard as she could at the dancer. It missed him, unfortunately, and went through the window into the street. A moment or two later the sound of the tinkle of broken glass upon a stone pavement and the cries of the indignant populace were wafted up from Piccadilly.

Aurora might be the daughter (indeed, was the daughter) of a frivolous, handsome, and inconstant child of Mayfair, but she was also the daughter of the hard-headed corset-manufacturer of Accrington, and she came straight to the point.

"I've got young Seeley," she said.

"Hell," said Dope.

Mr. Dowley reached for his cheque-book.

"Wait," said Aurora, "I'm not giving him back. I've come to get his contract cancelled."

The Persian Publicity-Director frowned. "What's the game, little lady?" he enquired, peering at her.

"If you don't cancel his contract, I'll take him down to Brighton with me for a week-end. That will rather spoil your Turtle-dove Tour of Domestic Felicity, won't it?"

Arthur Ed. rubbed his hands in respectful admiration. "Lady, you're great," he exclaimed. "I'll give you a hundred a week to join us as deputy publicity man."

"If you do," croaked Felida, "I walk out on you. Get that, big boy?"

"The Seeley contract, please," said Aurora, quietly side-stepping a deft flanking movement of the Argentinian and boxing his ear as he slouched past like an amorous leopard.

Mr. Dowley suddenly became intensely excited. His brown eyes blazed and he marched up and down the room with his hands behind his back. He gave the impression of being a kettle that is just on the verge of coming to the boil, or of a delicate lemon and gold narcissus that is about to open its petals to the sun.

He stopped, clapped his hands, and cried, "Lady, you're a genius. The boy can have his contract back. I'm tired of him. He's more trouble than he's worth. But you must sign a promise that you'll take him to Brighton, and then we'll have a grand little old divorce case. Eh, Felida? Eh, Dope? That's the style. What's more, we'll run a double divorce, one here and one in Reno, Nevada. Dope, get the story out to the Press boys: Miss Caliente, interviewed to-day, said, with a sob in her throat, 'Alas, it is true. The house of my dreams has fallen about my ears. For months now Michael has been maliciously debauching my intellect, and that is the cause why I am divorcing him in Reno. Before I met him I used to read—used to read——' "

Mr. Dowley broke off, snapped his fingers, and went on, "Fill in some good highbrow books there, Dope. I can't remember any just at the moment. Go on from there: But now I don't get a chance of reading anything except Harriet Beecher Stowe and Ballyhoo. Maliciously debauched intellectually, concluded the World's Adored.—Get that out good and quick, Dope."

"That's O.K. for America," replied Cokayne, "but it's no good here."

"It's got to be Brighton here," said Aurora, and Dope nodded sourly. His admiration for the splendour of Aurora's person in no way diminished his disgust at missing the reward of the thousand pounds.

"You've got to fix that, Dame," said Arthur Ed.

"Dope, draw an agreement. In return for Smith's contract to masquerade as Seeley, she agrees to spend a week-end with him at Brighton and to furnish us with the evidence. And he'd better swear an affidavit that he is Michael Seeley. That'll straighten things up."

Mr. Cokayne banged away on his typewriter while Mr. Dowley studied Aurora's appearance with the frankest and liveliest interest, and the Argentinian dancer held his head and whimpered softly in a corner. Felida ostentatiously turned her back on the room and studied herself intently in a pier-glass.

The agreement was typed in duplicate, carefully scrutinized by Dowley and Aurora, signed and exchanged.

"And the repository ticket for the rest of Mr. Smith's property?" said Aurora.

"Not in the agreement," snapped Ed. promptly.

"It doesn't require an agreement," murmured the girl with the gentleness of a cat that is sure of its kill, "to get one's own property restored. Though it sometimes requires a writ."

"Got us," observed Cokayne succinctly.

Mr. Dowley fumbled in his pocket-book rather sulkily and produced the ticket and handed it over. Then his face brightened. "Dame," he said in a most insinuating tone, "will you lunch with me?"

Felida whizzed round. "I'm lunching with you, you big stiff," she barked.

"Then lunch with me," interposed Cokayne before the manager had time to extricate himself from the dilemma.

"No, no, no," cooed the Argentinian, now somewhat recovered. "The divine señorita will lunch with me, and I will tell her the poem which I have just composed about her."

"Huh!" commented Felida with a remarkable amount of meaning in the monosyllable.

But Miss St. Hilaire was not to be blandished into acceptance. She had earned eleven hundred guineas in a single morning, and she was anxious to get home, and collect the cheque, and draw the money.

Miss St. Hilaire went home, collected both the cheque and Hugo, paid the former into her bank, took the latter out to lunch, and then drove him to Somerset House to swear his affidavit that he was Michael Seeley and married to Felida, and then, after they had returned to her flat, she explained the terms of her bargain with Mr. Dowley.

Hugo was appalled. During the anxious hours of waiting for news while Aurora was at the Ritz, the pendulum had swung completely to Uncle Eustace. Sitting in Miss St. Hilaire's flat, Hugo had had ample time for reflection, and by midday he was regarding the lady as a mixture of Joan of Arc, St. Theresa of Avila, and Florence Nightingale. She had gone out to fight his battles like a feminine Sir Lancelot. For him and for him alone (no one could suggest that so beautiful a character had been in the very least bit influenced by the beggarly honorarium which he had promised her) she had gone single-handed to tackle a gang of unscrupulous toughs in their lair. Indeed so profound did Hugo's admiration become, and so high soared the pedestal upon which his lady was placed, that by a quarter to one he was regarding the Ritz Hotel as if it was as dangerous a trap as the basement of a Chinese laundry in the Ratcliffe Highway, E.15, and Aurora as if she was a feminine counterpart of Mr. Sherlock Holmes.

When she had returned from the Ritz, waving the contract over her head, Hugo had fallen on his knees in front of her and kissed the hem of her skirt. But now, when he found that the price which she had agreed to pay for his liberty was nothing less than the fate which Uncle Eustace had always emphatically stated might be all right for Frenchwomen and that sort, but for an Englishwoman was a great deal worse than a lingering death from cancer, the unfortunate youth was paralysed with horror. It was utterly impossible for him to accept such a sacrifice. The very fact that she had been prepared to make it raised the pedestal to such dizzy heights that Hugo began to feel that he had been guilty of sacrilege in touching even the hem of her skirt. A golden halo seemed to crown her glorious hair. Faint voices of a celestial choir vibrated upon the air of Chelsea. An odour of incense was wafted in at the open windows from the direction of the Lots Road Power Station and the Cremorne Arms public-house.

Hugo stood up, took his hat, and said, "I shall never forget this as long as I live. Good-bye."

"What do you mean?" asked Aurora in surprise.

"I am going to give myself up to Mr. Dowley."

"But, good heavens, why?"

"Because I cannot accept your sacrifice."

"What sacrifice?"

Hugo fell on his knees again. "It's so like you to pretend that it is only a trifle. But you cannot deceive me. I know better.

"Nonsense," said Aurora, tapping the floor with her heel. "We'll enjoy ourselves at Brighton."

Hugo shook his head. "Lovely goddess, I cannot do it. You know I cannot. I worship you too much."

"Oh hell," said Aurora petulantly.

"You do understand——"

"And what about my agreement with Mr. Dowley?" asked Aurora grimly. "You say you don't want to make a loose woman of me. Do you want to make me a fraud?'

"No, no, of course not."

"Very well, then."

"But surely," Hugo expostulated, "it's a very odd state of affairs when I have to drag a wonderful creature like you through the sordid beastliness of the law-courts in order to get a divorce from a woman I'm not married to?"

"It seems a bit queer," admitted Aurora with a delicious laugh. "But I've promised on your behalf that you will."

"Can't I just go to the judge and say that Felida and I want to be divorced?"

Aurora threw up her hands. "My poor pet, don't you know the laws of England? If husband and wife both want to part, they aren't allowed to. But if one does and the other doesn't, then they may. Collusion to get married is one thing. Collusion to get un-married is another."

"Miss St. Hilaire," said Hugo with a sort of tragic seriousness, "I've only been in the civilized world for a very short time, but I think everybody in it is utterly mad. I haven't met a single sane person or sane institution or sane idea."

"Never mind about that," said Aurora. "Are you coming to Brighton with me to save my honour?"

"But how in heaven's name will it save your honour to go with me to Brighton for a week-end? Uncle Eustace always said that a woman's honour is the brightest jewel in her moral diadem."

Aurora wrinkled her brow. "Your Uncle Eustace said that?"

"He did."

"But what about my honour if I break my pledged word?"

"That isn't honour as Uncle Eustace meant it," said Hugo.

"Then what did he mean?" enquired Aurora.

Hugo blushed feverishly and began to stammer.

Aurora interrupted, "So you're going to make me a fraud?"

"Sooner that than a——"

"Yes?"

"Oh, you know."

"Hugo Bechstein Smith," cried Aurora, "you are no better than a damned prig."

"I'm terribly sorry——"

"Look here, young man," she interrupted. "You've got to go to Brighton with someone, or Dowley will be after me with a bucketful of writs. You see that, don't you? If you won't go with me you've jolly well got to pretend you've been with me."

"Why must it be Brighton?" asked Hugo.

"It always is," she answered impatiently.

"But don't the judges smell a rat, if the evidence always comes from the same town? I mean, wouldn't it be better if it was varied a bit?"

"If the evidence didn't come from Brighton, it would look jolly queer," Aurora explained. "They don't like innovations in the Law Courts."

Hugo sighed. It was all very difficult to understand. "Very well," he said. "I must take someone to Brighton. How do I get hold of one? Shall I advertise?"

"If you do, you'll get ten years penal servitude and twenty strokes with the cat for being engaged in the White Slave Traffic," was the grim response.

"But, good gracious me!" exclaimed Hugo. "Do they flog people for trying to comply with the law?"

"They might. You never know."

"Miss St. Hilaire—Aurora—I beg of you to help me. What am I to do?"

Hugo's voice was getting quite plaintive.

Aurora lit a cigarette and made a dainty twirling gesture with it in the air, expressive of care-free independence. "My dear child," she said airily, "if you won't go with me, you surely don't expect me to provide you with a rival demoiselle. And incidentally," she went on with a sudden change to severity, "it is a criminal offence to try to persuade a girl to find you a victim for your unbridled licentiousness. You could get thirty strokes with the cat for that."

Hugo almost burst into tears. "But I'm not licentious," he protested. "I'm being exactly the opposite."

"You don't have to tell me that," said Aurora coldly.

"I think, if you don't mind," said Hugo, his voice suddenly faint, "that I'll go home now. I'm not feeling very well."

"Good-bye," said the tawny-haired goddess.

Hugo slunk out, muffled his face once more in his scarf, and went to a hotel in Sloane Street in a taxi.

The posters of the lunch editions of the evening papers were announcing:

PEER'S DAUGHTER

FINDS

MICHAEL SEELEY

Sitting on his bed in his small room at the Sloane Street Hotel, Hugo reflected bitterly that freedom in this crazy world was just as bad as slavery to the Dowley circus. Indeed, in some ways the prospects were even blacker now, even though he had won his liberty and had a very large sum of money deposited in a London bank. The fearful experience of the parachute and the Welsh Harp became a trivial episode when compared to the terrors and dangers which lay ahead. He checked off the position on his fingers. In order to save one girl's honour, he had to ruin another girl. Furthermore, he had to find a girl who was prepared, for a consideration, to be ruined. In order to find that girl, he had, apparently, to run the risk of interminable imprisonment and innumerable lashes. And when that other girl had been found and the Brighton ordeal had been successfully undergone, he had then to face the miserable and prolonged proceedings of the Divorce Court, all of which would be based upon his perjured affidavit that the Caliente was his lawful wedded wife. Hugo shuddered when he contemplated the penalty for perjury, and he shuddered still more when he wondered what penalties would be inflicted on a man who was found guilty, simultaneously, of perjury, of conspiracy to defeat the ends of justice, of persuading a girl to procure him a girl, and of engaging in the White Slave Traffic. And he was involved in all these hideous crimes through no fault of his own. The pitfalls which lay in the path of a man who wished to be divorced from his wife were deep enough, thought Hugo, but they were shallow indentations in the ground compared with those which yawned for the man who was planning to be divorced from a lady who was not his wife.

He went out into the balcony of his room and

gazed across the expanse of houses in the Cadogan-Brompton area. In every single one of those tall, narrow, heavily porched houses dwelt a family that had money invested in Consols. So Uncle Eustace had told him. The whole of South-West Three and South-West Seven was poised upon the basement system for the domestic staff and the three-per-cents for the remainder of the occupants. The whole district was a single solid fabric. And all the inhabitants were respectable. All were unspotted from the world. The hideous dangers of imprisonment, fines, and flogging which confronted poor Hugo had never ventured to raise their heads in the Onslows, the Ovingtons, the Hans and Ponts, the Pelhams and the Thurloes and the Beauchamps.

With a fearful oath Hugo rushed downstairs, flung himself at a cab and shouted to the driver to take him to any railway station that would get him out of London. The cab-driver, being a Scotsman, drove him in a leisurely way to Liverpool Street Station and thereby secured a seven-and-threepenny fare. But Hugo did not mind. He booked a first-class single to Saffron Walden—simply because the name appealed to him—secured a place in the restaurant car, and drank seven double whiskies-and-sodas in forty-eight minutes.

The restaurant car attendants respectfully scratched out the previous record of five double whiskies-and-sodas in forty-four minutes, a record which had stood for some years, and entered Hugo's feat upon their tablets.

R

CHAPTER XVI

THERE is peace to be found in the county of Suffolk, and for a couple of weeks Hugo found it. The nightmare life of London dropped away in a moment, just as real nightmares drop away when the sleeper awakens out of darkness into the sunlight. Felida and Mr. Dowley, and the terrifyingly unscrupulous Dope, receded into a dim obscurity. The hue-and-cry for Michael Seeley had died down the instant Aurora claimed the prize, and the great honest heart of the British Public was concentrating now upon the exploits of the Borealian cricket eleven, which was touring the country. The lustre of the high-dive into the Welsh Harp had already been dimmed by the innings of three hundred and forty not out which a young gentleman from Kicking Mule Gulch, Murrumbidgee County, Borealia, had scored in three hours against the unfortunate citizens of Glamorgan, Britain, and the roseleaf curve of Felida's lips was rapidly fading before the sensation at Nottingham when the Might of England (a technical journalistic expression for eleven cricketers) was overthrown in a single innings by the redoubtable Wheatstalks.

And so poor Hugo found some peace in Suffolk at last. It was a conclusive proof of his worn and battered condition of body and mind that he should have selected for his retreat one of those counties which Uncle Eustace so heartily despised. If Hugo had been his normal self he would never have dreamt of staying, deliberately, of his own free will, in a county which was not good enough to compete in the First-Class County Cricket Championship, but only pottered about in the Minor Championship. But he was so tired that he did not care. And any faint twinge of conscience that he may have felt, was softened by the fact that although he went into Suffolk every day, he slept every night in Saffron Walden in the First-Class County of Essex.

It was early June, and Suffolk is very lovely in early June. It is a county of corn-growing, rich red ploughland in the spring, and in the summer rolling fields of ripening grain. The kindly earth is full of promise for the harvest. The villages are small and the farmhouses far between; here and there a derelict windmill stands in the summery haze, with a brave old defiance against all modernity. And everywhere are the great parish churches that might easily be taken for small cathedrals, splendid survivals of the days when East Anglia was a humming little world of cloth-workers, when the villages of Kersey and Woolsey sold their wares in markets that lay within sound of the carillon of the Beffroi of Bruges, when Worsted was a prosperous townlet of Norfolk, and the Cloth Hall at Ypres was symbolical of other things than savage destruction.

Hugo wandered in a dream through the long village of Long Melford, past the old Bull Inn to the

Green and the stately church beyond it, with its stained glass and its painted frescoes in the Clopton Chapel. He woke up for a moment or two when he found himself in the tiny church at Acton gazing down at the brass effigy of Sir Robert de Bures, the second of the four great brasses of England, lying there in its chain-mail as Sir Robert himself must have lain six hundred and thirty years ago. And near the armed knight was the brass of Alice de Bryan, a widow lady, in a simple gown. He went to Clare, a small, sleepy, tired village that has given its name to a Cambridge College and a county of Ireland, to the Dukedom of Clarence and the Clarenceux King-of-Arms. And from Clare he drifted through the magic lanes to Stoke-by-Nayland with its rose-pink church tower, and the busy little town of Sudbury, birthplace of Gainsborough and scene of the Eatanswill election, and to East Bergholt where Constable was born, and so wandering he came past many churches till he came to the greatest of them all, the dark grey, dominant splendour of the church at Lavenham.

It seemed to Hugo to be a land that has been forgotten by Progress. He saw no gangs of housebreakers picking away at the Tudor Hall at Melford, to replace it with blocks of flats. He saw no tearing down of moated granges to make way for offices in concrete and steel, to be filled with glass furniture and overworked typists. Development, that blessed word which used to mean only the change in a photographic negative from absence of visible picture to presence of visible picture, and which now means change from ancient loveliness to modern hideousness, had not yet reached Suffolk. This, felt Hugo, was the England that Uncle Eustace had known and loved, the England of beer and Queen Victoria and Doctor W. G. Grace. No one in Suffolk would throw him out of aeroplanes. No one in Suffolk would stick revolvers into his ribs. No one in Suffolk had ever heard of Tabriz in Northern Persia, home-town of Arfa-ed-Dovleh.

So Hugo wandered in the enchanted land, and leant on stiles, and smelt the honeysuckle, and gazed at the sheets of brass where the buttercups glittered beneath the willows, and talked to innkeepers. He drank the beer of Greene King, whose plaque, like a bas-relief of Lucca della Robbia, on the walls of many inns, is a sure proof to the thirsty wayfarer that good beer is obtainable within. He learnt, among other strange bits of lore, that people only go to Clare to die, and even at that they are not very successful, and that at Lavenham people only get out of bed on Thursdays. He learnt that kittens which are born when the brambles are out are weakling kittens, whereas kittens which are born when the whitethorn is in bloom are rare little devils for the mice. He watched a man making brooms for sale in Saffron, a man whose great-grandfather had made brooms for sale in Saffron, and he found an old lady who was making a smock. But who was likely to wear the smock was not so easily discoverable.

And on wet afternoons Hugo strolled, awe-struck, through the rooms of the Saffron Walden Museum and gazed at the skeletons of long-forgotten mastodons, and the strange fauna of long-melted glaciers, and the trophies of many a long-dead Anglo-Indian colonel. Hugo never mastered, nor could he find any-one to help him to master, the connection between the bones of prehistoric mammalia and the sweet cornlands of English Suffolk. But there they are, room after room of them, jostling and jumbling each other so closely that is is often difficult to distinguish be-tween the bones of the yak which Smithers Sahib shot near Gilgit in '84, and the bones of the rat which Smithers Sahib, then of course a much older and more highly seasoned man, strongly denied having seen on the floor of the Officers' Mess in Amballa in '99. But come yaks, come rats, it is all one to Saffron Walden. Few of the citizenry above the school leaving-age visit that dread mausoleum. The town rests content upon its bulb of Saffron-crocus which was brought by the palmer from Jerusalem, con-cealed in a hollow in his palmer's staff, the very first bulb of the coveted yellow dye to be smuggled into England.

One morning, a June morning, a morning of bird-song and hedge-scent and the far-off cries of hay-makers, Hugo was drifting along an enchanted lane. Clematis was flowering in the thorn-bushes and the edges of the lane were thick with the flower that the English call ladies'-lace and Socrates called hemlock. There was even a faint touch of dust in the air, and in these days you have to be a long way from rushing cars, and tar-macadam roads, and concrete racing-tracks, and A.A. Scouts, to get a touch of dust in the air. The corn was beginning to turn from dark jade to pale lemon, and there was no wind. Bees and butter-flies wandered hither and thither so slowly that it seemed as if they thought their span of life was eternity and not a little hour.

Suddenly Hugo stopped. A sound had come through the belt of beechwoods, a staccato sound, a crisp, brisk click. There it was again. And again, click.

It was unmistakeable. Hugo had never heard it before, the real authentic sound of willow upon stitched leather. But he had often enough heard the sound of palm-wood upon a primitive ball of cocoa-nut fibre with goatskin stretched round it, and he knew that beyond that belt of beech-woods a game of cricket was in progress.

A game of cricket! Kalataheira sprang before his eyes. Scarlet parrakeets flapped across the Suffolk corn; tom-toms were beating in the vestry of that old stone church with the rose-pink brick tower; the murmurous lapping of small waves upon coral came whispering through the woods. And there, in the en-chanted lane, stood the ghost of Uncle Eustace, shaking a finger and talking. What was he saying? The words were almost audible, those oft-repeated, well-remembered words, "If the batsman shows a tendency to draw away from the wicket, put three men on the leg-side and send him down a fast yorker on the leg-stump." Dear Uncle Eustace, with your great beard and your deep, strong laugh, and your simple mind. Get the man out in any way you can, so long as you keep within the letter of the law.

Dear Uncle Eustace, that was the fifth of your five gospels. Hugo smiled a gentle, reflective smile. The old boy did not seem to know very much about women, but he did know about cricket.

Click! There it was again. Hugo began to hurry. It was only half-past eleven, and the match probably had not yet begun. If he was quick, he might not miss a single ball, he, brought up to cricket from infancy, and never yet a player or a spectator in any match. He broke into a run, and soon came round the corner of the beeches on to that loveliest of English sights, a country-house cricket-ground, surrounded by trees, in the sunlight. The wickets were pitched, the outfield was mown, the sight-screens were sheets of white against the trees. Rows of deck-chairs were filled with shimmering summer-frocks and pale silk stockings, and surmounted with gay, dragon-fly parasols, and in front of them the players themselves were practising, some batting, some bowling, others throwing catches to each other. Hugo with a thrill recognized the blazers of the Foresters, the Hogs, the Dumplings, the Stragglers, I Zingari, the Nomads, and many another Joseph's coat.

He crossed a buttercup-meadow until he reached the fence of the cricket-field itself, and then he leant upon it and looked across at the beautiful, shimmering kaleidoscope. A quarter to twelve struck upon an invisible clock. Hugo wondered when they were going to begin. The practising was slackening off, and the men in flannels were clustering in small groups and talking. Then a telegraph-boy arrived with a telegram, and there was a lot of shouting and running to and fro. Still the game did not begin. Finally the captains tossed and one side came out to field. It consisted of eight men in white flannels, a gardener's boy in corduroys and a grey flannel shirt, a chauffeur in blue breeches and black, shiny leggings, and another man in flannels who followed a few minutes later amid shouts of "I'll relieve you when you like, Jim." This was obviously a substitute lent to the fielding side by the batting side.

By a curious chance the very first ball of the match was hit sharply to the boundary almost exactly where Hugo was watching. In order to save a long run for one of the fieldsmen, Hugo picked it up—the first real cricket-ball which he had ever handled—and flicked it full pitch exactly into the wicket-keeper's hands with the effortless ease of one who has been accustomed to bring down a humming-bird with a cocoanut at eighty yards range, five times out of six.

Two overs later the same thing happened, and a tall middle-aged man, wearing an Eton Rambler scarf and an air of authority, strolled across the ground between two overs and called out to Hugo:

"You a cricketer, sir?"

"Well—er—er——"

"Care to turn out for us?" went on the man. "We're three short."

Hugo was enthralled. To play cricket — a real game—with real cricketers—if only Uncle Eustace had been there to see. And how Uncle René would have smiled.

"They'll fix you up with kit at the house," said the

Rambler. "Tell them I sent you. Vernon is the name."

"I'd love to," exclaimed Hugo enthusiastically.

"Good man," said the other, and he went back to his place.

A quarter of an hour later, Hugo, feeling very self-conscious and very proud, was standing in an alert position at extra-cover-point.

There was plenty of fielding to be done, for the opening pair of batsmen soon found their form, and it turned out that two of the three missing players were the star bowlers of their team. The score mounted rapidly and Hugo was kept busy. But Uncle Eustace's teaching, and those laborious hours of practice on the scented evenings by the lagoon, bore fruit on this Suffolk playing-ground, and Hugo won many little tributes of applause by the brilliance of his picking-up and the lightning accuracy of his throwing.

At one o'clock play was stopped for luncheon, with the score standing at 131 for no wickets. Mr. Vernon walked across to Hugo and asked him his name. Hugo hesitated. If he said Smith and someone recognized him as the film star, it would lead to awkward explanations. On the other hand, now that the excitement and the hue and cry had died down, there could be no harm in boldly taking advantage of the prestige of the name of Seeley on an ephemeral occasion like this. Hugo therefore replied firmly, "My name is Seeley." He was rather surprised, and a little disappointed, that the Eton Rambler registered no sign of ever having heard the name before. Nor did the other members of the team to whom he was introduced. Among the ladies, however, there was a most gratifying buzz of recognition. Several fair ones, who had been asleep in their deck-chairs for some time, awoke suddenly. Others instantly abandoned the knitting or sewing upon which they were relying to pull them through the tedium of watching their "men-folk" at their dull and stupid game. Others, again, shut their novels hastily, while only a group of three or four young ladies of about seventeen years of age paid no attention to him, but continued to stare with rapt adoration upon the two incoming batsmen, both of whom, it appeared, had played cricket for Middlesex.

The enthusiasm with which the ladies clustered round Hugo at first puzzled Mr. Vernon and his elegant colleagues, for they were not accustomed to being ignored in this way on their majestic return to the luncheon-tent, but when Hugo's identity was revealed to them, they became extremely sulky. It was true that the fellow's fielding had been astonishingly brilliant, but that was just the sort of monkey-trick which these fellows were taught in their profession. Just like doing acrobatics on the balcony of the Ritz and jumping out of aeroplanes and so on. In a very few minutes Mr. Vernon and his colleagues and his opponents were feeling like the Guardsmen in *Patience* who found that in spite of their "uniforms handsome and chaste the peripatetics of long-haired aesthetics are very much more to their taste."

Hugo, however, was delighted. The excitement of his first match, the applause which he had won, the strength of the home-brewed ale, the beauty of the countryside, and the unaffected admiration of so many charming ladies, not so beautiful perhaps as Felida but far less sophisticated, all mounted to his head and made him forget his natural shyness. One or two slightly *risqué* bits of repartee, rather in the style of Uncle René, brought peals of silvery giggling and numerous dark and heavy scowls. Hugo began to wonder if he might not find some charmer at this very table who would masquerade as Aurora in a Brighton hotel, and scrutinized each of his immediate neighbours in a way which they found enchanting and the cricketers licentious. But they all looked so very simple and gay and innocent that he soon abandoned the notion. These pretty creatures of the country were very different from the experienced, self-reliant women of a great city like London. Hugo felt that it would be a crime to make temporary love to any of them. It would leave behind a broken heart and a blasted life. He directed his attention, therefore, more towards the old ale and the steak-and-kidney pie and less towards his companions. The temperature at his end of the table cooled; the ladies drooped disappointedly. At the other end, among the cricketers, a definite thaw set in, and one of the players thought for a moment of addressing a comparatively civil remark to the mountebank who had so let down the prestige of the Old School by becoming a film actor.

After luncheon the game was resumed, but knitting, sewing, novels, even the charms of gentle sleep, were all abandoned, and every feminine eye was fixed upon the swift and graceful extra-cover-point.

The County players settled down again and the score had risen to 180, when Vernon held a brief consultation with his wicket-keeper, then shrugged his shoulders like a man who has to make the best of a bad job, and went up to Hugo.

"D'you bowl at all?" he asked curtly.

"I think so," replied Hugo.

Vernon looked at him sourly as if to say, "More monkey-tricks, eh?" and then said, "Next over. That end."

And so began, with those four brief words, the final chain of events, inexorable, inescapable, fore-doomed, that was to bring Hugo to ultimate disaster.

Poor Hugo. He did not know it. At that moment the world was perfection for him. There was no hint that Nemesis might be at work. Only a voice kept repeating somewhere inside him, "You're going to bowl in a real cricket-match, you're going to bowl in a real cricket-match."

Treading on air, Hugo walked to the far wicket at the end of the over and rolled up his sleeve and took the ball. "Right hand over the wicket," he told the umpire, and then he paced out his run. "Eight yards, never more," Uncle Eustace had said so often.

Then he began to place his field.

The spectators watched in breathless silence.

Hugo bowled with a sharp off-break, and his bowling was the fastest ever seen on that ground or any other ground in the county of Suffolk. In four overs he clean-bowled nine batsmen, broke two stumps, hit the tenth batsman on the body and broke a rib, and broke three fingers on the wicket-keeper's left hand, and severely bruised both hands of the deputy wicket-keeper.

In an awed silence the fielding team returned to the pavilion. The total was 186. Hugo had taken nine wickets for four runs. The four runs were a snick through the slips that reached the boundary in a flash.

Mr. Vernon, by this time distinctly more respectful in manner, approached Hugo and asked him if he would bat first for the home team.

"I'm afraid," replied Hugo, "that I am not a good batsman. I can only keep my bat straight," and then he added automatically, "on and off the field."

Mr. Vernon looked at him suspiciously, as if he was afraid his Old Etonian leg was being pulled, but Hugo's air of unconscious simplicity was most disarming.

"Very well," he said. "I'll put you in sixth. You'll find pads and gloves in the pavilion."

Hugo batted sixth and kept his bat so rigidly straight that his defence was quite impregnable, and he retired undefeated at the end of the innings, having compiled seven runs in an hour and twenty minutes.

While the teams were packing their belongings into cricket-bags, and drinking beer, and talking in little groups, and carrying trays of cocktails to the ladies, Hugo perceived an animated discussion in progress between the two Middlesex batsmen who had batted first for the visiting team, and an older man in a Zingari blazer. All three were talking in vehement undertones, though once one of the county players raised his right hand as high as possible above his head and exclaimed loudly, "Marvellous, I tell you."

A few minutes later the man in the Zingari blazer came up to Hugo and said, "Would you care to come up to London to-morrow, Seeley, and have a net at Lord's?" '

"At Lord's!" exclaimed Hugo with a thrill of excitement. "Do you really mean that?"

"Of course I do," replied the other, "and perhaps you'll be my guest at luncheon in the Pavilion afterwards. Shall we say half-past eleven? Good."

Hugo resisted with some reluctance and a great deal of difficulty the combined pressure of the ladies to stay to dinner and spend the night in the red-brick, battlemented, moated manor-house that here and there appeared through the trees. He wanted to spend a quiet and abstemious evening, and to go to bed early, so as to be as fit and as fresh as possible next morning for his net on the famous ground which he had heard Uncle Eustace describe so often as literally the Mecca of the cricket world. He found it easier to resist Mr. Vernon's invitation to stop and take pot-luck at supper. The moment he had begun to indicate that his answer was likely to be in the negative, Mr. Vernon had brightened perceptibly and had interrupted, "Got to rush off, have you? Well, many thanks for turning out. So long."

The famous film star bowed to each of the saddened ladies, and strolled home across the meadows through the scented English evening, his feet upon Suffolk buttercups and his head among the eternal stars.

There was no match at Lord's on that June morning, and Hugo gazed in silence at the empty arena. How well he knew it, although he had never seen it. There was the Mound Stand over which Victor Trumper had hit Schofield Haigh in the first over of a Test Match. There was the wicket on which Spofforth, the Demon, had routed the strength of England in a single day with his tremendous bowling. There was the Pavilion over which only Albert Trott had ever hit a cricket-ball. There were the steps down which the mighty figure of the Doctor had walked year after year, on his way to smite, year after year, the bowling of the Players of England.

Who shall resist all resistless Graces?

as the poet asked in despair. To Hugo the ground was full of ghosts—Thomas Lord who made it, and those who came after and adorned it, Alfred Mynn and Fuller Pilch, Silver Billy Beldham and Felix and Squire Osbaldestone and Lambert and that fiery parson the Lord Frederick Beauclerk, and Shaw and Shrewsbury, and Spofforth, that grim Australian, and Trumble, and Kumar Shri Ranjitsinjhi, and Tom Hayward, and Tom Richardson, and the immortal band of Yorkshiremen. All these were household names to Hugo, freshly remembered. Tears came into his eyes, as he looked at the silhouetted figure of old, long-bearded Father Time on the top of the new stand, taking the bails inexorably off the stumps, and instinctively he found himself murmuring:

For the field is full of shades as I near the shadowy coast,
And a ghostly batsman plays to the bowling of a ghost,

And I look through my tears on a soundless-clapping
 host
As the run-stealers flicker to and fro,
  To and fro,
   Oh my Hornby and my Barlow long ago.

Then he gave his eyes a furtive dab with his handkerchief and went round to the Pavilion, handed in
his name, and was taken off at once to a changing-
room.

The cricketing-nursery at the east end of Lord's
was humming with its usual activity. Young professionals were bowling away at middle-aged members of the M.C.C. and the air was filled with the
sounds of bat on ball, and the sounds of ball upon
stumps, and the gently laudatory cries of "Well
played, sir." But Hugo was guided past these nets
to a mysterious enclosure of green canvas, and then
the "door" was carefully closed. Inside the enclosure
there was another net, with stumps ready and creases
marked out; a young man in flannels, pads, and
gloves, was leaning upon a bat; and behind the net
were standing three men, shining in morning-coats
and silk hats and gardenia buttonholes. As Hugo
came in, one of the three hooked an imaginary ball
off his left ear with an exquisitely rolled silken umbrella and the other two watched gravely. Near this
vision of masculine sartorialism were two other men,
in ordinary suits and soft hats and very solid, well-
made boots. Both were of medium height and both
were about fifty years of age. One was thin, with a
thin face and a long, bird-like nose, while the other's

s

face was round and red and rustic. They stood about two yards from the men in the silk hats, and the distance, neither too far nor too near, seemed to convey a certain deference to superiors, and at the same time a readiness to join in the conversation at any moment as independent equals.

Hugo was introduced to the prospective batsman. He could not catch his name, but he understood that he came from Gloucestershire. A handful of new cricket-balls was produced, and Hugo measured out his run. For half an hour he pounded away at the young man and was surprised, and indeed rather piqued, at his inability to bowl him out more than twice. On the other hand, the young man treated the terrific onslaught with the utmost deference, dodging the high-kickers, and leaping with extraordinary agility out of the way of the lightning expresses that pitched just outside the leg-stump. The five men behind the net watched every ball intently. At the end of the half-hour there was a pause, and Hugo heard one of the silk-hatted gentlemen call out to the red-faced man, "Like a knock, Wilfred?"

"Ah'm not such a fooil, Sir Francis. Try Jack here," said the red-faced man in a north-country accent and they all laughed, and the thin, bird-like man shook his head cheerfully. "Not me, sir. I survived Gregory and Macdonald and I'm not going to risk my life now."

The five men then put their heads together and talked earnestly for a minute. Hugo sat down on the grass for a rest, although his training was so good that he felt as if he could go on bowling for hours.

The batsman was summoned to the secret palaver and there was much nodding of heads.

Finally one of the immaculate gentlemen left the group and came across to Hugo. "I must introduce myself, Mr. Seeley," he said, as Hugo scrambled to his feet. "My name is Sir Francis Wilson, and I am the Chairman of the M.C.C.'s Selection Committee. Those two gentlemen are my colleagues, and the other two are our professional advisers. I don't think they need any introduction," he added with a smile. Hugo, who knew neither the names nor the faces of the two professionals, nor any reason why they did not need any introduction, thought it best to say nothing.

"We have unanimously decided," went on Sir Francis, "to invite you to play in the second Test Match against Borealia, which begins next Friday on this ground."

Hugo was staggered. The scene went dim. His voice vanished somewhere down into his chest, and he had no subsequent recollection of any circumstance whatsoever until he found himself, returned to ordinary clothes, on the top of a bus in the vicinity of the Marble Arch, staring down at posters of evening newspapers, which trumpeted out the tidings "Unparalleled Test Sensation," and "Mystery Test Cricketer."

The Great Day dawned misty but warm. There was dew on the grass at Lord's and the famous sparrows darted impertinently from one fairy mesh to another in search of incautious worms and crumbs left over from the match of two days before.

At 6 A.M. the queue of spectators with their three-legged stools stretched as far as St. John's Wood Road Station, and by 10 A.M. twenty thousand people were sitting on newspapers in the street. At half-past ten the gates were opened; at a quarter to twelve the Prime Minister took his seat in the Pavilion; and at one minute to twelve His Majesty the King, His Royal Highness the Prince of Wales, Gold Stick-in-Waiting, the Gentleman-Usher of the Black Rod, seven Grooms of the Bed-Chamber, the ex-Sub-Dean of the Chapel Royal and Deputy Clerk of the Closet, and the Master of the Horse, arrived and were greeted with the tempestuous cheering of forty thousand loyal citizens of the far-flung Empire.

At twelve o'clock precisely, in a warm sunshine and under a blue, windless sky, the English captain led his team amid another tremendous burst of cheering down the steps of the Pavilion and out to the wicket. The eleven men gazed wisely and intently at the pitch and one or two of them threw a ball idly from hand to hand. Then a third roar—much of it resounding from the section of the stands which had been allotted to the Borealian spectators—with a curiously pitched accent, heralded the appearance of Borealia's opening batsmen.

One of the umpires handed a new ball to the English captain, who handed it in turn to Hugo.

"You start, Seeley," he said laconically. "Pavilion end. What slips do you want?"

"One," replied Hugo firmly, "and five short-legs."

The English captain looked at him queerly. "They told me you were a fast bowler," he said.

"I mix 'em," replied Hugo, pinning all his faith in Uncle Eustace. For what was it Uncle Eustace had said so often? "When in doubt put five men on the leg-side and bowl at the leg-stump." That was the ticket.

As the batsmen were walking out, a great silence fell upon the ground, that silence which Elia says is multiplied and made more intense by numbers. But when the first two men took up their stations almost at the batsman's elbow, there came a muttering in the Borealian corner of the vast crowd, like the rolling of far-off thunder over downland, rising for a moment to a menacing growl, and dying away behind the slopes of grass, and rising again in a sullen boom. As the third short-leg and then the fourth and then the fifth took post, "You heard as if an army muttered; and the muttering grew to a grumbling; and the grumbling grew to a mighty rumbling," and then the noise died away into a sultry, tense, hot, silence.

There was not a sound. The stillness of forty thousand beings lay across the arena. But there was a deadly menace in the air.

The Borealian batsman was ready. The wicket-keeper, the slip-fieldsman, and short-legs crouched, and the other fieldsmen began to walk towards the wicket. Hugo ran up to the wicket and delivered a levin-bolt at the leg-stump. The ball jumped sharply and hit the batsman in the ribs. Instantly there was a roar of fury from the Borealian corner. It was a terrible sound, like a thousand hungry lions, or revolutionaries baying for the blood of aristocrats.

Hugo apologized to the Borealian and walked

back. Again he ran up the wicket, gracefully and yet compact with power and energy, and down flashed the ball again upon the leg-stump. The Borealian tried to defend himself against the bolt, and was easily caught by one of the short-legs, and then the Borealian spectators, ten thousand strong, let loose a terrific yell and surged over the ropes like the bursting of a gigantic sluice, and rushed towards Hugo. In a moment the air was full of dust, and queer-shaped felt hats with very large brims, and raucous cries in the strange accent that seemed to be partly American and partly Cockney, and whirling boomerangs, and oranges, and flagon-shaped bottles, and horrid black bottle-tops with a screw thread. Here and there pet kangaroos were leaping about the ground like maniacal acrobats. Wallabies howled at the Pavilion. Opossums, escaping from their masters, danced wild dances in front of the sight-screen at the nursery-end, while omnivorous bandi-coots lived up to their epithet by devouring impartially hats, paper-bags, oranges, and boomerangs. A flying squirrel perched on the score-board, and a root-eating wombat, balancing itself upon the railings of the Pavilion, wailed its mournful song into the unwilling ear of the oldest member of the M.C.C., who was jammed into a corner beside the rails and was unable to move.

It was, in short, a stirring sight, a wholly unprecedented sight, and, as seen by Hugo and his colleagues, a not altogether pleasing sight. However, its lack of pleasing effect was compensated for by its very short duration, for, after a single appalled moment, the English team took to its heels and bolted for the protection of the Mound Stand, leaving the playing-field, the pride and joy of old Thomas Lord, in the undisputed possession of the fauna, if not perhaps of the flora, of the great Dominion of Borealia.

Once lost in the dense masses of spectators which clung in festoons to every seat, railing, and square foot of space, on the Mound, the team began to feel a little safer, and after a short time they were smuggled down to one of the batmakers' shops below. In the meanwhile pandemonium was raging on the ground.

The Borealians, stern, lean men with brown, clear-cut faces and a not especially developed cranial development, were soon torn between two conflicting emotions. And one idea at a time is difficult enough for a simple son of backwoods and bushrangers and sheep-dips to assimilate; the simultaneous impinge-ment of two notions upon those classic brows was the devil and all. The cruel dilemma played Old Harry with the usually self-reliant Borealian power to make a decision. These ten thousand strong men, and to a somewhat lesser extent the kangaroos and bandi-coots and other pets, were thirsting for the blood of the iniquitous ruffian, the dastardly scoundrel, the monstrous villain, who had revived the "body-line" controversy by placing five men close in on the leg-side and bowling like lightning at the batsman. At the same time these ten thousand simple souls were longing to sing *Land of Hope and Glory* in front of the Pavilion, as a gesture of Imperial solidarity and good-will. They paused irresolutely in the middle of the ground. The bottles stopped flying through the air and came to rest on the turf, displaying their gay labels in the sun, Château Lafitte Paramatta, Château Yquem Wagga-Wagga, Coolgardie Beaujolais, and Bendigo Beaune, and many another delicious product of the Southern Vineyard. The kangaroos stopped bounding. The omnivorous bandicoots looked up from their meal of walking-sticks and early editions of the evening newspapers, and even the flying squirrel stopped tearing pieces out of the score-board and throwing them at the scorers.

A strange hush fell over the ground, broken only by the dreary wail of the root-eating wombat into the oldest member's ear. So melancholy was the dirge, so heartrending the long cadences, that it seemed to be an even-money chance whether the wombat died of a broken heart before the oldest member had a fit of apoplexy.

Then the tension was broken by a loud shout from the balcony of the Pavilion. It was the Secretary of State for the Dominions, megaphone in hand, a gay, gallant figure in morning-coat, striped trousers, grey top-hat, orchid buttonhole, and white spats. The crowd of Borealians instinctively crowded towards the Pavilion to hear what the ever-popular Cabinet Minister had got to say.

He lifted the megaphone and shouted, in the voice that had dominated a thousand meetings, "'Ere, why not start the blinking game again? We'll 'oof that blighter hout, and start fair. Wotchersay?"

A roar of applause made it clear what the Borealians wanted to say.

"Then get to it, me boys," roared the Cabinet

Minister, and the situation was saved. The Borealians as one man struck up *Land of Hope and Glory* and sang it right through, every verse of it, completely drowning, and thus profoundly discouraging, the melancholious wombat, and then strode, with that famous long, loose stride of the backwoods, to their seats, whistled in their pets, and prepared to enjoy the game once more.

The English team re-emerged, with the twelfth man substituted for Hugo, and the Second Test Match began for the second time.

In a small room in the Pavilion of the Marylebone Cricket Club, a grim scene was being played. The room faced north, so that no sunshine brightened the dark sombreness that shadowed the faces of the actors. Out of the window nothing could be seen except the fantastic excrescences of grimy red and still grimier white which are called, in St. John's Wood, blocks of residential flats. In that dreary vista there was no suggestion either of a glade of trees or of the holy apostle. Everything was drab.

Hugo, bewildered, harassed, dejected, sat all crumpled up on a hard wooden chair. The President of the M.C.C. stood leaning moodily upon a small desk. He was in a scowling rage, and was tapping the floor impatiently with his foot. He obviously was anxious to get back to his seat and watch the game. Some sort of permanent official of the club was hovering behind him. Two enormous policemen stood one on each side of the door, in identical attitudes of corpulent alertness. Opposite Hugo sat the Secretary of State for Dominion Affairs, talking, talking, talking. Hugo hardly listened. He could not understand what had happened. Apparently he had committed some hideous and unforgivable crime in getting that Borealian batsman caught like that. But what crime could it be? He had spent hours before the Test Match began in studying the 1934 Laws of Cricket to see if they differed in any way from the Laws in Uncle Eustace's time, and nowhere had he discovered that it was a crime to get a batsman out like that. And now that he came to think of it, during the second or two that had elapsed between the dismissal of the batsman and the irruption of raging, torrential Borealia upon the playing-field, there had been time for the umpire to remonstrate with him if he had been playing unfairly. But the umpire had said nothing. The umpire clearly saw nothing wrong, and did not the Laws of Cricket say, in Law 34, "The Umpires are the sole judges of fair or unfair play"? And if that was so, why did he have to fly for his life from the ground, and then, what was almost worse, have to listen to this portentously pompous statesman droning away interminably? And why policemen at the door?

What was the old fool saying? " 'Ow do you expect me to land a rebate on the tariff on whipple-sprockets that Birmingham is 'owling for," he was shouting, as he hammered the palm of one hand with the fist of the other, "if you play old blasted 'Arry like this with Borealian Suscip-suscibbi—well, you knows what I mean."

Hugo had not the faintest idea what he meant.

"And there's the contract for the rotary bevil-flanges for the new power station," went on the politician vehemently. "Coventry 'ad as good as got the job, and now I'll 'ave to slog like 'ell to save it from going to Krupps. And then there's the new suspension bridge. Oh my God!"—his voice rose to a wail—"I'd forgotten the new suspension bridge. Ninety thousand tons of Durham steel." He wrung his hands in despair.

"What on earth," asked Hugo wearily, "has a game of cricket got to do with ninety thousand tons of Durham steel?"

"Young man," said the Cabinet Minister with a dreadful emphasis upon every word, "that is not a game of cricket. It is a link of Empire. It brings together the mother and daughter countries in a way that nothing else can. Do you realize that if I had not been on that balcony just now, and had not exerted the full force of my personality, there would by now, already, be a very definite chance of the secession of Borealia from our far-flung Empire and her absorption into the Empire of Japan?"

"Good heavens!" The President of the M.C.C. started out of his fidgety apathy. "You don't mean that, sir?"

"I do, sir," was the stern reply.

The President seemed knocked all of a heap. "No more Test Matches," he muttered over and over again.

The Dominions Secretary turned his attention to Hugo again. "They tell me you're an 'Ollywood film star."

"No, I'm not," said Hugo sulkily. "At least, I am."

"You'd better make up your mind," said the Minister grimly. "Because you're going to be deported to the United States to-morrow."

"For getting a Borealian batsman caught at short-leg?" demanded Hugo indignantly.

"For hendangering hour himperial 'armonies, and for 'ampering hour hexporting hindustries," came the slow, magniloquent, overwhelming reply.

Hugo, more convinced than ever that he was dealing solely and exclusively with maniacs, from highest to lowest, shrank back in his chair from this terrible indictment, and thought it best to say nothing.

The interview was over. The Minister, the President, and the permanent functionary filed out, and the two policemen escorted Hugo to the dressing-room, and thence to a taxi, and thence to his hotel. They had orders, they explained, not to leave him until he was safely on board the American liner. As the trio left Lord's, they heard the loud, raucous, exultant cries of the Borealian supporters, as their champions smote the slow and medium-paced deliveries of the remaining English bowlers all over the field.

CHAPTER XVII

THAT afternoon, that hot, dusty, lazy, cricketing afternoon, was one of the most hectic that the evening newspapers in Fleet Street had ever known, and the sales of the later editions were prodigious. First of all there was the usual sirocco of excitement that swirls round every Test Match. Then there was the "mystery" player in the English team whose name had been kept secret till the very last minute. Then followed the terrific sensation when it was divulged that this "mystery" player was none other than a romantic, glamorous, film actor who had secretly developed into a tremendous fast-bowler.

Those three pieces of flaming, red-hot news were sufficient in themselves to crowd a really beautiful triple-murder in Islington into an obscure half-column on page nine, and to jam into an "Other News" paragraph an earthquake in China which had caused the deaths of about two and a half million people. But those three were not all. At seven minutes past twelve, the first incoherent babblings of hysterical cricket correspondents began to impinge upon the telephone-receivers of Fleet Street with the story of Hugo's bowling, and News Editors and Chief Sub-Editors were looking a bit glassy in

the eyes and were beginning to breathe rather
heavily.

And at three-fifteen that afternoon the real
Michael Seeley arrived at Croydon aerodrome, having flown with a friend from Yucatan to the Azores,
from the Azores to Paris, and from Paris to London,
all within thirty-six hours.

Mr. Seeley, who had been out of range of newspapers for four weeks, was naturally a little puzzled
by the kaleidoscope of posters which struck his eye
from every conceivable angle at Croydon. He had
often thought that there must be other Michael
Seeleys somewhere in the world, but it had never
in his most extravagant moments occurred to him
that one of those namesakes might have acquired a
fame in any way comparable to his own. He was, in
consequence, a little piqued at the prominence which
this fellow seemed to have secured with his "body-
line," whatever on earth that might mean.

However, the spectacular return of the famous
film-lover would soon, Mr. Seeley reflected, put the
other chap's nose out of joint, and it was with a completely restored equanimity that the young man
stepped into the waiting limousine and drove to the
Ritz. He had no idea where Felida might be, nor
did he greatly care. But the Ritz was an admirable
headquarters, and to the Ritz he drove. He walked
straight into Felida in the lounge. Felida was ex-
plaining to a crowd of reporters that Michael had
learnt his cricket in Beverly Hills, but that she herself had been born in a dinky, wee, winsome little
house near Kennington Oval, and that as a girl she

had often been taken to see the boys playing, and how the Prince of Wales had been their landlord, and how he'd always been very considerate.

Mrs. Michael Seeley saw her husband approaching, and such is the power of feminine intuition, and such the infallibility of the wifely eye, that she recognized him instantly.

"Micky," she cried in a voice so penetrating that the hall-porter came running in to see if anyone was hurt. The journalists spun round as one man.

"Why aren't you playing at Lord's?" they demanded as one man.

"Boys," Felida answered for him, "that guy at Lord's is one big fake. Phony. Bogus."

Pencils were whizzing across note-books like wildfire.

"This is my big, wonderful man," went on Felida crooningly. Mr. Seeley winced.

"Let's get out of this," he said sharply. "Where's Arthur?" He took Felida's arm and started to go towards the lift.

"Hi!" exclaimed the reporters plaintively. "What about the divorce?"

Mr. Seeley stopped. "What divorce?" he demanded.

The representative of a rather pompous daily newspaper stepped forward as the spokesman of the party. "Miss Caliente's divorce from ——" he stopped and looked puzzled.

A bright little illustrated sheet took up the running. "If Miss Caliente isn't married to this faker——"

"Of course she isn't," said Mr. Seeley crossly. It

began to dawn upon him that someone had been stealing his limelight. Stealing his wife was one thing. But stealing his limelight was a very different kettle of fish.

"Let's go and find Arthur," he went on impatiently, and, still holding Felida's arm, he pushed his way through the reporters.

The bright little illustrated seized a passing waiter. "Where's the telephone?" he demanded, and in a moment the throng had vanished.

Mr. and Mrs. Seeley went upstairs to the sitting-room where they found Mr. Dowley.

"I can explain everything," said Mr. Dowley, opening a box of cigars.

After the explanation was over, Mr. Seeley said only, "I had a first cousin who was supposed to be drowned at the age of two."

He then retired to a distant corner of the lounge and spent two hours in deep thought. Then he smiled an inscrutable smile and got up and went out.

Next morning the world was in possession of the amazing tale, and although at a million breakfast tables a million males explained, commented upon, and exclaimed over, the score in the Test Match for the benefit of their wives, mothers, and sisters, nevertheless those explanations, comments, and exclamations went entirely unheeded. For Feminine England was enthralled by the domestic drama of Felida, World's Adored, and her twin husbands, and not even the most lyrical description of the previous day's cricket could extract more than an absent, "Yes, dear, very nice." Feminine England, indeed, was torn by as pretty a problem in psychology as had faced it for some years. One-half answered the crucial question with a sniff and a tossing head and a flashing eye and the words, "Of course she knew, the hussy." The other half, mostly residing in that mysterious region called "below stairs," dried a tear with the corner of an apron and sighed that men should be so eternally wicked as to deceive a poor girl like that.

There was a very strange scene at the Universal and West Kensington Hotel at 10.30 on that morning of the second day of the Test Match. Hugo was in his bedroom packing his clothes, and a great gloom was upon him. For he was about to be deported from the gentle land of his birth and conveyed to a strange country without the slightest assurance, or indeed reasonable probability, that he would be admitted into that country. His papers would be carefully scrutinized and the forgery detected. At the worst he would be flung into some hideous penitentiary in the United States for attempting to evade the immigration laws; at the best he would be deported back to England. With a shudder he recalled the conversation which he had had with the captain of the yacht *Joseph Conrad Korzeniowski*—heavens! it seemed years ago—about the unfortunates whom no country will accept and who are forced to travel backwards and forwards to all eternity like shuttles on a loom. There was no chance of escape. The two gigantic policemen sat in hard, upright chairs, their helmets

T

on their knees, and gazed unwinkingly at their prisoner. They had their orders direct from the Home Secretary, to deliver Mr. Michael Seeley to the captain of the *Ruritania* at Southampton and obtain a receipt for him, and these orders they intended to carry out.

But at 10.30 A.M. a complication arose, for two clean-shaven men in bowler-hats and large-toed boots suddenly came into the room without the suggestion of a knock on the door. They seemed a little disconcerted on seeing the uniformed policemen, and the leader of the pair exclaimed, "Hullo, hullo, hullo, what's all this?" and then, without waiting for an answer, he addressed Hugo.

"I am an officer of Scotland Yard and I have a warrant for your arrest on a charge of perjury, in that you did swear an affidavit that you married Miss Maud Maggs in Sacramento, California, United States of America, on May 16th, 1933, knowing same to be false." He paused in his recitation, took a deep breath and delivered in a swift gabble the warning about evidence with which the detective-writers have so thoroughly familiarised the British public, and wound up politely with the words, "And now, sir, if you will put on your hat and come with me."

"Oi!" exclaimed one of the uniformed constables, and the other started up and also said, "Oi!"

"What's up?" asked the C.I.D. man sharply.

"You can't take him," protested the quicker-witted of the constables, the one who had said "Oi" first.

"Oh, I can't take him, can't I?" said the detective.

"No, you can't take him."

"And why can't I take him? Eh?"

"Because he's got to leave the country to-day. Deportation-order of the Home Secretary."

"He's got to be at Bow Street in half an hour. Magistrate's warrant."

"He's got to clear out."

"He's got to stay."

There was a long pause. Neither side would budge an inch, and Hugo sat down on the edge of his trunk. A third alternative to an American jail and an eternity of Atlantic voyaging seemed to be opening out—a period of languishment in a British jail. His head began to ache a little, as the two branches of the law wrangled and argued. At last the detectives went out to telephone for further instructions and there was a little peace. At eleven o'clock some more detectives arrived, and at a quarter-past a car-load of officials from the Home Office, and there was more arguing and discussing. By twelve o'clock Hugo had lost all interest in the proceedings. He did not care what they did with him. He was past the stage of human emotions. There was a new turn of events at about twenty-past twelve, when an entirely fresh set of detectives appeared with a warrant for Hugo's arrest under the Defence of the Realm Act in that he had committed acts likely to endanger the harmonious relations of His Majesty's Empire and Dominions beyond the Seas, and they were quickly followed by a small band of uniformed constables from the St. John's Wood police-station with a warrant that had been granted on the application of the M.C.C. on the charge of behaviour "liable to cause a breach of the peace."

By this time the crowd in Hugo's bedroom was so dense that by common agreement all the parties descended to the hotel drawing-room, and the dispute raged more fiercely than ever. Finally the officials of the Home Office were overborne by the sheer weight of warrants, and it was decided that the deportation-order should be withdrawn, temporarily at least, in order that the charges against the miscreant might be preferred.

At Bow Street Hugo was released on his own recognizances in £1000. At St. John's Wood Court the bail was £500, and at Marlborough Street.

Tired and exhausted after his round of police-courts, Hugo turned into a Soho restaurant for a belated lunch—it was now nearly three o'clock—and it was only by a matter of minutes that he was able to get a bottle of wine. And even so he had to drink the entire bottle before three o'clock had actually struck, in order that another branch of the laws of England might be respectfully observed. There was no time to wait for his *escalope de veau*. Hugo poured glass after glass down his throat, in a desperate endeavour not to be arrested again. He felt that he had been arrested often enough for one day.

The effect of the wine, so hastily consumed with so little solid food, was exhilarating and Hugo began to feel faintly care-free for the first time since that terrible opening of the Test Match. The wine, which had been vinted in Algeria, and chemicalized at Sète, and bottled at Bordeaux, and labelled Bordeaux, was raw and strong, and Hugo determined to lunch at this restaurant on the days of his various trials.

As three o'clock struck and the waiter removed the empty bottle, Hugo smacked the table with the palm of his hand and said to himself, "Dammit, let 'em arrest me again. I don't care."

The next moment he was arrested again. And this time the charge was a serious one.

If there is one thing which ought by this time to have impressed the readers of this history, it is the fact that Mr. Dowley was no fool. His enemies might have said that he worked too hard, or that he got up too early in the morning, or that he was sometimes too flamboyant in his methods, but none of them ever suggested that he was a fool. The moment Mr. Michael Seeley stamped, very peevishly, into the sitting-room at the Ritz and began demanding explanations of what that other goddam swob had been doing with the fine old name of Seeley during the last week or two, Mr. Dowley's brain had begun to click over at its fastest and smoothest. And like all great men, he put his finger upon the nub of the situation at the very start. He saw, in a flash, that an answer had got to be provided for the question which was certain, within a very few hours, to be convulsing the feminine heart of England, and he whisked Felida off to Somerset House, to a K.C.'s chambers, to the office of a Commissioner for Oaths, to the office of the King's Proctor, and to the clerk of the Divorce, Probate, and Admiralty division of the High Court of Justice, before each and all of whom she swore a solemn oath that she had been honestly and sincerely under the impression that the man Smith was really her lawful wedded husband, Michael Spottiston Seeley.

The result of this whirlwind tour of affidaviting was seen in the little Soho restaurant, when two large, clean-shaven, bowler-hatted gentlemen, with large-toed boots, arrested Hugo on the charge of rape.

Bail was admitted in the sum of £5000.

Just as Hugo was tottering out of the court, faint with hunger—for he had been ruthlessly parted from his *escalope de veau*—and somewhat intoxicated by his Algerian Bordeaux, he was re-arrested on the fatal, sinister, appalling charge of having committed Jactitation of Marriage.

The magistrate before whom he was haled to answer to this fearful charge was a kindly old gentleman whose main practice consisted of advising ladies to give their husbands one more chance in spite of that straight left to the boko on the previous Saturday evening, and of advising gentlemen to give their wives one more chance in spite of that smash across the ear with the half-skinned halibut, and he was greatly puzzled by the case. His clerk, however, was a bright young spark who stated that Jactitation of Marriage was an ancient but none the less grave offence against the Marriage Laws. The magistrate, blushing to the roots of his venerable hair, at once cleared the court. The clerk, who had whispered vehement but vain expostulations against this drastic procedure, then explained that the crime consisted in boasting of marriage with a lady, or, alternatively, with a gentleman, with whom "one was not, in point of actual fact," as the clerk observed, married. The charge against Hugo was that he had jactitated marriage with Mrs. Michael Seeley, *née* Maggs. He was remanded until the next day on his own recognizances in £1000. The Hackney Marshes branch of the Imperial Union Bank had to be specially opened at four o'clock to cash Hugo's cheque.

After this shattering series of experiences, it was the merest child's play to be arrested, as Hugo was, at 5.15 P.M. on the charge of being in possession of a forged passport when he landed in England; on the charge, at 5.25 P.M., of having made a false entry in the register of the Ritz Hotel when he signed himself "Michael Seeley"; and at 6.15 P.M., on the charge of obtaining money for a hospital for crippled children under false pretences, in that, when he visited it with Felida, he was masquerading as a celebrated film actor whereas he was nothing of the kind.

All these experiences passed over Hugo's head. They were mere dreams, feathers in the wind, ghostly phantasmagoria. Detectives came and went. He did not see them. Charges were read out. He did not hear them. If he was cautioned once against saying anything that might be used as evidence against him, he must have been cautioned a dozen times. There seemed to be no crime in the calendar except murder, simony, and barratry, that he had not succeeded in perpetrating during that last fortnight. Before the day was out there were seven charges of trespass from householders in the neighbourhood of the Earl's Court Road and Redcliffe Gardens, and eleven charges of unlawful entering after dark, and one of malicious damage to a slate roof. But all that was as the sound of thorns crackling under a pot. Even the writ, served upon him at about seven o'clock, for Loss of Professional Reputation by Masquerade, at the instance of M. Seeley, Gentleman, failed to rouse him from his apathy.

At about eight o'clock that evening, Hugo returned to the little Soho restaurant and ordered two bottles of the Algerian Bordeaux and two mixed grills.

The latter gave him muscle and stamina, the former gave him the fighting spirit. And when the crowning insult arrived, shortly after nine, Hugo was in no mood to take it lying down.

It was clear that he had been followed all day by sleuths, both public and private, for the blue-chinned man with the high stiff collar, shiny black stock, gold-rimmed glasses, and air of supernatural sharpness, came straight up to him in the restaurant.

"For you, Mr. Smith," he said, pushing a blue paper across the table to Hugo.

"I've not yet been arrested for assault," said Hugo, breathing heavily, talking thickly, and picking up an empty bottle by the neck, "but I don't mind if I am."

"Steady, steady," cried the blue-chinned man, backing away in alarm. "I'm not a detective. It's only a divorce writ."

"What!" shouted Hugo furiously, flinging the bottle at the man. The aim of a Test Match player with any sort of missile is bound to be pretty accurate, and Hugo's shot with the bottle was extraordinarily accurate. But even Test Match players are not accustomed to reckon with veteran writ-servers whom a long and sad experience of unpopularity has made uncommonly nippy on their pins, and it was with almost contemptuous ease that the blue-chinned man side-stepped the missile so that it continued on its way until it struck an elderly gentleman sharply in the waistcoat, with such an impact as to make him sit down in a rather perplexed manner on the floor.

Hugo examined the writ. It had been issued before the real Michael Seeley came back from Yucatan. Hugo was still wondering whether the Social Laws of England permitted a man to be divorced from a woman who was legally admitted to be his wife, and simultaneously to be severely flogged for raping her because she was legally admitted not to be his wife, when a policeman, who had been summoned by the restaurateur, came in and arrested him on the charge of committing a breach of the peace, in that he had thrown a bottle, et cetera, et cetera, et cetera.

Hugo gave it up. He refused to apply for bail, and spent the night in the cells at Marlborough Street. After all, he could not very well be arrested there.

CHAPTER XVIII

Next morning, as Hugo was sorting out his writs, summonses, and bail-receipts, and trying to arrange in some sort of chronological order his forthcoming appearances in the dock in order that he might surrender to his various bails at the right moment and in the right court, the door of his cell was unlocked and Mr. Michael Seeley was ushered in.

The two men stared at each other for a moment, and then the film actor said, meditatively, "We're first cousins, you know. That accounts for it. Your father and my father were brothers, and what's more, they married sisters. We certainly are devilish like each other."

"'Devilish' is a mild word," retorted Hugo with some asperity.

Mr. Seeley was surprised. "Don't you care about being like me?" he enquired. "I'm supposed to be rather good-looking."

"Well, I'm good-looking too, amn't I?" demanded Hugo crossly. He didn't see why this fellow should claim all the credit for their joint handsomeness.

"Of course you are," replied Seeley. "Haven't I just told you that you're exactly like me?"

"It's the first time," said Hugo, "that I've ever felt dissatisfied with my appearance."

Mr. Seeley considered this statement for some moments and then shook his head. "I don't follow that," he said. "It doesn't somehow make sense."

"Look here," he went on, "what are you going to do now?"

"Go to prison for about forty years, so far as I can make out," said Hugo savagely.

"You've certainly got yourself into a bit of a muddle," conceded the other. Hugo interrupted him.

"Got myself?" he shouted. "Got myself? I haven't done a single damned thing by myself or for myself for weeks and weeks. It's Dowley and you and Cokayne and the rest of the pack of scoundrels who've got me into this mess. Look at these," and he hurled his pile of dread official documents into the film actor's face. Seeley was unmoved. He picked up the papers and began to examine them with an over-acted air of casualness.

"By the way," he said, "they tell me your name is Hugo Smith."

"It is," was the sulky reply.

"It isn't really, you know," said Seeley. "My uncle—your father—had rather odd ideas about Christian names. My father was the worldly one of the two brothers, and he went bankrupt financing the Gaiety chorus; yours was a more serious sort of card from all accounts, and I'm afraid, old chap, if you go to Somerset House you'll find that your name is Reuben Obadiah, surname Seeley of course."

Hugo was about to burst into a torrent of polyglot

invective when a police-officer opened the door and announced that the interview was at an end.

Mr. Seeley picked up his hat and, in doing so, carelessly dropped all Hugo's papers on to the floor, However, he made amends by assisting to pick them up, and then he went out. His last words were, "Reuben, old boy, I think I can pull you through. Leave it to me."

Bitterly reflecting that the last person who had guaranteed to pull him through had been the perfidious Dope Cokayne, Hugo was marched off to the police-court and fined thirty shillings with costs. It was past eleven o'clock when the ceremony was concluded and he was released, and Hugo was due to answer the charge of having committed Jactitation of Marriage at half-past ten. He hurried as fast as an elderly taxi-driver, and an even more elderly taxi-cab, permitted to Westminster Police Court. Presumably there was some terrible penalty for arriving three-quarters of an hour late and he would be seized again by the minions of the law. But at the Westminster Police Court a curious incident occurred. Hugo gave his name—H. B. Smith—to an usher, and then, fearing that he had committed yet another crime, fumbled badly and amended it, in a nervous croak, to the hateful name of Reuben Obadiah Seeley. The usher looked at him queerly.

"You'd best go home and lie down, sir," he said in a compassionate tone. "And if you take my advice you'll send for a doctor."

"But I'm charged with—with Jactitation of Marriage," protested Hugo.

"Run along, sir, run along," said the usher. "The Jactitation case came up at 10.30. H. B. Smith pleaded guilty and was remanded for another week."

Hugo found himself outside in the street. The affair was quite incomprehensible. He hailed another taxi and drove to Bow Street to answer the charge of making the false entry in the register of the Ritz Hotel.

Again he found that the case had been heard already. H. B. Smith had appeared, had pleaded guilty, and had been fined ten shillings, with costs.

Suddenly Hugo understood. It was Michael Seeley's way of pulling him through. It was the dear good fellow's notion of doing him a kindness as some sort of recompense for all the trials which he had been through. Hugo's heart warmed towards his cousin. It was the first noble gesture that he had encountered in England, for Aurora's offer to visit Brighton with him, though dictated by a friendly heart, could hardly be associated with the quality of Nobility.

But Cousin Michael's action in representing him in some of the courts, and in taking some of the miserable burden of crime on to his own shoulders, was without any shadow of doubt the sort of behaviour which would have brought tears to the eyes of Uncle Eustace. And then Hugo remembered. Of course. Michael was an Old Etonian too. No wonder that he was acting in this generous fashion. Uncle Eustace would have done just the same. Choking down a lump in his throat, and humming a snatch of the *Boating Song*, Hugo drove to two more police-courts and found, as he expected, that the gentle-hearted Michael had been there before him.

The dear old boy, thought Hugo, his eyes dimming slightly as he examined his documents to see where his next appearance in the dock ought to be made. ·

He ran through them all, and then wrinkled his brows and ran through them again. There seemed to be one missing, but he could not remember which one it actually was. It was only in a subconscious way that he felt that one of the most important documents had disappeared. He went through them a third time, and it jumped to his eyes that the papers relating to the charge of rape were missing.

Hugo froze. A terrible chill struck him from head to foot. He shivered. His teeth chattered. His knees struck each other and his hands trembled. What—what in the name of Heaven was Michael saying and swearing at the Old Bailey? Was he a dear good fellow, who was helping him out of terrible diffi-culties, or was he a fiend incarnate who was trying with diabolical subtlety to saddle him with Felida for ever and ever and ever?

His doubts were solved the instant he entered the fatal court. There was the smug, sleek, hypocritical scoundrel standing in the witness-box. Someone was speaking to him:

"Is your name Hugo Bechstein Smith?"

And the villain answered with a gay smile of triumph, and in a strong voice, "It is."

Hugo staggered back into the lap of a bejewelled dowager and was restored to a perpendicular position by an usher.

"Have you ever been married to Miss Felida Caliente?" The questioning went on at a vast distance, and from a vast distance came the strong voice:

"Never."

"Have you ever represented yourself as Miss Caliente's husband?"

"Yes. I was convicted of Jactitation of Marriage this morning at the Marlborough Street Police Court."

Treachery could go no further. Hugo tottered out into one of the corridors, and collapsed into a chair and buried his face in his hands. People looked at him curiously as they hurried past him on their various duties. It was an awkward case, of course, but somehow they had not realized that film stars felt as strongly as other folk about such things. Poor Mr. Seeley was obviously hit pretty hard. As for that scoundrel Smith, in the dock, he must be a relation, a brother probably, of that Smith who drowned the Brides in the Bath. A ruffian, that's what he was. Capable of anything. There was a buzz of subdued sympathy in the corridor.

A pleasant Irish voice intruded itself melodiously upon Hugo's despairing attempt to picture a lifetime of matrimony with Felida and business with Mr. Dowley. He looked up at the brown face of Captain Timsy O'Sullivan.

"Well, Mr. Seeley," said the Irish airman, "do you want to do any more flying?"

Hugo sprang from his chair with a hardly suppressed yell. "Captain," he cried, "what would you do to earn twenty thousand pounds, in treasury notes, paid in advance?"

"Anything," was the Captain's comprehensive reply.

"Then listen," and Hugo began to whisper eagerly into his ear.

The Old Bailey was packed during the trial of the scoundrelly Smith. Mr. Dowley and Mr. Cokayne sat with the solicitors. Mr. Cokayne's nimble mind was busy on a scheme for signing up Smith with another film company and then forcing Mr. Dowley's Corporation to buy him out. After all, reflected the agile Dope, the film world couldn't hold two stars who looked identical. Aurora, magnificent as ever, was in the court and gazed thoughtfully at the prisoner. From the way the case was going, it looked as if some time might elapse before that week-end to Brighton would materialize. The Lady Honoria Jique was there, and Miss Crystallina Pontefract, and the Lady Bunty Spriggs, and Miss Euphrosyne Caerleon, and Mr. Cyprian Pontefract, and Mr. Valentinian Tracy, and the Lord Cholly Plumpton-stoke, and Mr. Evander Spruce, and, in fact, Society's brightest and best. Witness after witness testified to the prisoner's turpitude and to Felida's spotlessness. But the prisoner, to his own intense disgust, was acquitted at the end of it all, because the chief witness, Mr. Michael Seeley, the injured husband, could not be found when his turn came for giving evidence.

For by that time Hugo was sitting in Captain Timsy O'Sullivan's great long-distance aeroplane, flying at a vast height towards the south-east. The sparkling ribbon of the Rhône was spread out below them. Already the evening sun was touching the snows of the Alps with a red and golden glory, and the dark blue Mediterranean joined the African skies far away to the south.

In front of them lay Rome and Bukharest, the stormy Euxine Sea and the hills of Anatolia, and the deserts of Nineveh and Ecbatana, and the Arch of Ctesiphon, and the Persian Gulf, and Karachi. And east again they were going, east of Karachi, high above the scorching plains of India, eastwards to Rangoon and south to Penang and Singapore, and east again over the magical seas to the lagoon and the scented forests and the murmurous sounds of Kalataheira.

In Captain Timsy O'Sullivan's aeroplane Hugo had found one good thing in the world of Progress.

THE END

Printed in Great Britain by R. & R. CLARK, LIMITED, *Edinburgh.*

BY A. G. MACDONELL

ENGLAND
THEIR ENGLAND

22nd Thousand. Crown 8vo. 7s. 6d. net.

"An extremely friendly . . . satire upon the more gentlemanly aspects of English character. It succeeds in being almost consistently entertaining, contains some capital caricatures of recognisable English figures, and winds up with an exquisitely conveyed impression of Winchester."—COMPTON MACKENZIE in *The Daily Mail*.

"A joy to read . . . I cannot remember any passage (describing a cricket match) in a recently published book which has made me laugh so much. . . . It is a book which must certainly not be missed."—RALPH STRAUS in *The Sunday Times*.

"This is a book by a Scot, and it is the funniest book since Mr. Linklater's *Juan in America*. . . . It is a gloriously funny book and its humour is both dry and uproarious. It is the most triumphant onslaught upon the southern portion of Great Britain since the Romans built Hadrian's Wall."—SYLVIA LYND in *The News-Chronicle*.

"As fun it is immense. . . . You must get the book and read it."—GERALD GOULD in *The Observer*.

"One of the most amusing satires it has ever been my luck to read."—JAMES AGATE in *The Daily Express*.

"Rattling high spirits and irony and wit and keen observation and clean fun : this book's full of them. Also very accurate dialogue."—D. B. WYNDHAM LEWIS in *The Sunday Referee*.

"The richest international jest of the century."—*The Sunday Dispatch*.

"Surely, if there is anyone who doesn't like it, he must be decidedly grumpy and lacking in the proper sense of humour. . . . Every page is full of little and larger bits to make one smile."—*The London Mercury*.

MACMILLAN AND CO. LTD., LONDON

BY A. G. MACDONELL

NAPOLEON
AND HIS
MARSHALS

Second Impression. Crown 8vo. 7s. 6d. net.

"This book displays one of the most satisfying pageants of human nature that I have ever read. . . . Mr. Macdonell has essayed a task of the utmost difficulty and his presentation of that tremendous scene of conflict is a triumph of objective vision, unerring selection, and dignified emotion."—COMPTON MACKENZIE in *The Daily Mail.*

"This book, with its working men turning into kings, is a romance which makes Anthony Hope look tame."—SIR JOHN SQUIRE in *The Daily Telegraph.*

"*Napoleon and his Marshals* is a brilliant, if bitter, book. Mr. Macdonell very ably, very clearly, very ironically describes the major events of the Emperor's life in terms of his great commanders."—ST. JOHN ERVINE in *Time and Tide.*

"Mr. A. G. Macdonell has followed up *England, their England* with a book of a very different kind, but of equal delight. . . . It has been done magnificently."—HOWARD SPRING in *The Evening Standard.*

"Mr. Macdonell is, from the point of view of the general reader, a military historian of outstanding ability, a worthy successor to Mr. Belloc . . . he adds an eye for character, both in its heroic and in its comic aspects. His Marshals live, each of them an independent man, with his own qualities, weaknesses, eccentricities."—EDWARD SHANKS in *John O' London's Weekly.*

"The same qualities—much hard work, lightly hinted ; much knowledge, easily worn ; a fine economy of words ; the sense of humour that is really only a sense of proportion—go to this history that went to last year's satire (*England, their England*). . . . Mr. Macdonell's book is altogether as distinguished as it is enterprising."—*Birmingham Post.*

MACMILLAN AND CO. LTD., LONDON

21194041R00180

Printed in Great Britain
by Amazon